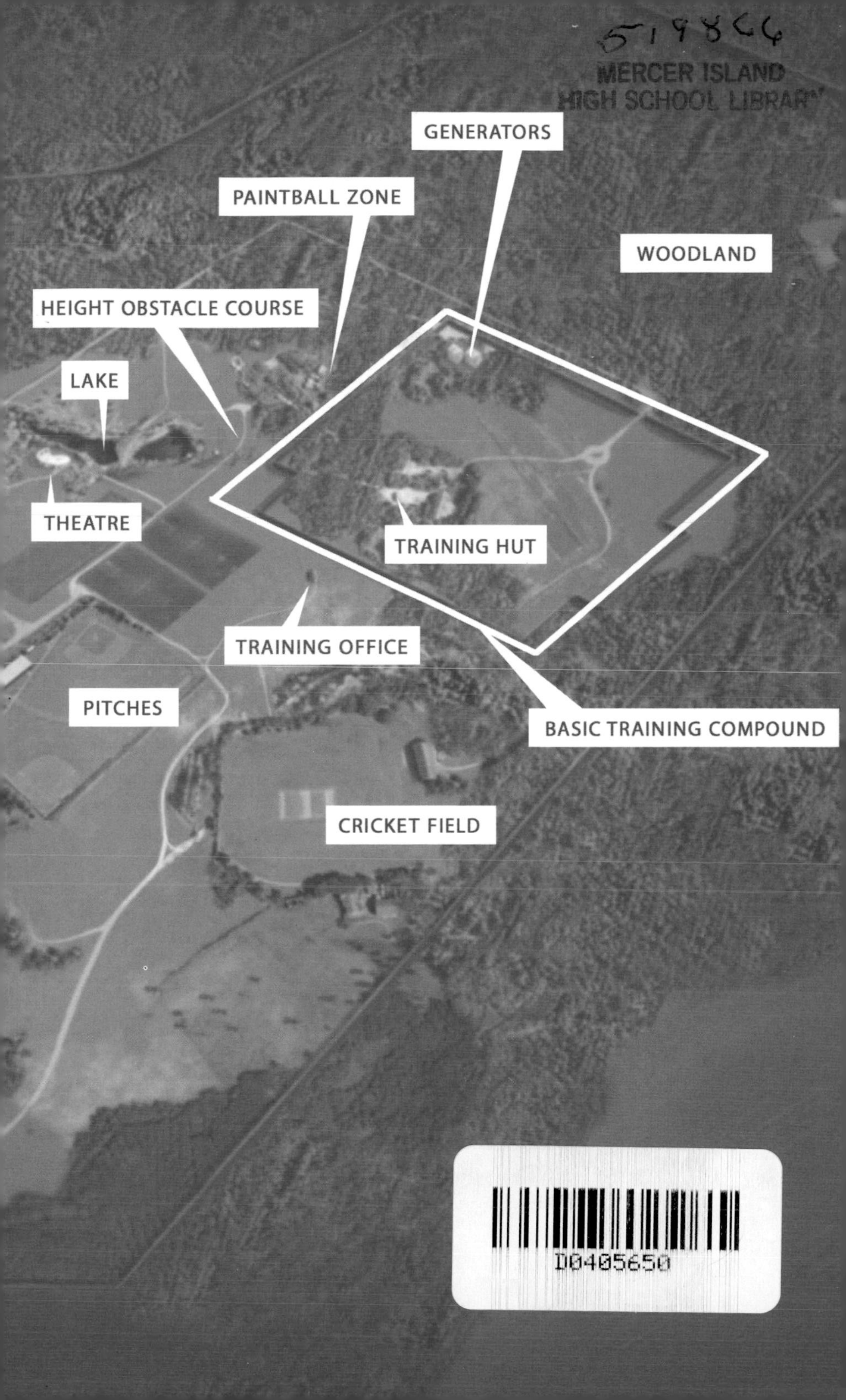
GENERATORS
PAINTBALL ZONE
WOODLAND
HEIGHT OBSTACLE COURSE
LAKE
THEATRE
TRAINING HUT
TRAINING OFFICE
PITCHES
BASIC TRAINING COMPOUND
CRICKET FIELD

Robert Muchamore was born in 1972 and spent thirteen years working as a private investigator. *CHERUB: Shadow Wave* is his twelfth novel in the series.

The CHERUB series has won numerous awards, including the Red House Children's Book Award. For more information on Robert and his work, visit **www.cherubcampus.com**

Praise for the CHERUB series:

'If you can't bear to read another story about elves, princesses or spoiled rich kids who never go to the toilet, try this. You won't regret it.' *The Ultimate Teen Book Guide*

'My sixteen-year-old son read *The Recruit* in one sitting, then went out the next day and got the sequel.' Sophie Smiley, teacher and children's author

'So good I forced my friends to read it, and they're glad I did!' Helen, age 14

'CHERUB is the first book I ever read cover to cover. It was amazing.' Scott, age 13

'The best book ever.' Madeline, age 12

'CHERUB is a must for Alex Rider lovers.' Travis, age 14

BY ROBERT MUCHAMORE

The Henderson's Boys series:

1. The Escape
2. Eagle Day
3. Secret Army
4. Grey Wolves

coming 2011

The CHERUB series:

1. The Recruit
2. Class A
3. Maximum Security
4. The Killing
5. Divine Madness
6. Man vs Beast
7. The Fall
8. Mad Dogs
9. The Sleepwalker
10. The General
11. Brigands M.C.
12. Shadow Wave

SHADOW WAVE

Robert Muchamore

A division of Hachette Children's Books

First published in Great Britain in 2010
by Hodder Children's Books

4

A Catalogue record for this book is available
from the British Library

ISBN-13: 978 0 340 95647 2

Typeset in Goudy by Avon DataSet Ltd,
Bidford-on-Avon, Warwickshire

Printed and bound in Great Britain by
Clays Ltd, St Ives plc

The paper used in this book is a natural recyclable product
made from wood grown in sustainable forests.
The hard coverboard is recycled.

Hodder Children's Books
A division of Hachette Children's Books
338 Euston Road, London NW1 3BH
An Hachette UK Company
www.hachette.co.uk

WHAT IS CHERUB?

CHERUB is a branch of British Intelligence. Its agents are aged between ten and seventeen years. Cherubs are mainly orphans who have been taken out of care homes and trained to work undercover. They live on CHERUB campus, a secret facility hidden in the English countryside.

WHAT USE ARE KIDS?

Quite a lot. Nobody realises kids do undercover missions, which means they can get away with all kinds of stuff that adults can't.

WHO ARE THEY?

About three hundred children live on CHERUB campus. JAMES ADAMS is our seventeen-year-old hero. He's a well-respected CHERUB agent with many successful missions under his belt. Hong Kong-born KERRY CHANG is James' girlfriend. His other close friends include BRUCE NORRIS and SHAKEEL DAJANI.

James' sister, LAUREN ADAMS, is fourteen and regarded as an outstanding CHERUB agent. She hangs out with boyfriend GREG 'RAT' RATHBONE and her best mate BETHANY PARKER.

CHERUB STAFF

With its large grounds, specialist training facilities and combined role as a boarding school and intelligence operation, CHERUB actually has more staff than pupils. They range from cooks and gardeners, to teachers, training instructors, nurses, psychiatrists and mission specialists. CHERUB is run by its chairwoman, ZARA ASKER.

CHERUB T-SHIRTS

Cherubs are ranked according to the colour of the T-shirts they wear on campus. ORANGE is for visitors. RED is for kids who live on CHERUB campus but are too young to qualify as agents (the minimum age is ten). BLUE is for kids undergoing CHERUB's tough one-hundred-day basic training regime. A GREY T-shirt means you're qualified for missions. NAVY is a reward for outstanding performance on a single mission. The BLACK T-shirt is the ultimate recognition for outstanding achievement over a number of missions. When you retire, you get the WHITE T-shirt, which is also worn by staff.

May 2009

1. BRIGANDS

Violent altercations at the biker music festival known as the Rebel Tea Party in August 2008 led to a brutal gang war between the Brigands Motorcycle Club and their bitter rivals the Vengeful Bastards. The stabbings, shootings and property destruction climaxed in October when Brigands national president Ralph 'the Führer' Donnington ordered a series of successful arson attacks on Vengeful Bastard clubhouses.

But the Brigands' triumph was short-lived. A random police stop on a suspicious vehicle unearthed homemade incendiaries intended for another Brigands attack. Two members of South Devon Brigands were arrested and a search of their London hotel room led to the seizure of firearms, sixty thousand pounds in cash and a laptop containing incriminating e-mails. The messages mentioned the arson attacks on clubhouses and contained financial records relating to South Devon Brigands' illegal weapons-smuggling operation.

Eight of the nineteen full members of South Devon Brigands were arrested and charged. Further searches led to more evidence of criminal activity and the arrest of twenty additional bikers, from other Brigands chapters and associate gangs.

Despite this success the Führer remains in control of the Brigands. But with many close associates in jail he can no longer separate himself from his gang's day-to-day criminal activities. After years of evading imprisonment the Führer is more vulnerable than ever before.

Excerpt from an internal police memo written by Chief Inspector Ross Johnson, head of the National Police Biker Task Force (NPBTF) January 2009.

*

James Adams cupped his hands under a mixer tap, splashed tepid water up towards his face and looked at his reflection in a mirrored bathroom cabinet. He'd let his hair grow shaggy and had straw-coloured bristles across his face. His acne was behaving itself, except for the red volcano near his Adam's apple.

James was going for the biker look, wearing wrecked Nikes, oil-stained jeans and a sleeveless AC/DC T-shirt. The effect was completed by an oversized chrome belt buckle shaped like a skull. He flexed his thick arms and felt good about the way he looked: muscular shoulders, big biceps and thick tufts of hair in his pits. A recent growth spurt would be his last and had left him dead on six feet tall.

'Hey there beautiful,' James told himself. Then he tried to look menacing. He shot a fist towards the mirror.

'What are you staring at?' he shouted. 'You wanna start something? See where it gets you, you Tottenham-supporting nerd. Bang!'

James laughed as the imaginary Tottenham fan crumpled to the ground, but there was no one else in the house to hear. He'd established his identity as James Raven the previous summer while living here with a mission controller and two younger agents, but he was living alone on this second phase of the mission. The back story was that he'd fought with his parents, quit studying A-levels and absconded to his family's Devon holiday home to pursue a career as a full-time rebel.

James grabbed a black leather jacket and slid it up his arms as he bolted downstairs. He then took his keys and mobile from a crystal bowl by the front door. *Hash sixty-nine* took him into the handset's hidden phonebook where he tapped the number for his mission controller, John Jones.

'No sign of the Führer yet, boss,' James told him. 'Gonna be at least fifteen minutes late.'

John's placid voice came back down the phone. 'When was the Führer ever on time?'

'Is everything at your end set?' James asked. 'Kerry OK?'

'Tickety-boo,' John agreed. 'Kerry knows her stuff.'

'We can't let the Führer off the hook,' James said seriously. 'I've been on his arse for more than ten months.'

'Any butterflies?' John asked.

'Sweaty palms, stomach churning,' James admitted.

'I've done enough missions now, but there's always a few tense moments.'

John laughed. 'Expect it'll be your last time if this goes down right.'

'Better go, they'll be here soon,' James said, feeling stunned as he dropped the Samsung into his jeans.

Your last time.

The three words made James feel like someone had smashed a brick around his head. He thought about his missions: Help Earth, KMG, Arizona Max, Leon Tarasov, the Survivors, the AFA, Denis Obidin, Mad Dogs, Street Action Group. Was the Führer his last target? Was today the final act of his CHERUB career?

The idea sent a sad ache through James, and remembering what he'd seen in the mirror upstairs made him sadder still. CHERUB agents were kids. They were effective because they were small and innocent and adults didn't suspect them. But James was no child. He was seventeen years old. He had the kind of imposing physique that people crossed the road to avoid and his stubbly face and bent nose looked about as innocent as a Russian battle tank.

A tear welled, but the adrenaline kick nixed it when he heard the Führer's Mercedes. It rumbled into his cul-de-sac, skimming past fancy houses before crunching up the gravel drive. The E-class saloon was a brute. Top of the line AMG sports model, with a V8, blacked-out windows, fat tyres and fancy alloys.

James recognised the three men inside as he grabbed a rear door on the passenger side. The Führer was in the driving seat, short and poisonous with his miniature Hitler-style moustache. The front passenger was Rhino, a biker and long-time Brigands associate who'd never actually joined the gang. In the back was Dirty Dave. Bald and with a thick moustache, he owned half of the strip clubs and massage parlours in South Devon.

'Morning all,' James said, as he lowered himself on to the tan leather.

He was surprised to get shoved back out by Dirty Dave. 'What's on your back?' he barked angrily.

James panicked as he realised he was still wearing his biker jacket. It bore the patch of the Monster Bunch, marking James out as a member of this feeder gang to the Brigands.

'Wear your patch in a car,' the Führer growled, shaking his head contemptuously as he reached under the dashboard and pulled the lever to open the boot. 'Shit for brains.'

For outlaw bikers the coloured insignia on the back of their jackets was sacred. They often travelled in cars, but it was against the rules to wear your club patch while travelling on more than two wheels.

James backed up and jogged to the rear of the car. The interior of the boot was huge. There was a pink golf bag belonging to the Führer's wife and two leather Brigands jackets folded lovingly so that the patches were on display. More significantly James saw two baseball bats, a pair of crowbars and a cricket bag bulging with guns and ammunition boxes.

'Let's go make money!' Rhino said cheerfully, as

James slammed his door and the eighteen-inch alloys spun in the gravel.

*

Their destination was Kam's Surf Club, a dozen miles east of Salcombe. Two storeys high, the restaurant hung precariously close to a cliff's edge, its blue planks weathered by salt spray off the sea below. Kam's food was a mix of noodles and burgers, with a fifties-style counter, vintage jukebox and surf memorabilia hanging off the walls.

The joint would be packed out come tourist season, but that was a couple of months off and the only customers at two on a Tuesday afternoon were German backpackers, cocooned in a romantic bubble as they shared a calamari platter and watched waves crashing in the rocky cove below.

'Service!' the Führer boomed, as he came through the door. 'Mr Kam, stop frying them rats and get your dirty yellow can out here.'

The Germans were unnerved by the presence of four aggressive looking bikers. James was last through the swinging doors, eyeing the tanned legs emerging from the female backpacker's cut-off jeans as he recognised Johnny Cash playing *Ring of Fire* on the jukebox.

The chef and owner came out of his kitchen. Kam was stocky, with his straight black hair tied in a ponytail and a striped apron around his waist. He smiled at the Führer, but body language made it clear he was the last person Kam wanted to see.

The Führer turned to James. 'Get the VHS.'

As James headed towards the service counter, Dirty Dave stepped up to the two backpackers. The girl looked at her boyfriend. He was chunky, going for the lumberjack look in his plaid shirt and Aran sweater, but he'd never thrown a punch in his life.

'I don't want trouble,' the German said in stilted English as he raised his hands.

Dirty Dave stopped half a step shy of the table. The Germans recoiled as he reached over and rammed a piece of battered calamari in his mouth.

'Tasty,' he said, nodding as he chewed. 'Dirty Dave likes a bit of the old octopus.'

The female backpacker glanced anxiously at her man. James spoke no German, but it didn't take a genius to translate *let's get the hell out of here*.

Dirty Dave reached towards his trousers. The German flinched, thinking he was going for a weapon, but instead Dave hooked his thumbs around his belt loops and yanked down his jeans. The woman caught the briefest glance of Dirty Dave's flopping penis before shooting back from the table and screaming.

'How's about some English sausage?' Dirty Dave sneered. 'Let me show you the real reason we won the war.'

The male backpacker took a twenty from his wallet and threw it at the table, before grabbing his girlfriend and the backpacks and hurrying towards the exit.

'Aww, come on baby,' Dirty Dave shouted, as he waddled after them with his filthy jeans around his knees. 'Why play so hard to get?'

Rhino and the Führer howled with laughter as James stepped behind the counter. Amidst the dishwashers and beer kegs was a dilapidated security recorder. James ejected the VHS and held it in the air.

'Got the tape, boss,' he called.

'Don't leave it behind,' the Führer ordered, then turned towards Kam wearing a sarcastic grin. 'Why the sour face?' he teased.

'How can I pay you when you throw out my customers?' Kam shouted furiously.

The Führer laughed. 'Two customers makes a difference? You had this place *heaving* all last summer. You owe me three weeks. That's seven hundred nicker.'

'Four fifty,' Kam corrected.

'Price shoots up when you don't pay me,' the Führer snarled menacingly, before grabbing Kam's apron and pulling him close. 'Don't think that I'm letting things slip, just because a couple of my men are behind bars.'

'I can't pay so much in winter,' Kam squirmed. 'You see how many customers I have.'

'These old wooden buildings burn easy,' the Führer threatened, as his hands made the shape of an explosion. 'Poof.'

'Who else is home?' Rhino asked.

'Just my wife and the translator you asked for,' Kam answered. 'Back in the kitchen.'

'Get 'em out here in plain sight,' Rhino shouted to James.

As James forced the VHS tape into his leather jacket, he stepped through an archway into a spacious and impeccably clean kitchen. The first woman he saw was Kam's wife, Alison. She was dressed to wait on tables in white pumps and a pale blue mini-dress. The other woman was Kerry Chang. Kerry was a sixteen-year-old CHERUB agent and James' current girlfriend, but he couldn't let on that he knew her and they avoided eye contact.

'You two bitches get out here,' James said forcefully.

Alison stepped out of the kitchen as James checked around to make sure nobody was hiding. As Kerry walked by, she gave James a tiny smile and silently mouthed, 'All good.'

'Aww, look at this little piece!' Dirty Dave leered, admiring Kerry as she emerged from the kitchen. 'Mag-bloody-nificent, though a boob job wouldn't go amiss.'

Kerry was self-conscious about her small chest and James felt like punching Dirty Dave's face in as the moustachioed biker sidled up to his girlfriend.

'So you're our little ching-chong Chinese translator?' Dave asked, placing one hand on Kerry's shoulder and sliding it down her back. 'You want my number baby? Me dig Asian girls.'

Dirty Dave made Kerry's stomach churn. He not only had cigar breath and BO, but she'd read police reports about girls who'd been abused inside his clubs, but were too scared to give evidence against a member of the Brigands. Kerry had the skills to flip Dirty Dave like a pancake, but she was on a mission and had to play her part by backing off and looking suitably repulsed.

'She's a bit young,' Rhino commented, as he looked

at Kam. 'You sure she's up to translating?'

'Why can't you do it?' Dirty Dave added.

Kam spoke furiously. 'Because I don't speak bloody Chinese. I grew up in Exeter, you understand? And my bloody mother was from the Philippines, not China.'

Kerry took a half step back as Dirty Dave's hand reached her bum. He jerked her back and made like he was about to kiss her. Fortunately the Führer stepped in before she had to push him away.

'Hands off, Dave,' the Führer warned. 'You've got enough pussy. We need this one for the meeting upstairs.'

Dirty Dave was put out by the rebuke. He couldn't take it out on the Führer, so he strode briskly across the floor and slugged Kam in the stomach.

'Nice shot!' Rhino laughed, as Kam doubled up in pain.

'Where's our money?' the Führer demanded. 'Little yellow bastard. I bet you've got a hundred grand under the bed, ain't you?'

'I'll pay as soon as I can,' Kam gasped.

'You see this boy here, Mr Kam?' the Führer shouted, pointing at James.

Kam nodded as he straightened up. James had no idea why the Führer was pointing at him.

'James is my up-and-comer,' the Führer explained, as he eyeballed Kam. 'He's young, but he's hard as nails and I'm putting him on your case. He'll be coming round here regular to collect your payments. If you don't pay, expect pain.'

'Why don't you leave him alone?' Alison shouted as

the Führer shoved her husband towards James.

'Show our man what you can do,' the Führer told James.

Two factors had enabled James to infiltrate the Führer's inner circle over the previous months: his advanced combat skills made him the ideal person to have on your side during a war between biker gangs, while his youth made the Führer think he was too young to be an undercover cop.

James had no problem when it came to thumping a member of another biker gang, but a hard-working civilian like Kam was entirely different.

'What shall I do?' James said awkwardly.

'Mess him up,' Dirty Dave urged. 'Your choice. Smash his fingers or something.'

James had to think fast. Most young bikers would do anything to impress the Führer. He didn't want to hurt Kam badly, but he couldn't back off without destroying his credibility.

'Can't break his fingers, can I?' James said casually, trying to buy time. 'Chef can't earn money with a broken hand.'

The solution came to James in a flash. He grabbed Kam around the back of the neck and gripped his right arm. Kam was stocky and almost as strong as James, but with no combat experience Kam had no idea how to defend himself as James expertly wrenched his arm behind his back.

From this position the easiest thing would have been for James to snap the arm, but instead he gripped Kam's bicep and violently twisted his upper arm, causing a crunching sound as his shoulder joint dislocated.

James had suffered this injury during combat training a couple of years earlier. A dislocated shoulder looked dramatic and was extremely painful, but was much less serious than a broken bone. A doctor could relocate Kam's joint. He'd be stiff for a few days, but fully recovered within a week.

Not that Kam appreciated James' consideration as he crumpled to the floor.

Alison charged towards James and screamed, as Rhino, Dirty Dave and the Führer laughed appreciatively. James didn't want to hurt Alison, so he intercepted her painted nails as she tried to claw his cheek and gave her a shove. She stumbled backwards into a table, tipping it up and sending condiments and a serviette dispenser crashing to the floor.

As Kerry rushed over to calm Alison down, James put on a show of menace, spitting on the floor in front of Kam's face and pounding his fist into his palm.

'I'd stay down if I was you,' James warned. 'And next time I see you, you'd better have our money or I'll be sticking your hand in the deep fryer.'

2. STRIFE

Kam sat on an upturned bucket in the Surf Club kitchen. He held a pack of ice cubes against his injured shoulder, while tears streamed out of his eyes. Dirty Dave was outside by the bar, while the other Brigands had gone upstairs.

'It's just dislocated,' Kerry whispered in Kam's ear. 'After the Brigands meeting we'll take you straight to hospital.'

Alison didn't like having Brigands in her restaurant, and was no fan of the attractive sixteen-year-old fussing over her husband either.

'What do *you* know about his arm?' Alison asked Kerry furiously. 'You don't look like any doctor I've ever met.'

Kerry quelled a mix of nerves and anger. 'I know first aid,' she said soothingly. 'I'm not an expert, but

I think it's a dislocated shoulder.'

Alison turned towards her husband and pointed an accusing finger at Kerry. 'Where do you know *her* from, anyway?'

'You'll understand when this is over,' Kam said, as he winced with pain. 'Stay calm and trust me.'

'Trust you?' Alison hissed. 'You've been shaken down and beaten up. You're in debt to the Brigands and now those lunatics are holding meetings upstairs in our restaurant. How can you expect me to stay calm? I told you to go to the police months ago.'

'Keep your voice down,' Kerry warned, as she pointed up at the ceiling. 'If they hear you making threats about the police they'll kill us.'

'Trust me, Alison,' Kam repeated firmly. 'On our daughters' lives, if this goes wrong I'll divorce you. You can have everything.'

'That's a bloody laugh,' Alison snorted. 'What do I get? The mortgage on the house? The debts on the restaurant? You're *so* stupid I can't even look at you.'

Alison stormed out of the kitchen into the dining area. Dirty Dave stood at the small bar, where he'd been helping himself to Wild Turkey.

'Looking nice,' Dave said, as he raised a shot glass. 'Sexy in that blue dress.'

Alison turned her nose up and gave Dave the finger before crashing at a table and burying her head.

'Must be on your period,' Dave sneered, then laughed at his own joke.

Back in the kitchen, Kerry looked accusingly at Kam.

'You should have told your wife what's going on,' she whispered.

Kam sighed. 'Alison wasn't supposed to be working today, but my waitress called in sick.'

'We've *got* to keep Alison calm,' Kerry said.

'I can't believe what that punk James did to my arm,' Kam groaned. 'I hope they lock the little prick up for a long time.'

Kerry smiled inwardly. Kam had agreed to cooperate with the police to stop the Brigands extorting money from his business. He'd been told that Kerry was a young looking nineteen-year-old police cadet, rather than a sixteen-year-old CHERUB agent, but he had no clue that James was also working undercover, or that it had been James' idea to set up a sting operation inside his restaurant.

Outside, two Chinese men stepped out of a big Lexus. The older of the two moved slowly towards the Surf Club entrance, in a stooped posture. As he rapped on the frosted glass above a sign that read *restaurant closed due to electrical fault*, his son opened the trunk of the limousine and lifted out two Louis Vuitton bags.

'Mr Xu,' the Führer said warmly, as he opened the door and shook the old man's hand. 'Come on upstairs. Traffic not too rough, I hope.'

Mr Xu barely spoke English and made no sound, except a sigh when he saw the two flights of stairs.

Xu's son Liam was completely different. He was in his mid-forties and looked like some kind of movie villain, with his tailored suit, dark glasses and a diamond-crusted

Breitling chronograph on his wrist.

'How's tricks?' Liam said as he put down his designer luggage.

The Führer had met Liam several times, but Liam's English skills didn't stretch beyond greetings and restaurant menus. As a substitute for words, the pair did a manly dance of back slapping, grins and laughter.

Kerry approached them and stood formally, feet together with her hands held neatly behind her back. 'I'm here to assist with any language difficulties,' she explained, before bowing slightly and repeating the phrase in fluent Mandarin.

As Kerry walked up behind Liam and the Führer, James came down from the top of the wooden stairs and offered an arm to a grateful Mr Xu. The Surf Club didn't do much business outside of summer season, so the top floor was closed for winter. The L-shaped dining-room had a desolate atmosphere, with chinks of light creeping around the edges of shuttered windows, plastic sheeting over the bar and chairs stacked on table tops.

Rhino sat in the centre of the room next to two tables pushed together. On top were five automatic weapons, clips and boxes of ammunition. The rest of the tables had been pushed back against the walls, creating a clear path to a metal target box at the end of the room.

Liam charged towards the guns, as James helped his frail father settle into a dining chair.

'State of the art,' Liam stated excitably, as Rhino offered him white gloves so that he didn't leave fingerprints.

'You've got a good eye,' Rhino complimented, watching Liam pick a small machine gun off the table. Kerry hurried to translate. 'That's the MP7 you asked for. Retractable stock and multiple sights, so you can use it three ways: assault rifle, machine gun, or even out in your hands as a pistol. The four-point-six-mil' round is small, but it's good up to fifty metres. It'll slip under the jacket of a big fellow like you, but packs enough punch to cut through thirty layers of Kevlar and kill a room filled with anyone you don't like the look of.'

'Beautiful,' Liam said admiringly. 'I know plenty of people who'll sell me a gun, but only you guys bring in this kind of fancy kit.'

'Nobody else has our contacts,' Rhino boasted. 'The Brigands over in the States were stealing weapons almost before they first mounted their Harleys. Most gun dealers have one connection. We have *dozens*, and we've been dealing with most of them for years.'

Liam turned the gun in his hand. 'What about the special ammunition? Can you get hold of it?'

The Führer took over Rhino's sales pitch. 'Would I sell you a gun you couldn't shoot?' he smiled. 'These are used by the German army. Now I'm not saying you can get bullets as easy as a standard nine-millimetre, but anything the German army uses can be had one way or another.'

'And we'll supply each gun with a thousand rounds,' Rhino added. 'Just to get you rolling.'

As Liam exuberantly pointed the machine gun towards the target and wished for a mirror so that he could see himself posing, Mr Xu leaned towards Kerry and whispered in her ear.

'Mr Xu asks about your recent difficulties with the police,' Kerry said stiltedly. 'He's interested to know how you continue to do business after all the arrests, and if it's safe for us to do so.'

'Parking tickets,' the Führer answered airily. 'I've been in this game for thirty-odd years. Bought, sold, ducked, dodged and I'm still here. I've seen people come and go, but the only trouble I've ever had is parking on a yellow line and doing fifty-five in a forty-mile-an-hour zone. And believe me, prison is a young man's game. I've got no intention of getting locked up at my time of life.'

The Führer sounded confident, but James knew it was a lie. Before the war with the Vengeful Bastards and the arrest of half his men, the Führer kept his weapons dealing at arm's length. Standing in a room with guns on the table, speaking to two men holding bags of cash was the kind of business he would have passed on to a subordinate. But gang wars aren't cheap and the Führer had to take risks.

'So we're all happy?' Rhino asked, as he slid an ammunition clip across the tabletop. 'Target box is set up if he wants to try shooting. The kid picked this place 'cos there's no neighbours within half a mile.'

Liam reached eagerly for the clip, but his father disapproved of his son's posturing with the weapon. The old man spoke brusquely in Mandarin and Kerry translated.

'Mr Xu says that the weapons are excellent. He wishes

to conclude business quickly and return to London. He trusts that the rest of the stock will be up to standard, and asks you to begin inspecting the money quickly to ensure that you're fully satisfied.'

Rhino leant towards one of the Louis Vuitton bags and unzipped it, but the Führer swatted him back.

'It's on trust,' the Führer said.

'Of course,' Liam smiled.

While working with the Führer, James had learnt that the level of trust between criminals became greater the higher up you went. The chances of street dealers ripping one another off in a small drug deal were high. But a half-million-pound weapons deal between the Führer and the Chinese crime syndicate for which the Xus worked went through on mutual trust, because the consequences of any dispute would be devastating for both sides.

'Here's a key, and a map showing the lock-up where the rest is being stored,' the Führer explained, as he handed Liam a padded envelope. 'Will you be wanting your luggage back?'

Mr Xu smiled as the Führer shook his hand.

'They're excellent fakes, a lucrative business of ours,' Kerry translated. 'Mr Xu says that your wife might like them, and that they're indistinguishable from the real thing.'

'Most kind,' the Führer smiled, as Kerry helped Mr Xu back to his feet.

James' heart accelerated as he saw the Xus heading for the top of the stairs. Everything was going to plan, but he was still edgy. The police had fitted the Surf Club with hidden cameras and microphones. They'd have the whole deal on tape, and the Führer's boast that he'd been dealing in guns for more than thirty years couldn't have been more perfect.

But now came the dodgy part. The police didn't want anyone to have a chance to destroy evidence or grab a weapon. They planned an overwhelming assault, moving in quickly with armed officers, arresting everyone in the meeting and grabbing the cash and the envelope with the location of the weapons.

None of the officers hiding outside knew that James was working undercover, so he could expect rough treatment. And with guns and ammunition lying around, the situation could turn into a shoot-out if the cops slipped up.

3. BLENDER

Kerry helped Mr Xu downstairs, with Liam and the Führer walking behind. The first sign of police was the clank of two aluminium ladders hitting the side of the building. Clad from head to toe in black, and sporting Kevlar helmets and sub machine guns, the firearms officers jumped on to the first-floor balcony and wrenched at wooden shutters covering the windows.

In theory, two shutters had been loosened in preparation for the raid, but it didn't work out. As the officers battled with sheets of chipboard screwed to the window frames, Rhino snatched an MP7 from the table top and slammed in a twenty-round clip.

At the same moment, another pair of officers hit the swinging front doors on the ground floor.

A shout went through a megaphone outside. 'This is the police, everybody down on the ground.'

'Fuzz,' the Führer shouted angrily, before acting with typical decisiveness.

He gave Mr Xu an almighty shove before doubling back up the stairs. Kerry held the old man's arm and couldn't free herself or get hold of the banister. She fell with Mr Xu, crashing helplessly down seven steps.

They would have hit the floor, but for the two firearms officers coming through the doors. One officer was supposed to aim her gun up at the men coming down the stairs, while her partner's job was to charge into the kitchen and deal with Dirty Dave. Instead, Kerry and Mr Xu clattered into the two officers, knocking them into an alcove containing a long dead payphone.

The hitch with the shutters and the bodies falling down the stairs only delayed the firearms officers by seconds, but it was the difference between a decisive take-down and complete chaos.

James was horrified. He didn't want to be near Rhino and the firearms officers when they started shooting and made a quick run before diving behind the upstairs bar. Daylight flooded the room as a shutter finally came loose.

Rhino hesitated with the MP7. Did he really want to take on two expert marksmen in full body armour? But there was no way he could drop the weapon before the officer started shooting at him.

So Rhino shot first. He was no marksman and he blew his twenty-round clip in two short bursts, hitting the floor, the ceiling and everything in between except for the police officer. The lucky officer kept his cool and took aim. Two shots punched through Rhino's chest, killing him instantly.

From behind the bar, James had no idea what was happening. He expected to hear either Rhino, or the sound of the firearms officers stepping in through the balcony, but all he picked up was the sound of metal cartridges rolling over the floor where an ammo box had been knocked off the table.

'I'm unarmed,' James shouted, as he bobbed up with his hands in a surrender gesture.

He saw Rhino. The force of the bullet had knocked the biker backwards out of his chair. Blood was beginning to pool on his chest, while his jaw had locked in its final shocked expression.

There was no sign of the firearms officers and James knew why: unlike soldiers, police officers are trained for absolute caution. They wouldn't enter any space without knowing exactly what they faced and had jumped down off the first-floor balcony at the first sign of confusion.

'This is the police,' a megaphone outside announced. 'You are totally surrounded by armed officers.'

'Screw you piggies,' the Führer shouted, as he charged around the top of the staircase. He saw Rhino, but didn't flinch. 'Poor bastard. You OK, James?'

'Had better days,' James said warily.

The Führer kept low as he raced between the tables. He grabbed one of the MP7s and picked up a couple of ammunition clips before pulling a wodge of twenty-pound notes from one of the money bags.

'What are you doing?' James gasped. 'Police

marksmen are deadly. They'll shoot you.'

Not that James minded the prospect of the Führer getting shot; he just didn't fancy being caught in the crossfire.

'Death or glory,' the Führer spat. 'Adolf never surrendered and I'm buggered if I'm going to. Now grab a gun and help me get the hell out of here.'

The Führer turned as he heard boots coming up the stairs. 'Stay back,' he shouted, before spraying bullets indiscriminately down the staircase. Then he looked at James. 'Why just stand there? Grab a gun or something.'

Despite years of training, James had lost concentration at a critical moment and squandered the opportunity to knock out the Führer before he'd grabbed a weapon.

'I'll stay here if it's all the same,' James spluttered. 'Take my chances, do a few years in young offenders.'

The Führer swung the MP7 towards him and smiled menacingly. 'I wasn't making a request,' he said. 'Fight or die, you little pussy.'

A chill went down James' back. It wasn't the first time he'd had a gun pointed at him, but he'd never felt so certain that the person holding the trigger would kill him at the slightest provocation, or maybe even for the fun of it.

There was more screaming downstairs as James rounded the bar. It sounded like Kerry. He stepped gingerly over the blood surrounding Rhino and reached towards the last MP7 lying on the table, but something hit the floorboards a couple of metres behind him and the room began filling with smoke.

'CS,' James shouted.

'Think you're clever?' the Führer screamed wildly, before firing the machine gun out of the window.

James' eyes and the back of his throat burned as the incapacitating gas swirled around him. It was like breathing hot soup, but the Führer managed to grab the collar of James' leather jacket and yank him towards the back of the room.

He opened a fire door with an almighty boot and James inhaled fresh sea air. They were on a wooden balcony overlooking the waves. In good weather it was Kam's most sought-after dining space, but today's wind was bitter and the sea crashed against jagged rocks stretching down more than thirty metres.

The cops had surrounded the three sides of the building that backed on to dry land. They'd assumed that nobody would be crazy enough to jump over the balcony on to the cliff face and the gas billowing out of the first-floor windows made it difficult for them to see what was going on.

'It's probably not as bad as it looks,' the Führer said, as he gave James a half smile. 'You jump first.'

*

Kerry fell awkwardly, turning her ankle as she slipped between the bodies of the two firearms officers and knocked her chin against the side of the payphone. For a horrible moment, the officers thought they were under attack.

'Don't shoot,' Kerry squealed.

In a state of confusion, one officer backed out of the building, while his colleague found her feet. She aimed her gun up the staircase as planned, but Liam already had his arms aloft in a gesture of surrender.

As Kerry untangled herself from Mr Xu she saw Dirty Dave holding Alison by the throat. He pulled back his arm and punched her in the face with his huge fist.

'You set this up, didn't you?' Dave roared, as he punched Alison again. 'This isn't over. We'll get you. We'll burn your daughters for this.'

Dave was powerfully built and Alison flopped like a doll as he threw her around. Kam stood in the kitchen doorway yelling at Dave to stop, but could barely move with his dislocated shoulder.

Kerry looked outside hoping to see a line of cops charging to the rescue. But the unarmed officers had retreated back in the road, awaiting an all-clear from the firearms team.

'Hey, dick wad,' Kerry shouted, as she stormed into the restaurant.

She ducked as she heard machine-gun fire upstairs. This was Rhino being shot dead, but Kerry had no way of knowing and was scared for James.

Dave laughed at Kerry's determined expression. Alison was barely conscious after the punches and Dave held her up by the hair, like a limp trophy.

'Were you in on this too?' Dave shouted. 'Come closer, see what you get.'

Kerry didn't need a second invitation. She hopped

forward and pivoted on the ball of her left foot. Before Dave knew it Kerry's right foot had swung through the air and smashed into his temple. As Alison slumped to the floor Dave crashed against the bar in a daze.

'Not such a big man now, eh?' Kerry screamed, and launched the hardest Karate chop of her life. It hit the base of Dave's skull with such force that his head snapped back, dislodging one of the vertebrae in his neck.

Dave now lay on the ground in between two bar stools, gasping desperately as he realised that he couldn't feel his legs. Meanwhile, the firearms officer had regained his composure and was coming back through the swinging doors.

'Hands where I can see 'em,' he shouted, approaching with his gun ready to shoot.

'We're all good here,' Kerry shouted as she raised her hands in the air.

'I can't move my legs,' Dirty Dave howled.

Kerry breathed deep as three unarmed officers rushed into the room to take control. Then she looked anxiously up at the ceiling, not knowing whether James was dead or alive.

*

James yelled as he made the three-metre drop from the first-floor balcony. He hit the rocks hard. The tough leather jacket saved his arms, but his jeans ripped and both legs bled as he rested on a natural ledge. It was another twenty-five metres down to the waves.

James had climbed steeper cliff faces during training, but this one was nasty. The sea spray created a perfect microclimate for the slimy green algae that covered most of the rock face. It was slippery as hell, and turned to an oily paste under your fingertips when you tried to get hold of anything.

Up above, the Führer tucked the compact machine gun into his belt and swung his legs over the side.

'Who wants to live forever?' he told himself, and jumped off the railing.

The results weren't good. James was seventeen, he had climbing experience and was in great shape. The Führer was almost sixty and carried a lot of excess weight. After bouncing painfully off the cliff face, he grabbed at a jutting rock, but couldn't hold on and gained momentum as he tilted sideways and plunged.

James dived to one side, narrowly avoiding the Führer's falling boot. He'd have bet his last pound that the Brigands' president was going all the way to the sea, but the Führer's leg hit a narrow gap between two rocks and became wedged.

The full weight of the Führer's falling body wrenched against the trapped leg. The thigh bone shattered as a jerking motion dragged the Führer's lower leg deeper into the gap between rocks. The Brigands National President patch on the Führer's jacket flapped in the wind as his body dangled upside down, supported by the smashed thigh bone speared through his jeans.

James had seen grisly injuries on missions and in training, but this looked the most painful by far.

'Please,' the Führer pleaded. 'Somebody help me out here!'

James considered climbing down, but the algae-covered rocks were lethal and his eyes and throat burned from the CS gas. Even if James made it there was no way he'd be able to lift the Führer. Instead, he studied the rocks, working out his best path back to the top.

After a precarious swing supported by a single finger hold, James had a simple climb of less than two metres before he reached a steeply sloping shelf. From there he crawled up to the road, troubled only by the last few plumes of CS.

'Please,' the Führer was bawling. 'Somebody get me.'

There were three cops waiting to arrest James when he reached the top of the cliff. He raised his badly grazed hands and they handcuffed him without any fuss. Hopefully John Jones would get him released before he reached the police station.

A smile from Kerry was some relief as he got frogmarched to a police van, but the cuts on his thighs made walking excruciating.

'How the hell do they get him up from there?' one of the cops asked as James walked past. 'Helicopter or something?'

'Let him stew,' an elderly officer standing close to the Führer's Mercedes replied cheerfully. 'It's about what he deserves.'

James thought of all the things the Führer had done – in particular the way he'd killed the entire family of fellow CHERUB agent Dante Welsh – and decided that he wouldn't mind if the rescue team took its time.

4. NURSE

It was dark by the time Kerry approached the automatic doors of South Devon Hospital. The stress of the mission was off. She was tired but cheerful as she crossed scuffed blue floor tiles and smiled at the nurse reading *heat* magazine behind a counter top.

'James Raven,' Kerry said. 'He's in room sixteen J.'

Sometimes you know you're going to get nowhere and the nurse's thin lips and raised eyebrow told Kerry this was one of them.

'Visiting hours is between three and six-thirty.'

'But I took *two* buses,' Kerry lied.

She was on a mission. Her expenses would be paid, so she'd taken a taxi.

'Rules are rules. Patients need to rest.'

'But I was told I could see James at any time because he's in a private room.'

'Who told you that? Whatever, they're wrong! Nothing after six-thirty.'

Kerry gritted her teeth. 'I checked the hospital website before leaving home.'

'Oh, the website,' the nurse said, as she cracked a mischievous smile. 'You can't take any notice of *that*. It hasn't been updated since we opened three years ago.'

Kerry groaned as she backed away from the counter. 'Thank you for being *so* helpful,' she said sourly.

The nurse was used to unhappy customers and took no notice. Outside, Kerry squatted against a bollard and pulled out her phone, intending to call James and tell him that she couldn't get in. But before dialling she got distracted by the ambulance rolling up at the accident and emergency unit.

A patient and her oxygen bottle were wheeled through another automatic door. Kerry glimpsed a crowded waiting room inside and a glance up the face of the building confirmed that accident and emergency was in a separate building to James' room, but a covered walkway linked the two.

Kerry hesitated. Her natural instinct was to be good, but she wanted to see James and she'd spent ages working out how to download the news footage of the Führer on to her mobile phone so he could watch it. And besides, this was hardly major crime. The worst that could happen was a security guard kicking her out.

The accident and emergency waiting room was as hot as hell. Druggies and drunks staggered around, sick kids screamed and there were old people who looked like they should be dead already. The only thing missing was the kid with the potty stuck on his head like you always see in movies.

Kerry's CHERUB training kicked in. The first rule of any break-in was to case the joint. She found a seat in between a kid with a badly gashed knee and an overweight man with breathing difficulties and started looking around.

There was a numbered ticket system for non-urgent patients, but the figures on the dot-matrix board never seemed to change. The receptionists were stressed out with forms and ringing telephones. The PA system paged doctors, requested cleaners, or ordered porters to take patients upstairs for X-rays.

Kerry had come to cheer James up, so she'd dressed skimpily in open sandals, short black skirt and a denim jacket over a tight white T-shirt. Trouble was, it also pleased the dude with barbed wire tattoos sitting opposite.

'If you stare any harder they'll pop out on stalks,' she said acidly, before standing up.

Amidst the chaos, Kerry decided to act confident and hope for the best. She cut purposefully around the main counter, walked between a row of cubicles with the sick and wounded inside, then peered down the corridor that led to the wards.

The door at the far end needed a swipe card, so she pretended to read a leaflet – *Are you entitled to a winter flu vaccination?* – until a porter strode towards it. She kept a few metres behind, then dived forward after he'd passed through the door, grabbing the handle an instant before it locked.

She held the door until the porter had disappeared, then passed through and turned in the opposite direction. For all her efforts, Kerry found herself standing by a lift, five metres from the receptionist she'd approached ten minutes earlier. Fortunately, the woman remained engrossed in a soap-star sex scandal and didn't glance up as Kerry waited for the lift to the fifth floor.

The rattly elevator was big enough for two beds. A helpful map on the back wall told Kerry where to go. The corridor into which Kerry emerged had large windows overlooking the car park and surrounding countryside.

James was in 16J, a single room, usually reserved for private patients. When he clambered off the cliff top, James was losing a lot of blood from the cuts on his legs and soon began feeling faint. He'd been ambulanced to hospital and admitted under his mission alias of James Raven. He was still under arrest and had a police guard sitting outside his room.

'I had a call from the boss to say you might be coming,' the young officer grinned, as his eyeballs walked up Kerry's legs. 'I'll have to pat you down before you can go in though.'

'Knock yourself out,' she said, before sighing and holding out her arms.

'Biker scum like that in there, doesn't deserve a pretty girlfriend like you,' the officer moaned, as Kerry let him look at the phone in her pocket and peek inside her little black handbag. 'These dudes might look cool on their bikes but . . .'

'Spare me the lecture, Granddad,' Kerry interrupted. 'Can I go in or not?'

'Can you believe this shit?' James called, as Kerry came into his room.

He angrily jangled a hand cuffed to the frame of his bed.

Kerry laughed, then shrugged. 'It was more important to get you stitched up before you lost too much blood. John said he's sorting out a helicopter to take you back to campus. You'll be James Adams again by tomorrow morning.'

'You know what the worst part is?' James asked. 'I can't go for a piss without that pig out there unlocking my cuffs. He falls asleep, so I was shouting for like half an hour. Then the pervert stands right in the room with me while I'm going. I hope I don't need to take a crap before they let me out of here.'

'Now there's a mental image I could have lived without,' Kerry grinned.

James wore a hospital pyjama top and boxers. As he sat up Kerry saw the dressings covering large cuts on his thighs.

'You look bloody amazing,' James said, sliding his free hand up Kerry's leg as she perched on the corner of the bed. 'You should dress like that more often.'

'Thought you'd like the slutty look,' Kerry smirked. 'But never again. Guys keep ogling me, it's creepy.'

'You should be flattered,' James said. He tried

pushing his hand up between Kerry's thighs but she clamped her legs together. 'Come on. I could *totally* nail you in that outfit.'

Kerry laughed as she pulled James' hand off and placed it on the bed. 'You're a randy goat. You'd want to nail me if I'd turned up wearing an Eskimo suit.'

'Yeah,' James grinned. 'But not as much.'

'Lauren said she texted you but you didn't reply,' Kerry said. 'Dante's well chuffed about the Führer. He says he owes you one.'

'Cops took my mobile when they arrested me,' James explained.

Kerry reached into her pocket. 'I've got something for you, actually.'

'Condoms?' James asked eagerly.

'No,' Kerry said, tutting and shaking her head. 'Do you *ever* think of anything apart from sex?'

'I do think about football a lot, but not when I haven't touched you all week.'

Kerry ignored James and played with the menus on her phone until she found her video clips. She cued up a news report and passed the handset to James.

The clip started with a helicopter shot of the Surf Club. As the camera zoomed in a voiceover explained how motorcycle gang leader Ralph Donnington had tried to escape from a police raid.

'The picture's all blocky,' James complained.

'I think you can get higher quality, but I was trying to do it quickly,' Kerry explained.

But once the zooming stopped, the picture improved

and James saw a close shot of the Führer dangling by his horribly fractured leg.

'Oh my god,' James gasped, as he looked away. 'That's *bloody* horrible. Was this local news, or national?'

'It started off on local,' Kerry said. 'But it got picked up. Now it's on the BBC, Sky, ITN, everywhere.'

The news reporter spoke through the phone's tinny loudspeaker. *'Donnington was left dangling for nearly three hours as an RAF helicopter and the local lifeboat crew tried to find a way of safely lifting the middle-aged biker clear of the rocks. Police also say that they've seized over four hundred thousand pounds in cash and a cache of automatic weapons from a lock-up garage near Bath.'*

James looked up from the screen as one of Kerry's sandals hit the floor beside his bed. She then swung her leg across James' waist and moved forward so that her long black hair dangled in his face.

'Knew you couldn't resist me for long,' James grinned.

'There's a cop right outside the door,' Kerry said. 'So you're only getting a snog.'

5. EWW

A week after the Surf Club shoot-out James Adams was back on campus. He had stitches in both thighs, so he walked awkwardly and had to wear shorts or loose-fitting tracksuit bottoms. It was a warm May Friday and most of the bedrooms off the sixth-floor corridor were at least partly open for ventilation.

Bruce Norris' door was an exception. James figured that his mate was getting dressed or something and charged in hoping to catch him out. A naked girl squealed as she hopped across the floor and wrapped herself in Bruce's duvet.

'Haven't you heard of knocking?' Bethany Parker shouted.

James' brain scrambled as he tried to process the scandal before his eyes. Bruce was sixteen but Bethany was two years younger. Bruce struggled with girls, so it was good to see him getting some action, but on the other hand he couldn't stand Bethany.

After considering everything through four seconds of awkward silence, James shuddered and uttered a single word.

'EWW!'

'What do you mean, EWW?' Bethany raged, as she threw one of Bruce's pillows at James' head. 'Haven't you heard of knocking? Piss off out of here.'

'Haven't you heard of turning the key?' James shouted back.

Bruce's head popped around the door of his bathroom. He looked guilty, but also grinned like a cat that just drank a big jug of cream.

'You brought that comparative faith answer sheet I asked for?' Bruce asked.

James raised a badly crumpled exercise book as Bruce stepped from his bathroom dressed in a green robe with a shamrock and *Ireland* written across the back.

'Tasteful dressing gown,' James grinned.

Bethany snorted with contempt. 'Bruce, why are you copying James' two-year-old religion homework? He's retarded, unless it's got maths in it.'

'We're both fairly useless,' Bruce explained. 'If I copy someone smart, people start asking questions. The trick is to always copy someone who's at least as rubbish at a subject as you are.'

At this point Bethany lost her temper. 'Bruce, I'm practically naked. Can't you *please* tell that moron to get the hell out of here?'

'Wouldn't want to outstay my welcome,' James smirked, but he was desperate to find a way to annoy Bethany some more before he left. 'She's probably crawling with lice.'

'Screw you,' Bethany stormed, charging towards James, holding the duvet up with one hand while shoving him back towards the door. The door slammed and James heard Bethany laying into Bruce as he walked down the corridor.

'Defend me then why don't you? Are you just gonna let that pig speak to me like that?'

As James headed back to his own room he worried that Bruce going out with a girl he couldn't stand would wreck their friendship. He sat on his bed and grabbed his laptop to check some Nikes he wanted to buy online, but Bruce arrived before he'd even found the bookmark with the web address.

He'd dressed hastily in baggy jeans and a black CHERUB shirt. James closed his laptop, raised an eyebrow and laughed.

'Cradle snatcher!' James blurted. 'She's barely out of nappies.'

'Seriously James,' Bruce said nervously. 'A few people know we're going out, but you can't tell anyone you caught Bethany in my room with no kit on.'

'You reckon?' James laughed. 'How'd you get off with her anyway? I can't even remember you talking to her before.'

'We did a mission after Christmas. Just a three-week thing infiltrating a bunch of drug dealers. But it was

January. We stayed in a flat together and the central heating was rubbish. Lots of cold nights and dark winter mornings. Hot cocoa, long cuddles. One thing led to another.'

'So what I saw wasn't just the result of heavy petting? You're actually shagging Bethany, right?'

'Yeah,' Bruce said defensively. 'But I wasn't even her first and you can't deny she's got a cracking little body.'

'Cracking little *fourteen-year-old* body,' James emphasised. 'You better be careful. If the staff find out you're having under-age sex, you'll both be kicked out.'

'That's why we're being so careful.'

'No, div head,' James grinned. 'Careful is when you *remember* to turn the key in the lock.'

'I was starting to feel like the last virgin on campus, anyway,' Bruce said. 'Everyone seemed to be at it except me. And she can't get pregnant; they've put her on the pill to regulate her heavy periods.'

James jammed his fingers in his ears and squeezed his eyes shut. 'Let's talk about something else.'

'Bethany says Lauren won't admit to anything, but one time she walked in on her and Rat and they'd both just showered and they both turned bright red when she asked what they'd been up to.'

'Shut up,' James begged. 'From now on, the only sex life I'm interested in is my own.'

'You were the one who told me to change the subject,' Bruce grinned.

'I meant away from girls entirely,' James said. 'And Bethany's just saying that about Lauren to justify herself.

You can believe me, Rat's not getting *any* action.'

'We're getting new carpet out in the hallway,' Bruce said. 'Carpet is always a good unsexy topic of conversation.'

'I remember the good old days when we were all innocent and someone getting a snog would be the scandal of the week,' James said, half seriously. 'When did we all grow up? Another five years and we'll be getting married and buying lawn mowers out of the Argos catalogue.'

'Hark at you, going on about the good old days,' Bruce said, smiling. 'But let's face it, we were smaller, dumber and useless with girls. I'm glad I'm growing up. Childhood sucks.'

James rubbed his palms down his face and yawned. 'Yeah, I'm turning into a nostalgic old fart. But look at the big hairy lout I've turned into. Do you remember the feeling when you first passed basic training? You felt like you were the bee's knees. Then you had your first mission. You didn't really have a clue what you were supposed to be doing, you were half scared to death, but everything was new and insanely exciting.'

Bruce nodded in agreement. 'I know what you mean. Like, when I see Kevin and Jake and those little kids running up and down the corridors. It seems like it's a million years since we were like that.'

'Oh well,' James said, 'at least we've got the wedding tomorrow.'

Bruce looked mystified. 'Well whoop-de-do. An hour sitting in the chapel listening to some vicar.'

'Yeah, well that bit's gonna be shit, obviously. But

loads of old faces are coming in. Kyle's gonna be here.'

'Dana said she might come,' Bruce grinned.

'Oh Christ, I hope not,' James grimaced. 'But campus is big enough to steer clear of her. I'm gonna eat like a pig, drink as much booze as I can get my hands on and party until I fall flat on my face.'

'You're a *classy* guy,' Bruce smiled.

6. CEREMONY

This was the first wedding in James' five years living on CHERUB campus. The only people allowed into campus were current or former staff and agents. Wives, girlfriends, university mates and work colleagues couldn't be invited, so campus weddings were almost always between two retired cherubs who now lived and worked on campus.

Chloe Blake was a twenty-eight-year-old mission controller who'd worked with James on a number of missions. Husband-to-be Isaac Cole was four years older. After leaving CHERUB, Isaac had a brief career as a professional rugby player before training as a child psychologist and returning to CHERUB to work as a carer in the junior block. His speciality was helping some of the youngest kids deal with their pasts and adapt to new lives on campus.

James had managed a few short visits to campus during the second phase of his Brigands mission, but he'd missed most of the pre-wedding build-up and hadn't appreciated what a huge deal it was for most of the girls on campus.

The ceremony wasn't until noon, but James was woken at seven by two recently qualified grey shirts. Dressed in night clothes, the girls were screaming in the hall outside his door and calling each other slags.

'What are you playing at?' James asked drowsily, as he stood in his doorway. 'People are trying to sleep, you know?'

'Bog off, Vanessa,' a short blond girl shouted, completely ignoring James. '*I* asked Kevin first.'

'Oh that's *such* a lie, Rhiannon,' an Asian girl shouted back. 'You hardly even spoke to Kevin until I did that art project with him. He's *my* friend. Just because you started trying to get off with him two nights ago.'

James was half asleep, but worked out that the girls were fighting over Kevin Sumner, who lived in the room directly across the hall.

'Girls, girls,' James said firmly, but they ignored him again.

'Take Ronan, he fancies you.'

'Ronan's gross,' Vanessa shouted. '*You* take him.'

'I'll knock and ask Kevin who he wants to go with,' Rhiannon yelled. 'I bet a million pounds that it's not you and your stupid hamster cheeks.'

'Hamster cheeks! You can talk, you flat-faced tramp.'

Vanessa lunged forward to knock on Kevin's door,

but Rhiannon shoved her back. At this point, normal twelve-year-old girls might have had a bit of a cat fight, but these were qualified CHERUB agents so what followed was a series of rapid-fire martial arts moves. The bout ended with Vanessa holding Rhiannon in a headlock, while Rhiannon was painfully bending back Vanessa's fingers.

'Pack it in,' James shouted. 'Now.'

Sick of being ignored, James barged forward, shoving both girls hard against Kevin's door. He then grabbed Vanessa's arm. After freeing Rhiannon from the headlock he ripped the girls apart and held them at arm's length. By this time, there were heads poking from doors all along the corridor, including Kerry two doors down.

'James, leave those girls alone,' Kerry shouted.

'Me!' James gasped. 'I'm just trying to stop them from killing each other.'

The prize the girls sought was also awake by this stage. Kevin stood in his doorway looking mystified. He didn't look much of a catch, dressed in one sock, a pair of Spiderman pyjama bottoms that were way too small and a ripped grey CHERUB T-shirt with half of last night's dinner down it.

'Kevin, tell Vanessa that you said you're going to the wedding with me,' Rhiannon demanded.

'Did I?' Kevin asked. 'Oh, well I guess I did.'

'Bull,' Vanessa shouted. 'You said in art class that you were going with me.'

Kevin looked confused. 'You asked if I was going to

the wedding. So I said, yeah if you wanted me to.'

Both girls looked flabbergasted. 'But you can't go with both of us!' Vanessa said.

Kevin scratched his neck. 'I just thought you were asking if I was gonna be there. I thought we were, but actually, most of us lads reckon it'll be boring. I'll probably go to the pool with Jake and them, and swing by for the flash meal and the party this evening.'

'But Siobhan said Jake's going to the wedding with her,' Vanessa said.

Kevin laughed. 'Yeah, Jake's really gonna sit through a wedding with *Siobhan*. He can't stand her. I'd bet my last quid he only said that to wind her up. It was Jake's idea that we all went to the swimming pool while everyone else was at the wedding.'

Vanessa and Rhiannon exchanged shocked glances. 'So none of you lot are going?'

Kevin managed to laugh. 'Not if we can help it. Who wants to dress up and sit through some boring church service?'

There was a sharp crack as Rhiannon slapped Kevin across the cheek.

'What was that for?' Kevin shouted indignantly.

He didn't get an answer, but he did get an identical slap from Vanessa.

'You're a total pig,' Vanessa hissed. 'And you'd better warn Jake to be on the lookout. When Siobhan hears that he's going swimming she's gonna beat the crap out of him.'

'Let's ditch this immature loser,' Rhiannon told Vanessa.

As the two girls walked down the corridor, apparently on the best of terms, Kevin rubbed the red welt on his cheek and looked up at James.

'Have you got any idea what just happened?' Kevin asked.

'Women are insane,' James explained. 'Don't even *try* to comprehend what's going on in their heads.'

*

Now that James was seventeen he had a real driver's licence and was allowed to use the campus pool cars when he wanted to go out. A condition of using the cars was that James had to take on some duties shuttling younger cherubs around when they wanted to go out bowling, or to the shops or whatever.

This was usually a drag, but he was happy to join a mini convoy of Volkswagen people carriers making the short ride out to the station to pick up guests arriving for the wedding. James' first pickup was a bunch of retired CHERUB agents from Isaac and Chloe's day and he didn't know any of them. The train an hour later brought another two dozen wedding guests, including some of James' old friends.

He knew that his best friend Kyle was on the train, but was astonished when he saw the long blond hair and tanned body of Amy Collins. Amy had been James' mentor when he'd first arrived on CHERUB campus and he hadn't seen her for nearly three years.

'Holy shit!' James shouted, ignoring Kyle and pulling Amy into a huge hug. Amy's older brother John stepped out behind her.

'Quite the hunk!' Amy giggled, as she stepped back and looked James up and down. 'Bit different from the chubby little brat that arrived on campus five years ago. I'd go as far as to say you're a catch, but the real question is, are you man enough to take me down?'

Amy launched a fairly genteel Karate kick. James dodged it easily enough, but in doing so clattered into a plastic dustbin and skinned his elbow. Kyle, Amy and John cracked up laughing as James grabbed his wound.

'Bastard arm,' he shouted. 'Jesus.'

'Sluggish response, low situational awareness,' Amy teased. 'Looks like you're still my bitch.'

'I didn't even know you were in the country,' James said, smiling through gritted teeth.

Amy's brother John explained. 'Chloe Blake and I go back a long way. We did basic training and a couple of missions together. We've always kept in touch and it seemed like a good excuse to get on an aeroplane.'

'And how's your diving-school business going?' James asked, as they began walking towards the car park.

'So-so,' John said, with a shrug. 'I get lots of work with the Japanese because I speak the language, but there's brutal competition. It's hard to make it pay.'

'I'm working in Brisbane now I've finished university,' Amy said. 'I mostly do translation and close protection work.'

'What kind of thing?' James asked.

'Oh all sorts,' Amy explained. 'Visiting business people. Pop stars doing Brisbane concerts, sports teams. It's not very exciting but plenty of people will pay lots of money to have a young female bodyguard.'

'Have either of you ever thought of coming back to work on campus?' Kyle asked.

'Too damned cold,' Amy said, rubbing her arms and shivering at the prospect. 'I love the hot weather. We've got a nice place by the beach, good clubs and restaurants nearby, surfing on the weekend. I can't see myself trudging through the mud on campus in the middle of January.'

'I'm thinking of going somewhere sunny when I leave campus,' James said. 'With my maths, I might be able to get a scholarship to a university in the States. California or Florida maybe.'

'Where does that leave Kerry?' Kyle asked.

James shrugged awkwardly. 'It's tricky. Kerry's a year younger than me. But American university courses are modular, so I can do one year, then drop out for a year and go travelling with Kerry.'

'And Kerry likes the idea of going to America?' Amy asked.

James nodded.

'If they're still together,' Kyle smirked. 'How many break-ups is it now? Five or six?'

James raised his hands. '*Don't* talk like that! It's different this time. We're more mature. We've both had other partners and stuff. But we've come full circle and realised we're best off with each other.'

By this time they'd reached the station car park. James blipped the key fob to open the doors of the big Volkswagen and John loaded bags in the back. Two more people carriers, plus a Mercedes 4×4 were also taking wedding guests back to campus.

'I'm really looking forward to this,' Amy said enthusiastically. 'Seeing all the old faces. Are there any new buildings or other changes on campus?'

'There's a library which is pretty cool,' James said. 'And they've refurbished the old gym.'

'And they've finally got everything working properly in the mission control building,' Kyle said.

'Nah,' James smirked. 'The iris recognition system's all gone wrong again and the roof leaks like a bugger.'

James fired up the engine and dropped the handbrake, but as he started backing out of the parking bay a man tapped urgently on the window beside him.

'Room for one more?' Norman Large grinned.

The disgraced training instructor appeared to have lost a lot of hair, but had compensated by growing his moustache into an enormous object that resembled a squirrel's tail.

'Ahh shit,' Kyle said. 'Who invited that wanker?'

James was tempted to drive off, but he'd been charged with picking up guests from the station and might have his driving privileges revoked if he mucked around.

Nobody liked Large and this fact hung in the air like a dog fart as James started the twenty-minute drive towards campus.

It was Kyle who finally broke the silence. 'So what does a retired CHERUB instructor do with himself?'

'Security work,' Mr Large revealed.

'Right,' Amy smiled. 'I do something similar myself

out in Brisbane. What is it, politicians, celebs, that sort of thing?'

'Asda,' Large said sheepishly. 'It's not glamorous, but it's easy work, regular hours.'

James couldn't help laughing. 'And woe betide any kid pilfering sweeties from your branch.'

7. CLOTHES

By 11.25 excitement had turned to hysteria. James stood by his bedroom window dressed in black trainers, black tracksuit bottoms and a white polo shirt. He looked down at the girls milling about on the path between the chapel and the main building. It was a fine day and they all wore their sparkliest shoes and party dresses, a stark contrast with the combat trousers and boots girls usually wore around campus.

Kerry's room was jammed with barefoot girls who'd been *almost* ready for the best part of an hour: Gabrielle, Amy, Lauren, Bethany and at least three others. Deodorant hung in the air and there was a racket coming out of the bathroom as girls did their make-up in the mirror. Rat, Bruce, Andy Lagan and Dante Welsh all squatted on Kerry's sofa, looking rather smart in jackets and ties.

'Ready when you are, Kerry,' James said, as he leaned into the room.

Female jaws dropped as Kerry gasped. 'James, you're *not* going dressed like that! Where's your suit?'

James pointed at his thighs. 'I've still got stitches in my legs from when I fell down that cliff. The only things I can put on without killing myself are baggy shorts or extra large trackies.'

'Well at *least* put on a proper jacket and tie,' Lauren suggested.

'I tried but it makes me look like a mental patient,' James said. 'Sportswear and formal don't mix.'

'You could have bought some looser trousers when we went shopping,' Kerry said, before sighing noisily.

James tutted. 'Unlike some people I haven't been planning my wedding outfit for three months and I'm buggered if I'm spending money on something I'll only wear once. The dress suits you by the way. Nobody's even going to look at me when you're so stunning.'

Disarmed by the compliment, Kerry broke into a smile. 'I suppose you're colour co-ordinated, at least.'

Rat tugged at the tie around his neck. 'Well if James doesn't have to wear one . . .'

Lauren killed Rat's mutiny with a swift cuff around the back of the head. 'Oh yes you will wear it,' she growled. 'If I've got to wear this stupid dress all day, you can wear a collar and tie.'

'You look really nice, Lauren,' Amy assured her.

Lauren perched a hat on her head as she slid her feet into a pair of ballet pumps. 'And as for this bloody thing . . .'

'It looks like you've got the wedding cake on your head,' James grinned.

A couple of the boys laughed, but Lauren looked upset and turned towards Bethany.

'I told you this hat didn't suit me. That's it. I'm not wearing it.'

Bethany gave James the evil eye. 'Lauren, it looks great. I mean, are you really going to take fashion tips from a boy who's going to a wedding wearing Nikes and the bottom half of a Primark tracksuit?'

'If we want decent seats we've got to move now,' Gabrielle said, as she glanced at her watch.

There was a mini panic as girls searched the room for hats and Kerry accidentally put on one of Bethany's shoes. Three more girls emerged from Kerry's bathroom and James reckoned that the only way so many could have fitted in there was if some had been standing in the bathtub.

'Just going for a quick piss,' Bruce said as he headed into Kerry's bathroom.

A scream went up as he stepped in and saw a girl sitting on the toilet with her dress gathered up and her knickers around her ankles.

'Get out!' she yelled.

Bruce turned bright red as he backed out and wished he could have come up with a smart line to diffuse his embarrassment.

Out in the corridor James smiled as Kyle emerged from his old room. He was immaculately dressed in a tight fitting blue suit, with flared trousers, a matching trilby hat, a wooden cane and a pair of huge Elvis-style aviator sunglasses.

'Kyle that is so *awesome*,' Kerry grinned, grabbing him by the arm. 'James can stay at the back, I'm strutting my funky stuff with you.'

'This is style,' Gabrielle said, pointing accusingly at the boys as she took Kyle's other arm. 'This is how you should *all* look.'

Dante shook his head and tutted as he walked down the corridor alongside James. 'I know you said Kyle's your mate,' he said cautiously. 'But *that* is the gayest outfit I've ever seen.'

Dante had gone from basic training on to one of the longest missions in CHERUB history, so he barely knew Kyle.

'Kyle *is* gay,' James explained. 'You think I'd let him walk off with my girl on his arm if he was straight?'

Kerry saw the crowd waiting for the next lift and decided to slip her heels off and walk the six floors down to the ground floor. The whole group followed and joined a mass of bodies leaving through the rear of the main building and heading along the gravel path towards the chapel.

On a normal day James would have known every face on campus, but weddings were always an excuse for a campus reunion and today there were three hundred retired CHERUB agents and former staff on the grounds.

James shouted at Kerry, as she walked five metres ahead of him. 'Oi darling, do you think *we'll* get married on campus some day?'

Kerry snorted. 'Who says I'm marrying you?'

There were a few laughs. James looked down and noticed the black scorch marks where his hand-built racing buggy had crashed and burned out eighteen months earlier. Two middle-aged women stood on the grass pointing towards the upper floors of the main building.

'I remember it all being built,' one woman said. 'That was my room at the end of the sixth floor. And in those days all the boys were up on the seventh and the top floor was mission preparation.'

More nostalgia, James thought to himself as he looked across at Amy. She was twenty-one and looked stunning in her strapless dress. But she'd lost the mystique she'd held six years earlier, when James was a new recruit and Amy seemed like an impossibly sophisticated and experienced black shirt.

These days Amy worked as a bodyguard, Kyle was a university student with a part-time job in a nightclub, while fearsome instructor Norman Large guarded frozen chickens in Asda. The prospect of life after CHERUB had never seemed duller and James felt depressed as he approached the rows of white plastic chairs on the lawn in front of the chapel.

A hundred and fifty specially selected guests would be crammed inside the small campus chapel. The rest would sit outside and watch the ceremony on a large video screen. If it had been raining, the chairs and screen would have been in the hall in the main building.

Kerry left an empty seat for James, but as he shuffled between the rows he was hailed by Meryl Spencer. His former handler had just been promoted to Chief Handler, which meant she was now in charge of campus life for every qualified CHERUB agent.

'Whatever it is, I'm innocent,' James grinned, as he stepped up to Meryl in the main aisle between the chairs.

'Cuts healing OK?' Meryl asked.

James nodded. 'Stitches out Monday. Hopefully I'll be able to wear some decent clothes after that.'

'You get on well with Joshua Asker and some of the other little red shirts, don't you?'

'Yeah. I've helped out with their swimming lessons and stuff.'

'Great,' Meryl smiled. 'We've got a couple of carers up the back who've worked with Isaac for a long time. They really deserve to be inside the chapel, but they're stuck out back keeping an eye on the little red-shirt boys. Would you mind sitting back and keeping an eye out so they can go inside?'

'Course,' James nodded. 'Just the boys?'

'Every girl aged between three and eight is a bridesmaid,' Meryl explained. 'All thirteen of them.'

The five little boys were fidgety so they'd deliberately been placed at the back. They looked cute dressed in matching shoes and jackets, though the littlest one was barely three and he'd already thrown off his tie and shoes.

Five-year-old Joshua Asker sidled up to James with a huge grin on his face.

'Can we do swimming again now you're back?' he asked eagerly.

James raised one eyebrow and shook his head. 'You're too smelly.'

'You're smelly,' Joshua shouted back noisily, before erupting with laughter and flicking James' arm.

A few people looked around, including Joshua's mum, Zara. As CHERUB Chairwoman, she'd be giving away the bride.

'*Behave*, Joshua,' Zara said firmly.

Joshua pointed at James. 'He called *me* smelly first.'

As Zara shushed Joshua a white Rolls-Royce emerged into the avenue of trees that led up toward the chapel. A few warm-up blasts from the organist came through the loudspeakers and everyone sitting outside swivelled around as the car stopped.

'I can't see,' one of the little boys moaned, as Chloe Blake stepped out of the car. The army of little bridesmaids gathered behind her in pale lemon dresses. Joshua put his lips against James' arm and puffed his cheeks out to blow a big raspberry.

'I wouldn't,' James warned. 'Your mum will *kill* you.'

Joshua raised his eyebrows thoughtfully before taking his lips away from James and sitting back in his chair. The giant video screen came to life, showing Isaac standing nervously at the altar. Chloe was a couple of metres behind James. She had too much make-up on and looked like she wasn't completely sure of what she was about to do.

'Please be standing for the arrival of the bride,' the

vicar announced from inside.

Chloe and Zara linked arms and paced slowly between the lines of plastic chairs to the sound of *Here Comes the Bride*.

8. BOPPING

James hadn't been looking forward to the wedding, but after the tedium of the ceremony he'd started enjoying himself. He'd stood in the afternoon sun playing plastic-bat-and-sponge-ball cricket with the little kids and a few mates while the wedding photos were taken, then he and Kerry had escorted seven retired agents on a tour of campus' newer facilities.

Most of the tour group were in their thirties or forties. James and Kerry swapped mission stories and campus anecdotes with these old-timers. James took a healthy interest in what they'd all done after leaving campus. Everyone seemed to agree that adjustment to ordinary life after the specialness of being a CHERUB agent was difficult. One bearded man even confessed that he'd found university boring, tried to compensate by using cocaine and narrowly avoided prison after getting caught up in a drug deal.

But the overall picture was encouraging. Even accounting for the party atmosphere, the group seemed like a happy bunch, with families and good jobs. Even the guy who'd narrowly avoided prison pulled out his wallet and showed James a photo of his three daughters, five cats and a hot Danish wife.

'You don't get into CHERUB unless you're in the top one or two per cent,' the bearded guy explained. 'The education on campus is outstanding, they'll make sure you get a top university place and the campus welfare department will support you emotionally and financially after you leave. So there's no need to look so anxious.'

James grimaced. 'Is it that obvious I'm worried about leaving?'

'It's etched in every line on your face,' the man smiled. 'But you need to think about all the other kids your age who haven't got half the advantages you've got.'

Once the tour was over, James and Kerry put their arms around each other's backs and took a slow stroll back towards the main building.

'If I go to university in America, will you *definitely* come too?' James asked.

Kerry sounded a little terse. 'I'll definitely think about it. But . . .'

'But what? You said you liked the idea of America.'

'Why don't we take it slowly?' Kerry asked. 'We've not been back together all that long and you've been on a mission for most of that time.'

'Kerry, I've got to start making decisions. I really fancy

living in California. The intelligence service has a long-term deal with quite a few countries. My post CHERUB identity can be British, Australian, American, Canadian. Pretty much anything I like as long as I can speak the language.'

'Make *your* decisions,' Kerry said softly. 'I don't really know what I want to do when I leave, so do what you think is best for yourself. If we're still together when I leave CHERUB next summer, I'm sure we'll find a way of working everything out.'

'I guess,' James said, before sighing sadly. 'Kerry Chang, always the sensible one . . .'

*

'I love you baybeeee!' Kerry sang boisterously as she danced frantically in the main hall.

It was past midnight and the room was heaving. Little kids who'd spent the night chasing around were crashed out along the side walls. Older kids were still going strong, with an epic boy vs. girl water fight, while the teenagers and adults sat around the tables talking, or bopped to cheesy music on the dance floor.

'James, get up!' Kerry demanded, and grabbed his wrist.

James and everyone else around the table laughed as Kerry stumbled backwards and lost her footing in a puddle of spilled booze.

'You've had too much champagne,' James smiled, as he pointed at Amy. 'Give us a minute to get my breath. I've just been dancing with her.'

Kerry put her hands on her hips. 'Oh you can dance

with her, but not me?' she said jokingly. 'OK, who wants to dance with me then? Shak, you up for it?'

But Shak was at the far side of the table with his arm around Gabrielle and didn't even look around.

'Ignore me then ya bastard!' Kerry shouted, as she gave Shak the finger. 'Kyle, how about you? You're a good dancer.'

'Why don't you sit down for a minute,' James suggested. 'Drink some water and catch your breath. You're gonna have one hell of a hangover in the morning.'

'BLAGH!' Kerry hiccupped. 'I'm not drunk. Kyle, get your arse out of that chair.'

Kyle gave James a sort of *I suppose I'd better* look before letting Kerry drag him on to the dance floor as *Dancing Queen* by Abba started playing.

'That's my song!' Gabrielle shouted, stepping over James with her insect thin legs.

She dragged the much chubbier Shakeel behind and he knocked into the table spilling several drinks. At the same moment, Bethany was coming across from the table where she'd been sitting with Lauren and their crowd and grabbed Bruce.

'Gotta circulate,' Amy said, and she stood up, leaving James on his own.

James didn't mind at first. He drank half a bottle of water and laughed as he saw Jake Parker, Kevin Sumner and a couple of their mates sneaking past on the grass outside armed with water-filled balloons. But after a few minutes he started feeling lonely and stood up, looking for a conversation.

Lauren was sitting with Rat a few tables along, but James didn't have anything to say to them. He thought about sitting down again, but his shirt was drenched with sweat so he decided to head out and grab some fresh air.

As he edged around the outside of the dance floor he walked straight into his ex-girlfriend Dana Smith. She wore ripped jeans and a giant baggy smock, and sat with a couple of shaggy-haired blokes, who James vaguely remembered from his early days on campus.

'Look who it ain't!' Dana said.

James put on a false smile. 'Hey . . . Good to catch up. How's art college?'

'All right,' Dana replied. She closed in on James and whispered in his ear. 'Fancy a roll in the hay for old times' sake? I've got some great spliff in my bag.'

'Love to,' James said. 'But Kerry might kill me, and err . . . I've got to meet someone outside.'

James shuddered as he hurried away from Dana. He could hardly believe that he'd gone out with her for eleven months and been in love with her for at least three of them. Dana was quite butch, she didn't get on with any of James' mates and she always wore battered old Converse trainers that made her feet stink. On the other hand, she had boobs like basketballs and he missed them dearly.

James stepped out through the fire exit into the night air. He felt slightly drunk as he moved aimlessly between the smokers gathered around the door, then almost tripped over Dante, who was making out with some random younger girl who appeared to be wearing net curtain.

'Get a room you dirty bugger,' James laughed, and swiped the unopened Budweiser can on the grass besides Dante. 'You're too young for this. I'm confiscating it.'

Dante looked up as James started drinking the beer. His eyes flashed with anger, but he was more interested in getting his hands up a party dress than arguing with James.

It was spring and the wind had a bite that chilled the sweat on James' back. He kept walking aimlessly into the night until he could barely hear the pounding music inside the hall. Some girls screamed as Kevin and Jake launched their water-balloon ambush and two red shirts protested that they weren't tired as they got marched off to bed by one of the carers.

James squatted down on a tree stump and tipped his head back to drink some of the tepid beer. He'd barely moved ten minutes later when he spotted Kyle helping Kerry out through the fire door. She'd abandoned her heels, but was wobbly even on bare feet.

'You OK?' James asked, jogging across the grass towards them.

'She said she feels sick,' Kyle explained, as Kerry hung off his arm.

'It's all the rich food,' Kerry slurred.

James smiled. 'Four glasses of champagne and the illicit supply of Bacardi Breezers in the girls' bathroom can't have helped.'

'I think we'd better take you up to your room,' Kyle said gently.

'I'm just dehydrated,' Kerry said, as she shook her head. 'Just give me a . . . oh god . . .'

James jumped back as Kerry spewed up in the grass between her feet. Kyle was closer and looked horrified as the puke spattered his shoes.

'Sorry,' Kerry said, gasping tearfully.

As Kyle dashed inside to grab some water for Kerry to wash out her mouth, she crashed into James' arms and started to sob.

'You'll be OK,' James said soothingly, and gently rubbed Kerry's back. 'Better out than in, eh?'

After she'd rinsed her mouth, James suggested to Kerry that she go back to her room. She looked sad at the idea of leaving the party, but she was pale and shivery.

'You go ahead,' James told Kyle. 'Open the doors and keep lookout for any staff. She'll get punishment laps if they see her this drunk.'

'It's something I ate,' Kerry protested, as James grabbed her around the waist and threw her over his shoulder.

'Tell me if you feel sick again,' James said, as he started to walk. 'Don't you *dare* spew on me.'

Kerry found this prospect mildly amusing. 'I love your arms,' she sang, as James carried her the long way around the outside of the main building. 'Big manly arms, carrying little Kerry.'

Kyle opened the front doors into the main building

and called the lift. James waited outside, keeping Kerry out of sight until the lift arrived and Kyle gave the all-clear. Kerry's weight wouldn't normally have been a problem, but James' injured thighs strained as he got her into the lift, so he flopped her down against the mirrored back wall.

'I owe you Jamesey,' Kerry slurred dopily. 'And you Kyle. I'll do you both a special favour some day.'

As the lift cruised upwards, Kerry hiccupped and brought more sick up into her mouth. It wasn't much, but in the confined space it made James and Kyle heave and they gasped with relief when they burst into the sixth-floor corridor and breathed clear air.

Kerry seemed less shaky, so rather than letting James pick her up, she staggered along the hallway using the walls for support. When Kerry reached her room James expected her to go inside.

'Hey, you missed your door,' James warned.

'I don't want to be sick on my carpet,' Kerry said, and she opened James' door.

Kyle grinned as James shook his head in disgust.

'But it's OK to be sick on mine I take it?' James growled. He followed Kerry into his room and flipped on the light.

'Where's my shoes?' Kerry said, as she crashed backwards on to James' bed.

'Someone will bring them up,' James said. 'If not we'll find 'em in the morning.'

'Everything's spinning,' Kerry moaned as she tried to sit up. 'I'll use your shower. It'll sober me up.'

'I thought it was the food,' Kyle noted sarcastically, while James gave Kerry an arm-up.

James turned his shower on full blast, then unzipped the back of Kerry's dress. Usually James would have enjoyed this, but Kerry was stumbling around and humming to herself. Her sweat smelled like booze and her breath like puke.

Still wearing her bra and knickers, Kerry stepped into James' bathtub. She sat herself down under the jet of cool water. One hand hung over the side of the tub, while she used the other to inspect the soles of her feet.

'Muddy toes!' Kerry said whimsically, as she tipped her head back and let the shower nozzle flood her mouth. Then she spat a jet of water at James' crotch and laughed. 'Gotcha.'

'Oh that's nice,' James said. He reached up and flipped the temperature control around to full-on cold.

'Bastard,' Kerry squealed, as she flipped over on to her belly and turned the nozzle back to warm.

'Give us a shout if you want something,' James said, backing out.

Kyle was sitting on James' bed, wiping his puke-spattered shoes with a clump of tissues.

'Turning into a bit of a wild one,' Kyle said. He looked up at James. 'You look like you've pissed yourself.'

'Girls can't take their drink,' James sighed. 'Lauren's exactly the same. Three beers and she's running round nude trying to snog street furniture.'

As the boys spoke, Kerry said something from the bathroom.

'What?' James asked irritably, as he leaned through the doorway.

'You're a good boyfriend James,' Kerry said, giving James a thumbs-up before doing a great big sob. 'I don't give you enough credit, you know?'

'Cheers,' James said half-heartedly. 'All part of the service.'

'I see you've got a mission briefing,' Kyle noted, as he pointed to a folder on James' desk. 'I thought you were done.'

James shook his head dismissively. 'It's barely a mission: two days of babysitting, week after next. Some Malaysian defence minister is coming over to sign a massive deal for British armoured vehicles and jet engines and stuff. Me, Kevin and Lauren have to chaperone his kids. You know, keep them entertained and show 'em the sights, while making sure that there's no human rights protestors trying to blow them up or abduct them.'

Kyle looked far more interested than he ought to have been. 'Malaysian defence minister? You're talking about Tan Abdullah, right?'

James raised one eyebrow. 'How the hell could you know that? Did you peek while I was in the bathroom?'

'Me and Mr Abdullah have some history,' Kyle said mysteriously. 'You mind if I take a look at your mission briefing?'

James looked baffled and shrugged. 'Knock yourself out mate.'

Four years earlier

December 2004–March 2005

9. BEACH

Kyle Blueman had just turned fifteen and looked relaxed as he lay in the narrow hull of an open motorboat, with his head resting on his rucksack. It was early morning, but the sun was baking. The sky was clear and the sea still like a pond.

Only the boat's outboard motors disturbed the peace, as it carved through the water close to the dense forest and unspoiled beaches of Langkawi island, fifteen kilometres from the Malaysian mainland. Kyle felt grotty after thirteen hours inside a 747 and couldn't wait for a shower and clean clothes.

'How long now?' he asked, as he looked up at Aizat, the boat's young captain.

'Fifteen, twenty minutes,' the Malaysian answered.

Kyle guessed that Aizat was his own age, maybe a little older. With ragged shorts, shoulder-length hair and a stained Jimi Hendrix T-shirt, Aizat moved about with total confidence, oblivious to the motion of the boat as he placed his feet amidst the benches, ropes, fuel cans and fishing gear without ever having to look down.

'Is that your mobile?' Aizat asked.

Kyle grabbed the side of the boat and leaned forward, unzipping a Nokia from a waterproof jacket balled up near his feet.

'Hello,' Kyle said, but immediately regretted not checking the caller display before answering.

'You bloody traitor,' Lauren Adams roared furiously. 'I thought we were a team.'

Lauren was ten years old and had been given a hellish ditch-digging punishment for hitting instructor Norman Large with a spade. Kyle had been serving an identical punishment for smoking marijuana on his previous mission.

'Lauren, listen,' Kyle said soothingly.

But she wouldn't let him get a word in. 'I can't believe you sneaked off. Now I'm gonna be stuck out there, up to my waist in that stinking filth with nobody even to talk to all day.'

Kyle felt bad. 'Look Lauren,' he explained. 'It was Christmas morning. I was going upstairs after we'd opened our presents and Meryl Spencer was asking for someone to urgently fly out to Malaysia because one of the training instructors had been injured. Nobody else would go, because it was Christmas, but I snaffled it because it got me out of my last two weeks' ditch digging.'

Lauren tutted. 'Well bully for you, *mate*.'

Lauren made the word *mate* sound like an accusation and Kyle felt guilty.

'I should have told you, Lauren. But I literally had to pack a bag, get in a car and get driven to Heathrow. I knew you'd be upset and I didn't want to ruin your Christmas day, but I bet you would have done the same if the opportunity to get out of your punishment came up.'

'Maybe,' Lauren sighed. 'But I would have at least spoken to you.'

'I know we had some laughs, but your punishment won't last any longer because I'm not there.'

'I'm just so tired,' Lauren moaned. 'Having the odd laugh with you has been the only thing that's made it bearable.'

'I'll bring you back something nice, OK? Oh, and tell James that my notes on *An Inspector Calls* from last year are in the grey file box under my desk if he needs them.'

'Right,' Lauren muttered. 'Try not to enjoy yourself *too* much.'

As Kyle ended the call, he looked towards the island and spotted a luxurious resort, with a white sand beach and dozens of large huts linked by a network of bobbing pontoons. People could dive from the balconies of plush rooms straight into warm seawater.

'That looks awesome,' Kyle said admiringly.

Anger flashed across Aizat's face. 'If the governor has his way, our whole island will look like that soon enough.'

Kyle didn't know how to reply and decided that it was going to be one of those days where it's better just to keep your mouth shut.

Their destination was a beach at the extreme north-western tip of Langkawi. Beyond a sorry stretch of sand strewn with litter and seaweed lay two shabby storeys of the Starfish Hotel. It had peeling white walls and tatty plastic furniture below faded sun shades.

A girl in short and vest ran barefoot towards the sea as Aizat cut the outboard motors and let the boat drift into shallow water. As he lashed it to a wooden post and stepped into the surf, Kyle jumped from the opposite end of the boat. He ducked under a wave, happy to let warm seawater drench his clothes and wash away the sweat after his long journey.

'How was your flight?' the girl asked as Kyle waded ashore. Her accent was Scottish. Her brow poured with sweat and her face burned red, as if she'd been exercising hard.

'Long,' Kyle answered with a smile. He looked the girl up and down. She was eleven or twelve with blond hair down her back. Her limbs were well tanned, but sliced and bruised from ninety-seven days of basic training. He'd seen the girl on campus, but didn't know her well.

'It's Iris, isn't it?'

'Iona,' the girl corrected. 'Iona Hardy. Mr Large says he wants you to bring everything ashore, then come over to the pool to see him as quickly as possible.'

Aizat handed Iona a bag filled with camping equipment. It was too heavy for her to carry up the beach, so she dragged it, leaving a rut in the sand behind her. When they reached the hotel a porter loaded everything on trolleys and wheeled them into a lounge.

Kyle wanted to know if he could speak freely. 'Are there any other guests at the hotel?' he asked Iona.

'Just CHERUB people,' Iona said. 'Mr Large, Miss Speaks plus the six surviving trainees.'

'How's Mr Pike doing?' Kyle asked.

'His appendix burst,' Iona explained. 'They took him by boat to the mainland on Christmas Eve and that's all we've heard. Now I'd better run back, before Large starts yelling at me.'

Alongside the small hotel was a paved terrace with a dilapidated swimming pool, surrounded by sun loungers and a decrepit diving board. The enormous figure of Norman Large stood at the edge of this, staring through the fencing around two sand-swept tennis courts.

Mr Pike's exploding appendix had put a dent in Large's carefully laid plans for a tough climax to the hundred-day basic training program, but that hadn't stopped him from finding ways to make Iona and five other trainees suffer.

'Push-ups, twenty,' Large shouted. 'And make it snappy!'

It was nearly thirty degrees. The youngsters on the courts looked like they were about to collapse as they dived forward and started doing push-ups.

'Sir,' Kyle said.

But Large ignored him as he counted out exercises. 'That was horrible,' Large yelled through the fence when he'd reached twenty. 'Now I want you running around the court. Fifteen laps and the last one to finish gets to do it all again carrying a bag of wet sand above their head.'

Iona led the way around the edge of the tennis courts, but a dark-skinned boy named Reece held his stomach and staggered across towards Large.

'I need water,' Reece begged, as he clutched the chain link fence to hold himself up. 'I feel faint.'

'You're lucky I'm a kind and gentle man,' Large growled, and passed a water bottle through a hole in the fence. 'But that drink cost you and all the other trainees ten more laps.'

The trainees were too exhausted to groan as Mr Large turned towards Kyle and looked him up and down with contempt. 'So they sent *you*,' he sniffed. 'Still, you're a decent enough swimmer, as I remember.'

'I'm OK,' Kyle nodded.

'I devised a four-day final exercise,' Large explained. 'The plan was for the kids to each drag canoes and heavy equipment up to the highest point of the island and then sail down a river. I tried to get training extended, but Mac says a hundred days is enough and won't let me extend. So, thanks to Mr Pike and his appendix we'll be setting off this afternoon on a truncated two-day exercise. I'll need you to help set things up, and act as a safety monitor during the exercise.'

Kyle nodded, though in his mind he sighed because the immediate start meant he wouldn't have any time to get over his jet lag. But anything was better than digging ditches in the freezing cold.

'Miss Speaks is in the jungle with two of our guides, setting up a few nice little surprises for the trainees. Right now I need you to take our quad bike along the beach and pick up fresh food from the fishing village. When you get back . . .'

Large stopped talking because the ground lurched, throwing him off balance towards the tennis-court fence. The water in the swimming pool behind sloshed like a giant bathtub, and an ankle-deep wave lapped over the edge, running across paving slabs and charging onwards across the tennis courts.

'Earth tremor?' Kyle said curiously.

A collection of plastic loungers and tables got washed into the pool as grateful trainees broke off their run to scoop cool water and splash it up over their bodies.

This outraged Large so much that his eyes practically popped out. 'Did I give you permission to stop running?' he bawled. 'You do not stop training, just because the planet does a little fart. Now get those legs moving you useless bloody lot.'

'Never felt one of those before,' Kyle said.

'Just an aftershock,' Large sniffed. 'We had a couple of bigger ones about an hour ago.'

The overheated trainees splashing in the water had pissed Large off and he pointed back towards the hotel.

'Quad bike's out front,' he told Kyle. 'Get on it. Collect the vegetables and fish. Then I want your arse back here helping me sort out the canoes and equipment.'

10. PARADISE

Kyle drove the quad bike three kilometres, towing a trailer across soft sand, but occasionally having to cut on to a single track road where the tide was in. The first sign of the village was Aizat's motor boat, which had been dragged across the sand and now rested keel-up beside the largest hut.

There were eleven huts in total, each mounted on stilts to protect from flooding. Young boys played football in the sand, their ball only half inflated and fishing nets hanging off bamboo canes for goalposts. Nearer to the huts two old women sat under a tarpaulin watching a quiz show on a tiny Sony TV.

'Excuse me,' Kyle said.

'No English,' one woman explained, before shouting, 'Aizat!'

Aizat came out the side of a hut. He'd taken off his

shirt to reveal a muscular chest and his hands were blackened with engine oil. Kyle took one look and decided that he wouldn't have minded a roll on the beach with him.

'Are you in charge of *everything* around here?' Kyle asked, smiling as Aizat jumped down into the sand.

'Pretty much,' Aizat agreed. 'You got old-timers and kids, but almost all of our parents live and work away from the village. In factories on the mainland, or the hotels. That leaves me and a couple of old men to fish, farm and generally run the show.'

'I don't know what I'm here to collect,' Kyle explained.

'I've packed it all up,' Aizat said. 'Vegetables, cooked rice and dried fish. You look thirsty, want a shot of my grandma's beer?'

Kyle knew Mr Large wanted him back quickly to start preparing the equipment for the two-day trek, but he liked the idea of spending time with Aizat.

'Quick one can't do any harm,' Kyle said. 'Even if it is a bit early in the day.'

As Kyle hopped up on to the balcony around Aizat's house, the higher vantage point gave him a view of some metal scaffolding less than a hundred metres beyond the village.

'Building something pretty big up there,' Kyle noted.

'Another hotel, almost finished,' Aizat spat. 'Five stars, air condition, three restaurant, two pool. I learn good English, so if I'm lucky they'll give me a job washing pots or cleaning toilets when it opens. In the meantime, the builders drink our wells dry and throw waste into the sea, killing our fish.'

'Sounds rough,' Kyle said, as he stepped inside. 'Can't you complain or something?'

Aizat's answer was a contemptuous tut.

The hut was shady and surprisingly cool. Aizat's eight-year-old sister Wati was curled up on a big cushion listening to her Walkman. All around were photos and piles of junk, while one of the outboard motors from Aizat's boat was spread across the floor in a dozen oily pieces. Pride of place went to a football shirt pinned to the back wall.

'Arsenal fan,' Kyle noted.

'The greatest,' Aizat nodded. 'Premiership champions, unbeaten in thirty-eight games. Do you follow football?'

'Not much,' Kyle said, shaking his head. 'But my mate James is a *mental* Arsenal fan. I expect you'd get right along with him.'

'Here we go,' Aizat grinned, as he grabbed a green wine bottle off the shelf, pulled a cork and poured out two beakers of a thick, cream-coloured liquid.

Kyle grabbed the beaker – which had Garfield and Odie printed on the side – and gave an exploratory sniff. 'Is this beer?'

'I just call it that,' Aizat said, and took a long swig.

Kyle took the liquid into his mouth and swallowed a small mouthful. The sensation that rose up his throat was like the time a wasp stung his neck, mingling with the hottest chilli he'd ever tasted.

'Holy mother!' Kyle gasped, his voice reduced to a

croak. 'That's fire water.'

Aizat's sister took off her headphones and howled with laughter as Kyle turned red, clutched his stomach and erupted into a rasping cough.

'Good eh!' Aizat beamed. 'One of my uncles went blind after drinking this stuff.'

'I'm not bloody surprised,' Kyle croaked. 'I feel like my head's on fire.'

Kyle took a second sip, but there was no way he could drink the rest. Aizat had downed his own glass without fuss, and now snatched Kyle's and drank it in three quick mouthfuls.

'You'll be drunk again,' Wati said bitterly.

'Who asked you?' Aizat shouted back, and threw the plastic beaker at his sister. 'Sitting on your arse all day, when the place is a pig sty.'

The girl poked her tongue at Aizat, then picked up her headphones from the floor and disappeared through a bead curtain into a side room. Kyle looked along a set of bookshelves and was surprised to find lots of very deep stuff: Marx, Freud, Kafka and other highbrow writers, mostly written in English.

'These yours?' Kyle asked.

Aizat nodded. 'I like to read. I have lots of pen friends too. One in China, a girl in Italy, a boy in United States. He's really cool. We've been writing each other since we were seven and he burns CDs with all the latest stuff on it. You like the Foo Fighters?'

'I can take 'em or leave 'em,' Kyle shrugged. He glanced at his watch, and imagined Large yelling at him for coming back late with booze breath.

'A British pen friend would be good too,' Aizat said. 'But you always say no.'

'Who says no?'

'Mr Large comes here, once or twice every year,' Aizat explained. 'Each time he brings different kids for the jungle expedition. When I ask one of them to be my pen friend, they always say no.'

Kyle understood now. Cherubs are discouraged from speaking with any outsiders they meet during basic training and Large would go bananas if any trainee was found with a stranger's address in their backpack during kit inspection.

But Kyle wasn't a trainee, and he thought Aizat was cute. 'I'll be your pen friend,' he said. 'Can't promise I'll write very often, but I'll try anything once.'

'Nice one!' Aizat smiled. He hunted for a pen and a notepad to exchange addresses. 'The post isn't great, so I use web cafés on the mainland.'

'No problem,' Kyle said, as he jotted his e-mail address on a piece of paper. 'Now we'd better start getting these supplies on the trailer, or Large will go ballistic.'

*

The tide had gone out surprisingly fast, enabling Kyle to drive the quad and trailer quickly over a plane of flat, wet sand, without diverting on to the road as he'd done on the outward journey. As he approached the Starfish Hotel, he was surprised to see Iona charging out towards him.

'Get moving,' she shouted, as Kyle pulled up in front

of the hotel. 'There's an emergency.'

'What's Large's problem?' Kyle moaned, stepping off the quad. 'I came as quick as I could.'

'It's not Large,' Iona said. 'The water splashing out of the pool wasn't just a normal earth tremor. We got a call from campus on Large's satellite phone. What we felt was an aftershock from a huge earthquake off the coast of Indonesia. A massive tsunami has already hit their coast and now the wave might be heading towards us.'

A chill went down Kyle's back as he looked around at the sea. He'd seen a video about tsunamis in the education block on campus and realised he'd have been defenceless if a giant wave had hit while he'd been out on the sand.

'That's why the tide went out so fast, I guess,' Kyle said. 'We did it in geography. The earthquake lifts up the entire sea, sucking all the water away from around the coast. Then the water comes back as a massive tidal wave, at over five hundred miles an hour.'

'Are you sure?' Iona asked thoughtfully. 'The tide here always goes out really quickly.'

'Well, I only got a C on that module,' Kyle said, half smiling. 'What about the locals? Is anyone warning them?'

'We tried ringing while you were at the village,' Iona explained.

'One signal bar,' Kyle said, as he pulled the phone from his pocket. 'Probably none at all in the village.'

'A couple of hotel staff have called their families, or

rushed off to be with them. We've moved our bags and everything up to the roof.'

'Kyle,' Large shouted, leaning over the wall built along the hotel's flat roof. For once his tone was purposeful rather than mean. 'Get that food up here pronto, we might need it. Then come and speak to me.'

Kyle and Iona, along with her training partner Dante, grabbed the boxes of food and carried them up to the hotel's rooftop restaurant. Everyone was scared, but it didn't play on their minds while they were occupied.

Large sat at a dining-table on the flat roof, with his laptop computer and the satellite phone on the slatted wooden table alongside him. Mrs Leung, the elderly lady who owned the hotel, sat nearby, staring anxiously out to sea.

Two trainees had been stationed on the corners of the roof with binoculars, looking for any sign of a large incoming wave, while the other pair sat on sun loungers, shattered after their workout on the tennis courts.

'What do you know about tsunamis?' Large asked Kyle, as he pointed towards a map of South East Asia on his laptop screen.

'Only what I picked up in GCSE geography,' Kyle replied.

Large tapped the western tip of Indonesia and spoke with uncharacteristic honesty. 'Kyle, this is a serious situation. Every decision I take could be a matter of life and death. You're the only trained agent here. Speaks is out in the jungle, so I need you as my second-incommand. I'm not infallible. I want you to speak frankly if you think I'm wrong about something.'

'OK,' Kyle nodded, then gulped at the sense of responsibility.

Paradise had turned to hell in the space of a few minutes. Kyle put his hands in the pockets of his shorts to stop them from trembling as Large continued the explanation.

'According to the control room on campus, the earthquake hit two hours ago in the ocean around this spot here, north-west of Indonesia. The resulting tsunami reached the Indonesian mainland within thirty minutes. Early reports say it's ripped up the entire coastline. God knows how many have been killed, but it'll be hundreds, if not thousands.

'The shockwave is now radiating outwards from the epicentre. There are tsunami warnings all along the western coast of Thailand. They're expecting it to hit within the next twenty to forty minutes and we won't be far behind. The waves that hit Indonesia were up to twenty-five metres high, but the shockwave gets weaker as it radiates outwards, so hopefully what hits us won't be anywhere near as bad.'

Kyle squinted and touched the laptop screen. It was shielded under a large sunshade, but the LCD still wasn't easy to view in the bright sunlight.

'So the earthquake's here and we're on Langkawi here . . . Which means the Indonesian mainland lies between us and the epicentre of the quake.'

Large nodded. 'Hopefully being out of the

shockwave's direct path will do us some good, but I can't get clear information on that. The control room on campus is trying to contact the meteorological office in London to work out what we can expect, but I've not heard from them.'

'But Norman!' Mrs Leung blurted, as she pulled off a pair of giant sunglasses on a chain. 'It may not be twenty-five metres like Indonesia, but even two or three metres of water coming up the beach will flood my pool, wreck my ground floor and do god knows what to the fishing villages.'

'Is there higher ground inland?' Kyle asked.

'There is,' Large nodded. 'But it's thickly forested once you go beyond the beach and the coast road. There's no guarantee that we'll be able to get to ground before the wave hits.'

'But this building could wash away completely if the wave hits hard enough,' Kyle said.

Large nodded seriously. 'Damned if you do, damned if you don't. But my gut's telling me to stay here where the hotel building gives us some protection.'

Kyle saw there was no correct decision. 'OK,' he nodded. 'But I don't think we should be out in the open. I say we go back into the building and hide in the highest room without a window we can find. That will minimise our chances of being washed away, or of getting hit by flying glass or debris.'

'Good thinking,' Large agreed, then looked at the owner. 'What's the highest room without a window?'

'Food storeroom behind us,' Mrs Leung said, and

pointed towards the rooftop bar and kitchen behind them. 'We'll all fit in there.'

Large clapped his hands. 'OK kids, follow Mrs Leung. Get yourselves into the back of the kitchen.'

'Grab some foam sofa cushions or something,' Kyle added. 'They'll protect you if you get knocked around and they'll act as floats if the water comes over the top of the building.'

'Good thinking, Kyle,' Large said, looking impressed as he snatched the binoculars from one of the lookouts. 'Everyone inside, I'll take lookout.'

The trainees ripped foam cushions from the wicker sofas in the restaurant's waiting area, and followed Mrs Leung into the back of the kitchen.

'You too, Kyle,' Large said, as he looked out to sea with the binoculars. 'I'll shout a warning if I see the wave coming.'

'If you're sure,' Kyle said, as he started to walk away.

The storage room at the back of the kitchen was stiflingly hot, with a bare bulb swinging from the ceiling and sacks of rice and vegetables piled against the back wall. The trainees had gathered several cushions each, and made themselves comfortable, sitting on them and clutching them for comfort. Also present were Mrs Leung, along with the hotel's only chamber maid, in her black dress and frilly apron.

As Kyle stepped in, sixteen eyeballs swivelled up to look at him. He was scared and kept picturing scenes from disaster movies, but everyone, including the adults, seemed to feel that he had some kind of authority after seeing Large ask his advice and agree with his suggestions.

'Give us a cushion,' Kyle said.

Dante passed a spare across and Kyle sat on the cushion with his back resting against tins of curry powder. The unventilated room was well over forty degrees and the trainees smelled ripe after their workout. The four girl trainees held hands, looking small and vulnerable as they tried not to think about the danger they were all in.

'So,' Dante said, with a slight grin on his face. 'I guess this is where they'll find our bloated drowned corpses in a couple of weeks' time.'

Iona didn't appreciate Dante's black humour and slapped his bare leg. '*Don't* say things like that,' she snapped. 'We've got to be positive.'

Another girl trainee agreed. 'We could sing a song or something.'

Dante grimaced. 'If you girls start singing, I'm outta here. Tsunami or no tsunami.'

'Come on,' Kyle said firmly. 'We could be in here for a long time. Don't start fighting.'

There were a few seconds of quiet before the chamber maid made an announcement in a mixture of Malay and English. 'They just say it reach Phuket. Big wave, very bad.'

Kyle hadn't noticed that she had the earpiece from her mobile phone in her ear, listening to the local radio station.

'Is that far off?' Iona asked.

'Less than a hundred kilometres north,' Mrs Leung said. 'At these speeds, it should be here in a few minutes.'

'Dun, dun dunnnn!' Dante added.

11. CRASH

After ninety minutes in the dimly lit shelter, Kyle fought to open his eyes as he walked into the dazzling sunlight on the hotel roof. Large hadn't moved, sitting at the dining-table with the binoculars around his neck.

'The maid has a radio on her phone,' Kyle announced, holding his hand over his brow to shield the light. 'It hit the Thai coast more than an hour ago. If it was coming here, I think it would have happened already.'

'Agreed,' Large said, as he scratched his moustache thoughtfully. 'News reports I've been reading on the laptop indicate that the Malaysian coast and the southernmost points of Thailand have been untouched. The Indonesian mainland acted like a giant breakwater, shielding us from the shockwave. I'm waiting on confirmation from the control room on campus before I give the all-clear.'

'Right,' Kyle nodded. 'A couple of the girls are getting desperate for the bathroom. Shall I tell them they can go?'

'Might as well,' Large said, 'but tell them to go back to the shelter for the time being.'

But by the time the girls had used the toilet, Large had received his call on the satellite phone. Everyone came out on to the roof and the trainees exchanged relieved hugs, smiles and high fives.

If there was one thing Mr Large disliked, it was seeing his trainees smiling and happy. He slammed down the lid of his laptop and spoke in a booming voice.

'We're now *very* late,' Large shouted. 'You should be setting off on the exercise about now. Instead you haven't even started preparing your equipment or reading your mission briefings. Your first orders are to carry the equipment that we brought up here back downstairs where it belongs. Then I want you lined up on the tennis courts, with your gear laid out ready for kit inspection and a briefing on your final exercise. You have twenty minutes, so *get* moving.'

As the six trainees sprinted into action and began lugging food and luggage down to the ground floor, Kyle turned towards Large and smiled with relief.

'Looks like we caught a break on that one.'

Large looked up at Kyle, made a huffing noise and then grunted. The nervous, almost human, character who'd valued Kyle's opinion in the face of disaster was gone and the badass training instructor was back with a vengeance.

'Why did you take so long bringing the food back, anyway?' Large shouted. 'There are six wooden canoes lashed to the back of a Land Cruiser in the car park behind the hotel. Drag them around to the tennis courts, along with the oars, safety vests and the rest of the equipment. I'll be in the hotel office. I've got to print off six revised mission briefings for the brats.'

'Gotcha, boss,' Kyle said.

Large's eyes bulged. 'Pardon me?' he roared.

Kyle looked mystified. 'What?'

'You may not be a trainee, Mr Blueman, but I still expect to be treated with respect at all times. If I ask you to do something, you respond with *yes sir* or *yes Mr Large*, not *gotcha boss*.'

Kyle reckoned Mr Large was a complete arsehole and felt like reminding him that he'd voluntarily flown half way around the world on Christmas Day in order to help him. But Large was the kind of man who bore a grudge and Kyle knew he'd exact sadistic revenge the next time he had to go on a training exercise.

'All right, sir!' Kyle said, daring mild sarcasm in the form of a military salute, before spinning on his heels and marching off down the stairs.

The wooden canoes weren't heavy over the hundred-metre walk between the car park and the tennis courts, but they would be for the ten- to twelve-year-old trainees who'd have to carry them on their backs over several kilometres of steep and overgrown terrain, along with backpacks containing rations and equipment.

Each time Kyle went past the pool, he got a smile from

the young maid who'd been tasked with fishing out the plastic furniture that had fallen in during the last earth tremor. Once the six kid-sized canoes were lined up on the tennis courts, he made sure that Large was out of sight before giving the trainees a hand cleaning their kits and laying them out for inspection.

'Stand to attention you idle shit-clusters,' Large shouted, as he approached bearing six freshly laser-printed mission briefings. 'Your four-day final exercise may have been cut down because of Mr Pike's exploded appendix, but you can be sure that I've crammed in more than enough extra hardship and misery to make up for it.'

Kyle smiled at the blasé expressions on the youngsters' faces. After surviving ninety-seven days of basic training they were largely immune to Large's insults and threats.

The sun was bright, and as Large began briefing the trainees on their final exercise, Kyle realised that he'd left his sunglasses behind when he'd been sheltering behind the upstairs kitchen.

Mrs Leung gave Kyle a smile as he jogged towards the bottom of the staircase. 'Norman likes to boss the kids,' she grinned. 'But he's a very sweet man.'

Kyle grinned. 'The man has a heart of gold,' he lied.

As he bounded upstairs to the flat roof Kyle couldn't help feeling that Mrs Leung was mainly fond of Large because he booked out her shabby twenty-room hotel for several days every year.

Kyle found the sunglasses where he'd expected, but as he headed out on to the flat roof he heard a roaring noise, more like the drone of a jet engine than the normal rolling of waves. When he looked out to sea, he saw a bulge in the still water half a kilometre out. It wasn't tall, but it was closing at a spectacular speed.

'Mr Large,' Kyle shouted, as he leaned over the edge of the roof. 'Get everyone–'

The wave hit the beach before Kyle finished his sentence. It peaked at less than one metre high, but the trainees down on the tennis court were bowled off their feet. The canoes and equipment laid out on the green rubber surface were thrown violently towards the hotel, as a wall of water ripped up fence posts.

There was a tremor and a deafening crash of glass as the wave hit the Starfish Hotel. Thousands of birds shot up out of the trees behind, as the sand-filled water crossed the coast road and rushed on into the jungle. Kyle leaned over the edge of the hotel, helpless and aghast.

After a minute the water slowed, then turned to a swirling pool thick with clouds of brown silt. After this pause it began rolling out more gently than it had arrived, powered by gravity rather than the colossal shockwave that had forced it up the beach.

Down on the tennis courts, Kyle was relieved to see all six trainees untangling themselves from the mangled fences and finding their feet. Large had stayed upright, clutching a buckled post. The only injury was to a girl who'd been whacked by a canoe and had a bloody graze across her shoulder and the back of her neck.

As Kyle looked back towards the building he noticed the maid floating face down in a tangle of plastic tables where the swimming pool had been. He bolted downstairs, jumping the lower half of each flight.

The hotel's ground floor was knee-deep in filthy water, with a fast flowing torrent running back towards the sea. Glass shards hung from every window frame, the electricity was out and Mrs Leung stood by the reception desk, her usually coiffured hair sprouting in a hundred directions and looking like she was about to collapse in shock.

After pushing through lightweight wicker furniture blocking the French doors leading out to the pool, Kyle waded on, fearful that the fast moving torrent would knock him down. The edge of the pool was invisible beneath the brown water and he arrived a step sooner than he'd guessed.

Kyle plunged forward, getting a mouthful of sand and filth. But he was a strong swimmer and the current pushed him quickly across the hidden pool towards the maid. Rather than fight his way back, he grabbed her gently around the neck and dragged her with the current until his feet found the opposite edge of the pool.

The maid was unconscious, nose broken and face bloody. A couple of the trainees had watched the rescue and waded against the current to help him. As Kyle grabbed the maid under her armpits, Dante grabbed her ankles and the pair lifted her up on to a brick barbecue, above the height of the receding water.

All CHERUB agents had to get an advanced lifesavers certificate, but while Kyle knew the theory there was a huge difference between a plastic dummy lying at the poolside on campus and a real, unconscious human with the knowledge that she'd die if he got it wrong.

Kyle thrust down on the maid's chest with both palms. Nothing happened the first couple of times, then brown water dribbled down her chin. The next thrust brought up a deluge and the maid coughed.

'You OK?' Kyle asked.

She sat up suddenly, banging her skull against Kyle's chin.

'Jesus,' Kyle shouted, and staggered back clutching his face.

He wasn't concussed, but his vision blurred momentarily and Dante was forced to take over, thumping the maid on the back and making her take deep breaths to get the remaining water out of her lungs.

Once Kyle had his wits back, he looked around and was staggered by the view. The water had mostly drained off and the white beach had turned to a mud pool, covered with glass shards, broken hotel furniture, tree branches and hundreds of shimmering fish, dying or already dead.

Large had not only stayed upright, but the satellite phone in his top pocket had stayed dry enough to keep working. He was on to the control room on CHERUB campus, wanting to know why they'd given him the all-clear, only for them to be hit less than thirty minutes later.

'What do you mean there's no tsunami in this region?' he shouted. 'There bloody well is! It just hit us, took all my equipment and . . . No the kids are fine, well one minor injury. But I want you to find out who gave that all-clear. I *demand* an explanation. I want to know if we're going to get any more waves in these parts and tell the meteorologist who gave us the all-clear that when I get back to Britain I'm gonna chop his balls off, put them on a big skewer and roast them on an open fire.'

12. SHADOW

Large squelched into the freshly deposited silt over the tennis courts and looked around forlornly. Two of the wooden-hulled canoes had disappeared, along with every piece of the trainees' kits, which had been laid out ready for inspection.

The six youngsters began a search, picking up random items – water canteens, soggy clothes and firelighters – until Large ordered them to go back up to the roof because there was no way of knowing if another wave was coming.

As Kyle led the trainees upstairs, they seemed hopeful. Mac had refused permission to extend basic training beyond the hundred-day limit and now, with all of their equipment destroyed, there seemed a real possibility that their final exercise would have to be called off.

'What do you think Kyle?' Iona asked, as they sat at

rooftop tables overlooking the devastated beach. 'Is there any way we can run the exercise?'

Kyle smiled. 'Knowing Large, I wouldn't go getting your hopes up. He'll find some way to make you suffer.'

As Kyle spoke, a car stopped at the rear of the hotel. Large's burly training assistant Miss Speaks sat at the wheel. She'd been out in the jungle with two local guides, setting up equipment for the trainees' final exercise. They'd been heading back along the coast road in a Land Cruiser when the wave hit. A front wheel had a slow puncture and the bodywork had been battered by debris thrown up by the giant wave.

'Thought we'd had our chips there,' Speaks explained, as she walked towards Kyle and the trainees on the rooftop. Her deep voice sounded troubled as she described what had happened. 'The waves lifted the whole car off the road. Almost toppled the Land Cruiser, but the road is overgrown and the dense undergrowth pushed us back. Then a huge backwash drained on to the road and started coming at us, more than two metres high. I thought we'd get washed out to sea. Luckily the rear end was heavy with all the equipment in the back and dug itself into the sand when we hit the beach.'

'Mr Large tried calling but your phone wasn't receiving,' Kyle said. He liked Speaks no more than he liked Large, but he'd never seen her in such a state before. Her hands were visibly shaking, so he offered her a drink.

'Something strong,' Speaks nodded. 'Scotch, vodka.

Make it big whatever it is.'

Speaks continued her story as Kyle stepped behind the rooftop bar and poured Japanese whisky into a tall glass.

'When the water receded, we were buried in half a metre of silt. The three of us dug out the back wheels and wedged planks under the tyres. The coast road is in a real state: deep silt, trees and debris blocking the carriageway. It's a good job we had a four-wheel drive. No ordinary car would have got through – thank you Kyle.'

Miss Speaks downed half a tumbler of whisky in two gulps. 'Calms the nerves,' she said, before passing the glass back to Kyle. 'Same again, barman.'

As Kyle walked back to the bar, Mr Large walked out on to the rooftop with his gargantuan moustache bristling furiously.

'Shadow wave,' he shouted. Then he saw Miss Speaks. 'How you doing? Did you get caught up?'

'Getting better,' Speaks replied, as Kyle handed her a second whisky.

'Shadow wave what?' Kyle asked, as all the trainees turned to listen in.

'I just spoke to the campus control room and they've been in contact with the meteorological service in London,' Large explained. 'Apparently, a tsunami works exactly like the ripples when you lob a big stone into a pond. The shockwaves radiate outwards and when they hit the side of the pond they reflect back in the opposite direction. What washed over us is known as a shadow wave, a reflection from the shockwave that hit the Thai coast. It may have looked scary, but it would have been less than a tenth as powerful as the direct hit on Thailand. Maybe a thousandth as powerful as what hit the coastline of Indonesia a few hours back.'

Kyle had just been through one of the scariest mornings of his life. He could barely comprehend what it must have been like for the people in Indonesia dealing with a wall of water a thousand times more powerful.

'So what's our situation?' Speaks asked. 'Supplies and equipment?'

Large tutted and shook his head. 'Trainees had their kits laid out for inspection, so we lost the lot. But if it's still clear up there in the jungle, I was thinking we could take the trainees in without kit for a rudimentary survival exercise.'

The trainees sitting nearby deflated visibly at this prospect.

Miss Speaks shook her head. 'With the greatest respect, Norman, I think it would be irresponsible. With this disaster, all the emergency services are going to be at full stretch. We can't risk taking kids into the jungle. What if something went wrong? There might be no rescue boats or helicopters available to pull them out after an accident, and if we made it to the hospital there'd be no beds available.'

Large thought about this for a couple of seconds. 'I guess you're right,' he sighed. 'We could give them shovels and make them run around digging holes in all this silt for two days.'

'What's in the silt though?' Speaks asked. 'I don't

want to give the trainees an easy ride any more than you do, but for all we know some of what's on that beach was in a Thai sewage plant three hours ago, or an industrial facility pumping toxic chemicals, or Christ knows what else.'

'And it's more than likely full of broken glass,' Kyle added. 'And there's still going to be no hospital beds or evacuation support if a trainee got injured or suffered heat stroke.'

The trainees looked at each other hopefully, but didn't dare smile in case it sent Large into a rage. In the event it didn't need anything more to set him off.

'So what do you expect me to do?' Large shouted, throwing his arms into the air as he scowled accusingly at Kyle and Miss Speaks. 'Mac won't let me extend training and from what you're saying, we might as well give the six of them their grey T-shirts right now.'

The two giant whiskies were beginning to affect Miss Speaks. She'd stopped shaking and her beefy shoulders were noticeably relaxed as she shrugged. 'We're in the middle of a huge natural disaster, Norman. Thousands of people could be dead. CHERUB training *has* to take a back seat.'

Iona caught Dante's eye and the training partners couldn't help smiling at each other. Then Reece, who'd been struggling on the tennis courts earlier, punched the air and shouted, 'Yes!' triumphantly.

Within a few seconds the trainees were all standing up and hugging each other. Dante crashed back to the floor tiles with his feet in the air.

'Think you're smart, do you?' Large shouted as he eyeballed his trainees. 'Think you've got away with it? But you're all *young*. I can't train you here, but I'll have *plenty* up my sleeve next time one of you lot reports for a training exercise.'

But whatever threats Large threw around, he'd never have the power to take away their status as grey shirts. Kyle remembered the massive relief he'd felt when he'd passed basic training and couldn't resist teasing the jubilant trainees.

'You never really went a hundred days though,' Kyle grinned. 'You're not *real* grey shirts.'

'Shove it up your bum,' Dante said, as he gave Kyle a two-fingered salute.

'Can we have our grey shirts *now*?' Iona asked pleadingly.

Kyle thought Large was going to explode at this suggestion, but instead he crashed out in a dining chair and turned to Miss Speaks. 'Sod it,' he said, with a wave of his hand. 'I could do with a rest after all that's happened this morning.'

Miss Speaks looked at Iona. 'The grey shirts are in my room, in the blue equipment bag. You'll have to get my room key from reception. *Don't* just rip everything out and make a mess.'

Iona put her hands on her cheeks and squealed, 'Thank you so much, Miss!'

None of the other trainees were prepared to wait for Iona to fetch their shirts back up to the rooftop, so they charged after her towards the staircase.

'It's good to see them happy like that,' Kyle said, grinning as he momentarily forgot that he was sitting with the two meanest training instructors on campus.

'They were a good bunch,' Speaks agreed. 'They'll all do well when they start missions.'

Large wasn't so charitable, and he pointed at Miss Speaks' empty glass. 'Get me a bloody drink, Kyle.'

'Keep 'em coming,' Speaks agreed. 'But try to find some ice.'

As Kyle stood up, he spotted a small figure running desperately through the silt towards the hotel. Exhaustion made her steps clumsy and she'd fallen over at least once, spattering her body with mud.

'Are you OK?' Kyle shouted from the rooftop, but he could tell from the way she was waving her arms that she wasn't.

'Help!' the girl shouted, as Kyle realised that it was Aizat's sister Wati. 'Come quickly.'

13. ROOF

It was the middle of the day and the high sun reflected off puddles in the newly deposited silt, blinding Kyle as he drove the Land Cruiser towards the village. Speaks sat next to him. She hadn't taken the wheel because she'd just downed three large measures of spirits.

In the back seats, hotel owner Mrs Leung sat with the mud-spattered Wati on her lap. Squeezed alongside were Iona, Dante and two other trainees, while the cargo area behind had been hastily packed with first-aid kits and emergency medical equipment from supplies meant for the aborted canoeing exercise.

The three-kilometre drive took them on a slight curve. The wave that Kyle saw hitting the Starfish Hotel head-on had swept towards Aizat's village at an oblique angle, having first hit the adjacent construction site.

The village's traditionally designed houses were

elevated on wooden poles and their lightweight flexible structures withstood storms and tidal waves better than western influenced designs made from brick and metal. But they'd been less able to cope with debris and construction equipment washed off the building site, including a four-storey scaffold carried across in the rush of water.

Of the eleven huts in the village, the four closest to the construction site had been seriously damaged. The rest had all suffered some degree of damage from floating boards and sheets of corrugated metal.

'What's the situation?' Kyle asked urgently, as he pulled up in front of Aizat's hut.

Aizat's boat lay broken between two distant palm trees, while a cement mixing machine had damaged several of the hut's main supports and lay wedged deep under the building.

Aizat's legs were spattered in mud. He'd dragged two elderly women from a damaged hut and laid them out on a metal sheet from the hotel site. Both were cut and one had an obviously broken arm. The lads who'd been playing football earlier stood about with no sense of direction and stared hopefully at the new arrivals.

Aizat pointed at the four severely damaged huts. 'I haven't even walked over that side yet. Are we expecting more waves?'

'We don't think so,' Kyle said. 'We're listening to the radio and we've got satellite phones working. But nobody warned us about the last wave, so you can't be sure.'

A jolt of adrenaline had sobered Speaks up and she quickly checked out the two elderly casualties. Once she saw there was nothing life-threatening about their injuries she turned towards the trainees.

'Use your first-aid training,' Speaks ordered. 'Clean the cuts. Seal any that are bleeding badly with compression plasters, splint and wrap the broken arm. Give her pain relief if you think she needs it.'

As the four trainees grabbed kit from the back of the car and became medics, Kyle and Speaks followed two teenage villagers who were particularly anxious to show them one of the wrecked huts. They barely spoke English and Kyle and Speaks knew no Malay, but it didn't take much to work out that the girls thought there were people trapped under the collapsed roof.

The scaffold had hit the hut at speed, ripping off the veranda and knocking the entire structure backwards on its supporting stilts. The wooden frame had caved in, leaving a tangle of planks topped off by the remains of the metal roof. The only reason the structure hadn't collapsed entirely was that the front of the house now balanced precariously on part of the buckled scaffold tower.

Kyle pushed against the side of the building to see if it was stable. The entire structure creaked alarmingly, making one of the girls scream in panic.

'Just checking it out,' Kyle said, backing away and raising his arms to calm the girls down.

Miss Speaks held up her fingers like she was counting. 'How many people?'

The taller of the two girls held up two fingers, but then she linked hands and rocked them from side to side indicating that one or both was a baby.

Kyle looked at Speaks. 'It's too unstable to clamber under that roof. We've either got to brace the structure or knock it down.'

He'd hoped that Speaks had a better plan, but she stayed quiet.

'Knocking it down is easier, but if it shifts it could crush anyone trapped inside,' Kyle added.

Speaks leaned under the structure and made a thoughtful inspection of the steeply angled rear posts. 'The scaffolding at the front is wedged at an angle. If it collapses, it's going backwards. So, what if we get the Land Cruiser up here and back it up against the building, so that it can't topple?'

'Will that hold it?' Kyle asked.

Speaks nodded. 'It's a heavy car. It'll hold for a while if you're gentle on the throttle.'

'Me?' Kyle gulped.

Speaks inflated her huge chest and bulky arms. 'Unless you want to get up there and try lifting up that roof. But I reckon that's my department, don't you?'

Speaks wasn't just muscular, she'd been a champion weight-lifter which made her pretty much the ideal person to have around under the circumstances.

Kyle hurriedly explained the plan to Aizat as he jogged back to the Land Cruiser.

'They're twins,' Aizat explained. 'Two boys, eleven months old.'

'It scares me that we can't hear them yelling inside,' Kyle said. 'We'll try, but I'm not optimistic.'

It was tricky driving the Land Cruiser up the beach and reversing over debris, down a narrow alleyway between the wreckage of the two most seriously damaged huts. Fortunately the families that owned them worked on the mainland and both had been empty when the wave struck.

By the time Kyle parked with the back of the Land Cruiser aligned to the rear of the teetering house a gaggle of villagers was watching, along with two painters from the construction site who'd come by to help.

Kyle leaned out of the car window. 'Ready?' he shouted.

Miss Speaks looked around at Dante, who'd donned a yellow safety helmet with a powerful rescue lamp fitted around it.

'I'm fine,' Dante said, before smiling nervously.

'Roll her back,' Speaks ordered.

Kyle switched on the Land Cruiser's low-ratio gearbox, giving it the kind of torque required for climbing muddy hills, or hopefully supporting the weight of a teetering pole house. He let out the handbrake and gave the accelerator the lightest of touches.

Kyle looked back over his shoulder as the house's wooden beams creaked. The Land Cruiser's back window shattered and the suspension sank into the mud as the rear end braced the weight of the wooden structure. This was the moment of truth. Would the car pushing backwards support the teetering house, or cause it to collapse and possibly crush the babies trapped inside?

'Enough,' Speaks shouted.

To Kyle's relief the big 4×4 seemed to be propping up the house, but sweat was pouring down his brow. The ground beneath the tyres was slippery and he had to strike a difficult balance between skidding forwards in the mud, or pushing the throttle too hard and knocking the house forward on to the scaffolding.

Speaks clambered up the side of the house and wedged her hands under a section of the collapsed roof. The corrugated metal roofing was light, but the wooden frame and joists to which it was attached needed all the strength in her beefy arms and tree trunk thighs.

As soon as there was a decent gap between floor and roof, Dante shot through into the hut's collapsed interior. The roof and sides seemed to be propped up by pieces of furniture. He found himself with a pair of cheesy thongs in his face, looking under a couch with his lamp illuminating empty cigarette packets and dead cockroaches.

'What can you see?' Speaks shouted, straining under the weight of the roof panels.

Dante's world shuddered as Kyle dabbed the Land Cruiser throttle a little too hard. At the same moment his nose caught an alarming whiff of cooking gas. According to the girls, their baby nephews had been asleep in a cot near the centre of the house.

Dante crawled in deeper. To his relief there was half a metre between his back and the roof over the middle of the house. His helmet-mounted lamp wasn't needed because sunlight blitzed through small gaps between the collapsed sections.

'I see them,' Dante gasped, as he rounded the end of the sofa and spotted a cot.

'Are they OK?' Speaks shouted.

Dante had a younger sister, so he knew about babies and was alarmed by what he saw. It was stiflingly hot, and the two tiny boys lay together, covered in a fine layer of dust. He slid his arm between the bars of the cot and touched one boy's hand. It felt warm and the tiny fingers reacted to his touch by curling into a fist.

'I think they're both alive,' he shouted.

Both boys had red faces, and Dante guessed they'd screamed themselves into a state of exhaustion and passed out in the heat.

'Bring them out quickly,' Speaks ordered.

But Dante cursed as he looked up and saw that the wooden sides of the cot were supporting the collapsed wall panel above his head. At a stretch he could reach around the top of the cot and get his arm in to touch the babies, but the gap between the top of the cot and the collapsed wall wasn't enough to lift their bodies through.

Dante pushed upwards, trying to raise the wall, but it was pinned down beneath the hut's roof and would take several strong adults to lift off.

'Get me a saw,' he shouted.

It was almost two minutes before Aizat brought a small hacksaw from his hut. During the wait Kyle had another accident with the throttle and Dante got horribly claustrophobic as he imagined the walls collapsing on top of him.

The only relief came to Miss Speaks, whose muscles were replaced by wooden props hammered in by the two painters to keep Dante's escape route open.

Once he had the saw, Dante crawled back to the cot and began using it to cut through a wooden side bar. The noise and dust disturbed the babies and after a brief instant of curiosity the pair began screaming in the confined space less than thirty centimetres from Dante's head.

The first rail twisted out of the cot frame once Dante had sawed through and he threw it down in the puddle of sweat that had dropped off his brow. He reckoned he'd need to take three rails out to make a gap big enough to get the babies through, but he was acutely aware that by removing rods he was weakening the cot frame supporting the roof over his head.

Back in the Land Cruiser, Kyle had been balancing throttle and brake pedals for five minutes. His knees hurt and his right calf was numb. Despite the pain he was getting a feel for what the car would do, but just as he thought he'd got the hang of it the biggest hornet Kyle had ever seen buzzed through the side window and dive-bombed his head.

Kyle instinctively flinched and in doing so jammed the accelerator pedal hard. The car shot back violently and the onlookers gasped as the entire hut groaned. At the front, one of the scaffolding sections twisted and began to buckle.

'Kyle, you crazy idiot,' Speaks shouted. 'What are you doing?'

He still had the hornet buzzing around his head and after several attempts to bat it away Kyle took a hand off the steering wheel and threw the driver's door open, hoping that the huge stinging insect would fly out.

Inside the house, Dante was terrified as the tangle of wood and metal over his head rumbled and began to shift. He thought about turning back, but he was tantalisingly close to freeing the babies. Then the props snapped, sealing his exit and bringing the roof even closer to his body.

As Speaks jumped on to the tilting structure and tried to lift the roof again, Dante saw a new opportunity. The jolt had shifted everything and a divine light shone through a hole directly above the cot.

Dante abandoned his saw, hurdled his way into the cot and stood up in the newly formed opening, being careful not to step on the babies down by his feet. The crowd gasped as they saw Dante's head, but this time it was horror not relief. The entire structure was shifting forwards.

'Somebody grab 'em,' Dante shouted, as he reached down into the cot and grabbed the screaming pair by their nappies.

Speaks was heavy and feared that her weight would collapse the roof, so Iona clambered desperately over the wreckage and grabbed the babies.

The two tiny boys screamed their heads off as they were manhandled and passed down into the waiting arms of Miss Speaks. Iona was about to jump down when she realised that Dante couldn't pull himself up through the hole and out on to the roof.

Iona was smaller than Dante, but basic training had made her strong and she yanked Dante out of the hole just as the scaffolding holding up the front of the house completely gave way. The onlookers dived clear as the section of roof on which Dante and Iona now stood began sliding towards the ground.

Dante considered jumping off the side, but Iona had a better tactic and he copied her, riding the metal roof panel on which they stood like a giant surfboard as it crashed down into the silt in front of the house.

The hornet had finally flown out, but Kyle couldn't see around the sides of the house. He had no idea what was going on and felt sick when he saw that the building was collapsing. Then he saw one of the other trainees giving him a thumbs-up.

'They're out. Drive off!'

Kyle flipped the Land Cruiser into a forward gear and the big car flexed with relief as it skidded off up the beach. In the chaos, Kyle had forgotten that his door was open and it smashed against a tree trunk, slamming shut and leaving a huge dent in the metal.

By the time he'd moved twenty metres clear the entire hut was straining. The scaffold at the front was dragging it one way, while the release of the Land Cruiser at the back pulled it the other. After several seconds making up its mind, both ends buckled simultaneously and the entire structure collapsed straight down on to its stilts.

Moments later Dante breathlessly approached the two teenage aunts who each held a screaming baby, while an elderly villager carefully wiped the dirt off their faces using bottled water and cotton wool balls, being extra careful that nothing ran into their eyes.

'You did good,' Miss Speaks beamed, giving Dante an almighty thump on the back. 'It's a shame you're not on a mission or you might have just earned the fastest promotion to navy shirt in history.'

14. FIRE

The afternoon brought tropical storms, with ping-pong-ball-sized droplets pelting the silt and turning the village into streams of ankle-deep mud. The village's only serious casualties were the broken arm and an elderly man whose back had been speared by a scaffold rod. One small girl had been washed several hundred metres but escaped injury, and a headcount revealed that the kids who'd been playing by the sea had all made it to the huts before the wave hit.

The coast road was blocked, so the two injured villagers were taken to the mainland in a large boat that belonged to contractors working on the hotel. Also aboard was the body of a painter, killed in a twenty-metre fall from their mobile scaffold and recovered from the jungle far behind.

The CHERUB party stayed to help the villagers.

Drinking water was drawn from a standpipe linked to a deep well, but the supply was contaminated with silt, so the trainees scouted for dry timber and built a fire to boil it.

Although Langkawi was rapidly developing, with modern infrastructure and tourist resorts, this north-western tip was insulated by the expanse of jungle in which the trainees would have conducted their final exercise. Aizat's motorboat was the village's main connection to the mainland and the rest of Langkawi, bringing post, fuel and supplies and taking the fish they caught to the twice weekly market.

Repairing the boat was number-one priority and Kyle provided muscle for two elderly villagers. In less than two hours they'd cut and replaced damaged hull sections with timbers from one of the collapsed houses. By pure luck, Aizat had been servicing the outboard motor and it had remained dry and undamaged on the floor of his hut.

Large and Speaks worked with another group of villagers. Three of the four huts hit by the scaffold were beyond repair, so they were cannibalised and their timbers used to shore up damaged sections of the remainder.

There was no need for plumbers, electricians or carpenters because the elderly men and women had a lifetime of familiarity with homes built by their own hand. The instructors and trainees marvelled at how everyone got on with things and realised how poorly British householders would have coped in a similar situation, huddling in the church hall waiting for the insurance company.

As hours passed and the most urgent jobs got completed, human nature surfaced. Villagers bickered over what job to do next, who would sleep where and whether a note should be kept of what materials had been taken and used from the destroyed huts so that the original owners could be paid. Two women rowed viciously over a DVD player and an almost-new gas hotplate being removed from one of the damaged houses.

But the community held together. As night drew in the sun had baked a dry crust on to the silt and there was a sense of the village getting back on its feet. Three women used the trainees' fire to steam rice and cook a huge fish curry.

The village's mains electricity had gone down, but the supply was always erratic and Aizat set up their portable generator, linked to a string of light bulbs.

A television and satellite dish were rigged up near the fire. Tired and aching, the CHERUB party and the villagers gathered around, gawping at images of much greater devastation in Thailand and Indonesia.

Kyle had made friends with a girl of about five, who lay with her tired head resting on his thigh. He noticed how the huts and people in the village where he sat bore extraordinary similarities to the destroyed landscape littered with dead bodies on the TV screen. Some of the worst damage had taken place on the Thai coast, less than a hundred kilometres away.

The presenter on the satellite news channel spoke in Malay, so Aizat translated anything important for Kyle.

'She just said Malaysia only suffered minor damage

from shadow waves. Less than a hundred casualties reported so far. Some damage to resorts along the northern coast of Langkawi island, and tourists are all being evacuated to the mainland.' Then he added, 'Good bloody riddance, hope they don't come back.'

Kyle smiled. 'You've got a thing about tourists and hotels, haven't you?'

'The government feels villages like this are in the way of progress,' Aizat explained, as he looked across and noticed that Wati was dozing off on the ground beside him. 'Don't fall asleep until you've eaten dinner,' he warned her. 'You'll wake up hungry and then moan at me.'

As Wati rubbed dirty palms in her eyes and yawned, Kyle watched graphics on the TV screen. You didn't need to speak Malay to understand figures on the maps: two hundred thousand-plus dead in Indonesia, thirty thousand in Thailand, more than ten thousand in Burma and untold thousands on islands across the Pacific. He'd been dragged to an Arsenal match with James once, and realised that it added up to six Highbury stadiums full of people.

The mood lightened as the women began serving bowls of fish curry and rice. Kyle wasn't used to eating food with his fingers and there was much laughter as he dropped scalding curry-coated fish down his leg and hopped about frantically as he rubbed it off.

Out at sea a large motorboat was coming in on the tide. A group of village natives who worked on the mainland had chartered the boat after hearing about the shadow wave. Kids abandoned their curry bowls and charged out into the surf to greet parents they usually only saw once or twice a month.

Kyle's little friend was soon in the arms of a mother and teenaged uncle, but Wati came back looking disappointed.

'Mum works in an office in Kuala Lumpur,' Aizat explained. 'That lot work in the factories.'

Wati looked sad as she watched kids with their parents. Most were treated to small gifts or chocolate bars from backpacks, before dragging their parents away to show them the damaged huts.

Many told the story of how Dante and the tourists from the Starfish Hotel had gone under the roof to rescue the twins. Earlier in the day there was work to do and people had got on with it, but now Dante looked embarrassed as he became a star, posing for shots on camera phones, shaking hands and smiling self-consciously.

Kyle stared through the crackling fire as the cooks steamed a fresh pot of rice and began frying fish to bulk up the curry for the new arrivals. Apart from a couple of restless naps on the plane, he'd not slept in more than thirty hours and his muscles ached from clearing debris and lugging wood. But the sense of the community pulling together to repair their homes and resume their lives gave him a warm feeling that made him forget his tiredness.

The tide was coming in and with the coast road unlit and blocked, Large gathered Kyle and the trainees together for the drive back to the hotel. They weren't flying out for two days, so Large promised that they'd come back and continue to help with the clean-up next morning, while Mrs Leung offered free rooms at the Starfish Hotel to anyone with nowhere to sleep.

The Land Cruiser looked rather battered. The crumpled tailgate wouldn't open after supporting the weight of the house, so three of the trainees had to clamber over the rear seats to squat in the boot. They were about to set off when a column of headlights appeared on the road behind the village. The lead vehicle was a wheeled bulldozer.

'Looks like they've cleared the road already,' Large said admiringly. 'They're pretty efficient in these parts.'

Behind the bulldozer were two vans filled with police officers and an empty bus. After helping out all day, the CHERUB group were curious about the arrival of the police. They all started getting out of the Land Cruiser again and heading up the beach to see if the cops had any useful information.

A stocky police officer jumped out of the lead truck. He had four stripes on his blazer and held a loudhailer. Villagers were strolling up the beach to say hello and tell him that they were getting by and didn't need any help, but instead of engaging them the officer yelled through the megaphone.

'He's telling the villagers that they have to leave,' Mrs Leung translated. 'All beach villages are being evacuated as a safety measure.'

Kyle was surprised by this, but he supposed that there was a slight risk of a second earthquake and it was fairly typical for people to overreact after a dramatic event.

'I'd better go up there,' Large said. 'They said about tourists evacuating on the news, so I'll see what they want us to do.'

Kyle, Speaks, Mrs Leung and most of the trainees began walking between the huts towards the road. By the time they arrived, the police chief was arguing furiously with several adult villagers.

'The villagers don't want to leave their land, but the police are insisting,' Mrs Leung explained.

As the senior officer argued, more men were coming out of the back of the van. They looked decidedly unfriendly, wearing riot helmets, body armour and carrying clubs or baseball bats. Most didn't wear uniform and they looked more like thugs for hire than police officers.

Mr Large pushed his way between the villagers and looked down at the tubby police chief. 'You speak English?' he asked.

'Tourists must return to their hotels and await instructions,' the chief said resolutely.

'Why do these villagers have to leave?' Large asked. 'They're capable of looking after themselves.'

'Safety,' the chief shouted, looking at Large as if he was simple-minded. 'Governor's emergency regulations. This is government land. The villagers must do as they're told.'

'This is *our* land,' Aizat shouted furiously. 'Our families have been here for hundreds of years.'

Several of the villagers roared in agreement. More had

joined the crowd until practically the whole village was lined up facing the police.

The chief turned towards a group of his men, then pointed at Large. 'Escort these tourists back to their hotel.'

A group stepped towards Large. He wasn't easily intimidated, but several of them had handguns on their belts and looked like the kind of chaps who'd use them. At the same time another group of thugs had broken off and begun encircling the villagers.

'The coach is waiting,' the chief shouted. 'You have five minutes to gather belongings. Anyone who resists the emergency evacuation order will be arrested and severely punished.'

Large turned back and looked at the trainees. If he'd been alone he might have put up a fight, but he had to look after his six charges.

'Go back to the car,' Large told them. 'We're leaving.'

'The hell we are,' Dante stormed furiously. 'Why do they want the villagers out?'

'Dante, you'll do as you're damned well told,' Large barked.

The police chief shouted something in Malay, and Mrs Leung translated as Large began backing off.

'He says they'll bulldoze a hut if they don't cooperate.'

On the edge of the crowd, several thugs began manhandling an old lady towards the waiting bus. This caused an explosion of outrage and male villagers ran towards the police. The armoured thugs charged, swinging their batons and clubs. Most of the villagers retreated, but one man stumbled and found himself down on the ground, being viciously kicked and clubbed by three men.

Large was shepherding the trainees down the beach. Kyle simmered with rage and tried to think up a plan, but it was Miss Speaks who waded into action.

Despite being unarmed she ploughed in, displaying extraordinary physical strength as she plucked two of the men clubbing the villagers off the ground and threw them towards a second group who were running to their rescue. The third man lifted a full metre off the ground as Speaks' enormous boot kicked him in the stomach. She belted him with his own club as he hit the ground.

But just as Large had calculated before her, Speaks knew that no amount of physical strength would keep the men with guns at bay for long. She grabbed the battered villager out of the dirt and threw him easily over her back.

As Speaks ran down the beach towards the Land Cruiser and the rest of the retreating CHERUB party, Aizat picked up a large rock. It belted the unhelmeted police chief full in the face, spattering his nose and slicing his bald head. As the police chief slumped back into the sand, one man grabbed Aizat while another swung a bat, hitting him full force in the stomach.

The other thugs were swinging indiscriminately, knocking down kids and busting old women's noses. When villagers fell, a second line of thugs fitted disposable plastic cuffs around their wrists and ankles before dragging them on to the bus.

Aizat thought he was going to die as the police chief wedged his handgun in his mouth. Instead, he ordered his colleagues to beat the boy before throwing him into a police van.

The CHERUB party, including Speaks and the man she'd saved from a beating, had reached the Land Cruiser.

'What's that?' Kyle screamed furiously. 'Why are they doing that?'

'Why didn't the villagers just get on the coach?' Iona asked.

'Tan Abdullah wants that land,' Mrs Leung said.

'Who?' Kyle asked.

'Tan Abdullah,' Mrs Leung explained. 'He's been island governor for more than twenty years. You can't build on this island without his construction firm getting a cut.'

'Why does he want the land?' Kyle asked.

'Tan passed a law saying all the beaches are government land. The villages have been here for generations, but they don't have title deeds or papers of entitlement. When he gets a chance he sweeps them away.'

'And a tsunami evacuation is the perfect excuse,' Kyle said, shaking his head in disgust.

'This civics lesson is all very fascinating,' Large shouted, as Speaks shoved the bleeding villager into the front passenger seat of the Land Cruiser. 'But right now, we need to get out of here.'

Large threw Kyle the ignition keys.

'We won't all fit,' Large explained. 'You drive with

Mrs Leung and the kids. Me and Speaks will run on behind you. It looks like the bulldozer has cleared the way so use the road once you're clear of the village.'

'Right,' Kyle said, as he climbed into the driver's seat. He looked at the bleeding man beside him before turning behind to look at the kids. 'Are there six of you back there?' he asked.

'Yeah,' Dante agreed, as he took a last glance up at the village. It seemed that the hard core of village men had been subdued. Now the thugs were rounding up the women and kids and dragging them off towards the bus. Because of the insurrection, they weren't even being allowed into their huts to gather up belongings.

The three-kilometre run back to the hotel was nothing for Large and Speaks and they were already running powerfully along the beach as Kyle started the engine and cut across the crusted silt before turning on to the coast road.

Iona and another girl were in tears after what they'd seen and Mrs Leung stretched her arms around their backs. Dante was trying to be a man and not show his emotions, but he felt intensely sad as he sat in the trunk with his face pressed against the shattered rear screen.

'This whole world is a crock of shit,' Dante fumed, as he kicked out at the rubber trim over the wheel arch. 'Stuff like this makes me wish I'd been murdered with my parents.'

15. CAMP

Large tried changing their flights home, but there were few UK-bound planes with empty seats and the earliest they could fly out was the morning of 29 December, only one day earlier than originally planned. With the village empty, the hotel pool out of operation and the silt covered beach potentially contaminated there wasn't much for the kids to do when they got up.

Newly qualified CHERUB agents are supposed to be jubilant, but seeing their repair work go to waste and the brutal evacuation of the villagers had dented their spirits. They stayed in their rooms, watching TV news and sweltering because the emergency electricity supply didn't provide enough juice to run the air conditioning.

Downstairs an army of hotel employees and Mrs Leung's relatives threw out the sodden furniture on the ground floor and shovelled silt and broken glass.

Mr Large chartered a boat from the mainland to visit Mr Pike at the hospital. The bored trainees came along for the ride, and Miss Speaks gave them some of the pocket money they'd accrued while in training so that they could tour the local shops. Officially they were shopping for souvenirs and gifts, but they ended up spending most of their money on pirate DVDs and PlayStation games.

Only Kyle stayed behind, recovering from his jet lag. He woke at noon, took a cold shower and headed downstairs. Mrs Leung sat on a stool by the reception desk drinking black coffee.

'You've been working hard,' Kyle said, faking cheerfulness as he looked at the cleanly swept tiles and faded paint which gave away the outlines of departed furnishings.

'The water wasn't here long,' Mrs Leung nodded. 'The heat will dry things out quickly. But I don't know if it'll be worth opening again. Do you want lunch? I can get the chef to fix you a sandwich.'

'I'm not that hungry,' Kyle said. 'I ate a bucket-load of fish curry in the village last night. Surely you won't close the hotel just because of this?'

'Not just this,' Mrs Leung sighed. 'Who'll want to stay in this old shack when the new hotel opens? Tan Abdullah is building an even bigger resort with an American hotel chain ten minutes' drive in the other direction. Now the villages are gone, this hotel is all that's stopping him from controlling a ten-kilometre stretch of coastline.'

'Villages?' Kyle said, emphasising the S on the end.

Mrs Leung pulled off her giant sunglasses and nodded seriously. 'Four that I know of, just on this stretch of coast. They've been trying to get the villagers off the beaches for years, and a tsunami threat made a perfect excuse.'

'Where do the villagers go?' Kyle asked. 'Is there any way to find Aizat and the others?'

'They built relocation camps for the villagers a few years back, but a judge ruled that they couldn't force the villagers out. They're set back in the jungle, out of sight of the beach.'

'Abdullah can't make you sell this hotel, can he?'

Mrs Leung smiled. 'I'm not like the villagers. I have paperwork stating that I own my land, so he can't just kick me off. But Tan's company has already made a half reasonable offer to buy me out, and he usually gets his way. If I don't sell, the health inspector will find cockroaches in my kitchen and close it down, my tax assessment will go through the roof, rubbish won't be collected, the electricity will fluctuate.'

'What about the newspapers or television?' Kyle asked. 'Do they know these villagers have all been thrown out?'

'It's old news to them,' Mrs Leung said, as she swept away a fly buzzing around her head. 'Eight, ten years ago there was a big fuss every time someone wanted to relocate a village. But Abdullah kept plugging away, saying tourism creates jobs and brings wealth. He said a thousand people in wooden huts can't stop progress for the whole island and that all villagers will be treated fairly and given new land.'

'And are they?' Kyle said.

Mrs Leung laughed. 'It might be the same acreage, but what use is land in a jungle clearing to a fisherman?'

'Not much, I guess,' Kyle said wryly.

'I'm past fighting,' Mrs Leung sighed. 'I'm sixty-seven years old and I don't have the money to make this hotel compete with Mr Abdullah's. I can buy a nice house, visit my grandchildren, make a garden and let handsome young men like you do the worrying.'

*

Both Land Cruisers were in a state, but the one with the dented sides and new front tyre looked a better bet than the one with the shattered back window, crumpled rear and what looked in daylight like serious rear suspension damage.

Kyle was small for his fifteen years and didn't look old enough to drive. He didn't have paperwork, so he'd be in trouble with the police if he got stopped and even bigger trouble with Mr Large if he was found out. But the villagers getting kicked out stuck in Kyle's throat and he reckoned it was worth risking trouble if there was something he could do to help.

The chamber maid he'd resuscitated the day before drew Kyle a map to the relocation camp. The route took him along the coast road towards the village. The bulldozers had done an excellent job of clearing the road. Traffic was rare, but Kyle passed several tradesmen cycling to the hotel site and had to reverse fifty metres and pull into a lay-by, allowing a truck filled with ruined hotel furniture to come past.

He slowed when he reached the village. The beachfront had been blocked off behind day-glow plastic mesh hung off wooden stakes hammered precariously into the sand. Three policemen with assault rifles slung across their chests manned the site.

Two stood guard, while a third dealt with a line of villagers who were being allowed in two or three at a time to recover belongings from their homes. Kyle wanted to stop and offer them a lift, but he didn't want to attract attention to himself with the police nearby.

Instead, he cruised on, pitying an elderly couple dragging all they could carry. The road changed abruptly, from a single unfinished track into two broad lanes of new tarmac with yellow markings. Alongside were narrower lanes, which confused Kyle until he saw a multilingual warning sign: *Golf Buggies Only*.

The road had been spared the silt, but the same couldn't be said for the lawns around the nine-storey hotel building. Acres of newly laid turf had turned to a brown bog and would have to be dug up and re-laid.

But the giant sign still proudly proclaimed *Langkawi Regency Plaza & Golf Resort – five star seclusion, opening March 2005*. Men hung from balconies painting the half-finished stonework, while a team on the ground threw rolls of sodden carpet into a mound outside the main reception.

The tarmac only lasted a kilometre, with greens and bunkers being dug out of the jungle alongside. Then the trees closed in and the road went back to a single lane.

Away from the police, Kyle felt safe to stop the car and pick up the two teenagers whose baby nephews he'd helped rescue the day before. The girls had thrown clothes and shoes into plastic sacks, along with a portable CD player, bundles of disposable nappies and a cardboard box packed with their few valuables and family photographs.

It was lucky that Kyle had picked up the girls because he almost missed the narrow turn-off leading towards the relocation camp. The unfinished road was steep and went for half a kilometre before opening out into a rectangle of cleared jungle filled with small metal huts. Along the way, Kyle stopped twice, collecting the belongings of three more villagers.

The camp was the size of a couple of football pitches, covered with identical, evenly-spaced tin huts. There were more than two hundred and their brightly painted exteriors reminded Kyle of Lego bricks. After every eighth hut there was a larger building with taps on the outside, and toilets and open-air showers within.

It was all clean and modern. A politician could argue that residents here had better facilities than in their villages on the beach, but nobody with a soul could compare the traditional huts stretched across golden beaches with this field of tin sheds with the jungle looming on all sides.

Kyle was greeted warmly by several displaced villagers as he opened the back of the Land Cruiser and let the locals take out the stuff he'd driven up the hill for them.

His main impression was how empty the place seemed, considering that four entire villages had been evacuated here the night before.

He helped the girls carry their stuff to a bright yellow hut, the interior of which was hot and stuffy, in exactly the way that Aizat's traditionally built hut hadn't been the day before. The heat made the twins grumpy and picking one of them up was a mistake.

'I don't think he likes me,' Kyle said anxiously, as he thrust the kicking baby back to one of the girls. 'Is Aizat here?'

The girls didn't speak English, but a couple of kids who'd trailed Kyle from the car understood and led him by the hand towards a green hut. As he walked he noticed half a dozen mosquitoes stuck to his bare arm and more swarmed around his head.

Aizat lay in the unfurnished confines of hut three, row nine, which had a bright blue exterior. He wore bloodied shorts, with his T-shirt balled up under his head as a feeble pillow.

The police hadn't bothered to arrest him, but his legs and torso were covered in welts and bruises. Two fingers on his left hand were broken and had been fixed up with a splint, while the backs of his arms were horribly swollen where he'd wrapped them around his head to fend off flying boots and clubs.

'Bastards,' Kyle said, as his eyes adjusted from the sunlight outside.

'I got off pretty light, considering that I bricked the chief of police,' Aizat joked, though his half-hearted laughter sent a shudder of pain through his body.

'Where is everyone, anyway?' Kyle asked. 'Mrs Leung said they evacuated four villages. I thought this place would be packed.'

'Would you stay here if you didn't have to?' Aizat asked, as he rolled painfully on to his side and propped his back against the wall. 'Abdullah's goons let anyone who wanted to leave collect their things first thing this morning. Then they brought in a ferry to take them to the mainland.'

'Do they have places to go?' Kyle asked.

'Mostly,' Aizat nodded. 'Almost everyone has a son, daughter, brother, sister or whatever who works on the mainland. Give it another week and all that will be left are old-timers and people with nowhere else to go. The sad part is, our village has been on that land for hundreds of years and it's gone in one night. Go back in two years and all you'll see are jet skis and cabana bars.'

'It's sick,' Kyle said shaking his head sadly, as he looked around the bare shed. 'You're in no state to get your stuff. Can I sort anything out? Fetch it up here in the Land Cruiser?'

'Wati's down there already,' Aizat explained. 'She'll collect some stuff, and I used to sell fish to one of the carpenters working on the hotel. He's gonna bring the rest up in his van during his lunch break.'

'So will you move down to Kuala Lumpur to be with your mum?' Kyle asked. 'City life will be different, but a bright person like you–'

Aizat interrupted starkly. 'I've no idea where my mother is. She left the village when Wati was a baby. Met this other guy. Married him maybe. At first we were going to move down there with them, but then she stopped calling. And her letters went down to once a month. Then once every few months. Haven't heard from her in over a year, but Wati doesn't know that. She'd get too upset.'

'So it's just you and your grandma?' Kyle said. 'What about your dad?'

Aizat didn't answer for several seconds, during which he seemed to be making his mind up about something.

'My mum worked as prostitute,' Aizat finally admitted. 'Ten blokes a night, paid for the motorboat and the best hut in the village. But nobody has a clue who my father is.'

This revelation hung in the empty hut like a bad smell. Kyle tried to say something to make it seem OK, but came up blank.

'I think that's why the village was so important to me,' Aizat said. 'Wati and my grandma are my only family, but even though I'm young I was someone in the village. I collected the mail, took the fish to market, fixed the electricity. Now what do I do? Apply for a job at Regency Plaza? Put on a silly uniform and say yes sir, no sir, to rich guys?'

'People in the village relied on you because you're smart,' Kyle said. 'I saw all those heavy-duty books you read. If you did get a job at Regency Plaza you'd probably be managing the place by the time you're twenty.'

'I'd sooner eat my own shit than work for a hotel,' Aizat spat.

'So is there *anything* I can do?' Kyle asked hopefully. 'I won't have time after today. We're flying out tomorrow afternoon, staying overnight in Kuala Lumpur and catching the early flight to London the morning after.'

Aizat shook his head. 'You're a good person, Kyle, but unless there's something you're not telling me – like you're related to the Malaysian prime minister, or you've got a billion dollars in the bank – I reckon my body's got to heal and my brain's got to work out how to get on with my life.'

'You're absolutely sure?' Kyle said, as he glanced at his watch. 'Because I don't mind helping if something needs doing, but I borrowed the Land Cruiser without permission and I don't want to go back to ditch digging unless there's a good reason for it.'

Aizat looked confused. 'Ditch digging?'

'Long story, mate,' Kyle said, feeling sad as he backed out of the metal hut. 'You keep safe and stay out of trouble. I bet you'll be fine.'

16. UNITED

It was the first of February, just over a month after Kyle's return from Malaysia. It was a Tuesday night, and the big projector screen was running in the main hall on CHERUB campus. There were fifty kids and a dozen staff in a room filled with shouts and cheering. Arsenal were beating Manchester United by two goals to one.

It was the fifty-second minute of the game. James Adams – aged thirteen – sat on a giant beanbag that usually lived upstairs in Kerry's room. Kerry sat alongside, dressed in one of James' old Arsenal shirts out of loyalty rather than because she was a fan. On James' other side was fellow Arsenal nut Shakeel, while behind was a big group of United fans, including James' mates Mo and Connor along with a bunch of older agents.

'United!' they chanted, before punching the air in unison.

'Champions,' the Arsenal fans shouted back.

'We're outplaying these Arsenal dicks,' Mo said. 'Cockneys have had all the luck.'

James overheard this and shot to his feet. '*We've* had the luck?' he shouted indignantly. 'What about Rooney? He should have been off before half-time if that ref didn't have forty pounds of shit in his eyes.'

'Piss off,' Mo shouted. 'It wasn't even a foul.'

A couple of little lads standing behind James wearing Arsenal kits pulled the back of their tracksuit bottoms down and mooned the United fans.

'United fans lick our bums,' one of them shouted.

He was only about seven. Kerry put her hands over her face in shock and turned to Kyle.

'How does football do it? Why do they act like that?'

Kyle laughed. 'I'm only here because Ronaldo's cute.'

'He is,' Kerry agreed, to James' obvious irritation.

'*Arsenal have to be careful here*,' the commentator said gravely. '*They may be ahead, but United are starting to take this game by the scruff of the neck*.'

'What do you know about football you bald git?' Shakeel shouted to the commentator. 'Come on you Gunners. Put another one in the net.'

James tutted as United took possession of the ball in midfield. Despite the bravado, he was chewing nervously on the cord that ran through his hood as he settled back on to Kerry's big cushion.

'Peanuts?' Kerry asked.

The room had been laid out with bottles of soft drink and snacks in china bowls. James kept his eyes on the giant screen as he scooped nuts into his palm. Then he put three in his mouth and spat them straight out.

'Bloody dry roasted,' he moaned, looking accusingly at Kerry.

'Well why don't you look before shovelling them into your gob?' she replied.

A cheer went up from the United fans as Ryan Giggs took possession of the ball in midfield and found space.

'Close him down,' James shouted desperately.

But the tackle came too late. Giggs passed to Ronaldo on the edge of the box. The ball ran on almost to the line, but as James thought it was going out for a goal kick, Ronaldo belted the ball past Arsenal goalkeeper Almunia and into the back of the net.

'NO!' James roared, burying his head in his hands as the United fans erupted in cheeers.

'United! United!'

'You're not singing any more. You're not singing any more, oi!'

And to the tune of Dean Martin's *Volare*, 'Ronaldo, oh, oh, oh!'

'You're so lucky,' James shouted. 'There's no skill shooting from that angle. It's a pure fluke.'

'*United are right back in the game now*,' the commentator said. '*And the way they're playing you just sense that they're going to nick it. Whatever happens, Highbury stadium is on fire and the last thirty-five minutes of this game are going to be something really special.*'

'Just look at Ronaldo's manly thighs,' Kyle noted, as Arsenal prepared for the kick-off.

James was now in a foul mood and didn't find Kyle funny. 'If you don't shut up, Kyle, I'm not gonna be responsible for–'

'You're bright red,' Kerry said, grabbing James' hand. 'You look like you're gonna have a heart attack.'

James gritted his teeth. 'I *hate* United so much. Especially that jug-eared chav Rooney.'

Kyle coughed and cleared his throat. 'Oh that's rich, coming from someone dressed in Nikes, football shirt and a hoodie!'

'That's better,' James said, applauding as Arsenal got hold of the ball and strung a few passes together. 'Come on boys, let's get back into this.'

'Normal peanuts,' Kerry said, as she held another bowl in front of James.

James had been going out with Kerry for almost five months. It was his first long-term relationship and he'd learned enough to know that even when you're wound up in the middle of Arsenal vs United you still have to be nice to your girlfriend. He scooped up some peanuts and gave her a kiss.

'I'm glad you came down,' James said. 'I know you don't really like football.'

'Hey, Kerry,' Mo shouted, as he stretched out the Manchester United logo on his shirt. 'You should come over here and kiss some real men.'

'Real men,' Kerry laughed. 'What, are they hiding behind you or something?'

James and the rest of the Arsenal fans laughed and a couple of older lads gave Kerry high fives.

'You tell 'em girl.'

But the Arsenal fans' moment of triumph was snatched as Ryan Giggs found space on the right.

'Get the ball,' James begged.

But as Almunia ran to the edge of his box, Giggs chipped the ball to the feet of Ronaldo, who fired another goal into the back of the net.

James' jaw dropped as the United fans jumped into the air and started hugging each other.

'Cristiano Ronaldo won't turn twenty until Saturday, but he's celebrating already. Two goals in four minutes for the young Portuguese striker, and the question is: is there any way back for the Gunners?'

'Jesus,' James screamed. 'What was Almunia doing? Who was supposed to be marking Ronaldo? This is dog crap!'

'Three, two!' the United fans were chanting.

Kyle saw that James was set to fly off the handle and put a hand on his shoulder. 'Don't let them wind you up, mate,' he said soothingly.

'No coming back,' Mo said. 'Your dickless team is out of the match *and* the title race.'

James puffed out his chest and gave Mo a shove. A few of the other United fans saw and jostled forward, while the slightly smaller Arsenal contingent faced them off.

'You wanna make a fight out of it?' one of the Arsenal boys shouted.

Kerry spoke in James' ear. 'Back off. You're making yourself look like an idiot.'

James was fired up, but there were a lot of older lads

in both camps and he didn't fancy getting sandwiched in a fight between them, so he backed off. Some staff who'd been watching the match over a beer at the rear of the hall had come forward to break the crowd apart.

'Just a game, people,' Mr Pike shouted. 'Settle down, or we'll switch the screen off.'

As the Arsenal and United fans retreated, Mo sucked air through his teeth. 'That's it James,' he teased. 'Back off like your little skank told you.'

'I'll stick your head through a wall if you call me that again,' Kerry warned.

'Three, two,' someone else shouted, which was more than James could take.

He wasn't brave or stupid enough to throw a punch, but he needed to vent somehow so he scooped the peanut bowl off the floor and lobbed its contents at Connor and Mo. One of the United fans instantly lobbed a Pringles tube back in the other direction, but the staff acted decisively.

'Enough,' Mr Pike shouted.

Three burly adults forced themselves between the rival supporters. At the same moment, James' handler Meryl Spencer grabbed him by the back of his shirt.

'What did I do?' James protested, acting innocent as Meryl shoved him towards the exit at the back of the hall to cheers and clapping from the United fans.

'You did enough,' Meryl answered as she shoved James against the wall in the empty corridor that ran the length of the main building's ground floor.

'I never started it,' James said indignantly. 'That

United lot have been winding us up all night.'

Meryl laughed. 'And the Arsenal fans weren't baiting anyone when you were ahead, were they?' Then her voice turned serious. 'There are seven- and eight-year-old red shirts in there. What would happen to them if bigger lads like you start throwing your weight about?'

James didn't have an answer for this. He glowered, pouted and finally huffed, 'Why single me out, they were all doing it?'

'You threw those peanuts, which could have made things ten times worse.'

'Everyone was having a go,' James whinged.

Kyle came out of the hall and began pleading with Meryl. 'They *were* really winding him up, Miss. Getting personal and that.'

'Who was winding him up?' Meryl asked. 'What were they saying?'

Kyle had come out to defend James, but he drew the line at grassing someone else up. 'Just all of the United fans.'

Meryl looked tired, and James could smell beer on her breath. He sensed that he might get off lightly if he acted sorry.

'I didn't think about the little kids,' James said solemnly. 'I'm really sorry. I swear it won't happen again.'

Meryl didn't seem entirely convinced as she turned towards Kyle. 'Escort James up to his room, where he can calm down. James, you're banned from watching matches on the big screen for the rest of the season and you're docked two weeks' pocket money.'

James nodded. 'Yes miss. I'm sorry.'

But James' contrition only lasted until Meryl had gone back to the match. He went into one as he stood waiting for the lift with Kyle.

'Meryl's such a bitch,' James protested. 'Two weeks. What was I doing that everyone else wasn't doing? And bloody Mo. I'm tempted to go in his room and take a great big dump on his bed.'

Kyle sounded irritated as they stepped into the empty lift. 'James, first of all it's a *football* match. Second, Meryl was pretty fair considering that you almost started a riot. I've seen people get punishment laps and laundry duty for a *lot* less than what you just did.'

'Take her side, why don't you?' James spat. 'Everyone's against me. And I *hate* Manchester bloody United so much. I wish their coach would crash on the motorway, or a nail bomb went off in their dressing room.'

'Jesus Christ, James,' Kyle laughed. 'Calm down you psycho.'

But James was so furious that he punched the aluminium strip above the lift buttons and hurt his fist in the process.

'Bollocks,' James shouted, as he clutched his knuckles and screwed up his face in agony.

Kyle knew that James would go bananas if he saw him laughing, but he was struggling to keep a straight face and he bolted off down the corridor as soon as the lift doors opened.

'What's with you?' James asked.

'Gotta pee,' Kyle lied.

James' room was just across the hall, so when Kyle got to his room, he dived on to his bed, buried his face in his pillow and howled with laughter as his mind replayed James' tantrum in the lift and the absolutely epic expression on his face when he'd hurt his hand.

He laughed even more as he heard James slamming his door, and crashing around in his room, slagging off Mo, Meryl and reserving his most special contempt for Cristiano Ronaldo.

17. WINDOW

When Kyle had his laughter under control, he looked at his bedside clock and saw that it was gone nine o'clock. He flipped on his TV to watch the last minutes of the game, but while he'd enjoyed the tribal atmosphere down in the hall, he wasn't interested enough to give it his sole attention. Instead, he sat at his desk and tapped the space bar on his laptop to wake it up.

The only e-mail in his inbox was from his English teacher, warning him that his latest essay was below par and had to be rewritten before the end of the week. This was too depressing to contemplate, but as he walked away a Windows messenger speech bubble popped up in the corner of the screen:

Aizat FIGHT THE POWER says – 'Hello!'

Life on CHERUB campus was hectic with lessons, training and missions plus all the social stuff. Kyle felt a twinge of guilt as he realised that he'd barely thought about the events in Malaysia since his return.

He opened up a chat window and typed a reply to Aizat.

BLUEMAN 69 says – Hello back. Howz life?
Aizat FIGHT THE POWER says – Pretty shit TBH
BLUEMAN 69 says – Wassup?
Aizat FIGHT THE POWER says – Everything. Stuck in the tin shed. Everyone here being sick, some kind of bug in the water supply. Grandma spent a week in hospital. And now Arsenal are losing to Man Utd.
BLUEMAN 69 says – Have you been doing much?
Aizat FIGHT THE POWER says – Did some work for the carpenter who used to buy fish from the village. Made door frames for Regency Plaza Hotel.
BLUEMAN 69 says – Sell out!
Aizat FIGHT THE POWER says – Exactly. But no choice. He pays me OK, but only casual work. No regular hours. Grandma had to sell necklace to buy antibiotics when Wati got sick.
BLUEMAN 69 says – V. sad.
Aizat FIGHT THE POWER says – Some of us at the camp are setting up a protest group. No big deal but you've got to try, haven't you?
BLUEMAN 69 says – Anything I can do to help?

Aizat FIGHT THE POWER says – Ideas, money, publicity, books!!!!!!!!!!!
BLUEMAN 69 says – Publicity and ideas, I'll have a think. Money, I'm a tight wad. Books, what books?
Aizat FIGHT THE POWER says – Political campaigns. Che Guevara. Guerrilla tactics.
BLUEMAN 69 says – Are you starting a campaign or a war?
Aizat FIGHT THE POWER says – Maybe both. AAAAAAARGH!
BLUEMAN 69 says – What?

But Kyle knew because he heard James shouting and throwing something in his room across the hall.

Aizat FIGHT THE POWER says – O'Shea 89 minute. Arsenal 2 United 4. Hate United sooooooooooooo much.
BLUEMAN 69 says – You should meet my m8 James some time. You have much in common.
Aizat FIGHT THE POWER says – So can you send me some books? Or help at all? We're just a bunch of hot heads with no ideas ☺
BLUEMAN 69 says – Guess so. But you scare me a bit. Don't do anything crazy!
Aizat FIGHT THE POWER says – Don't worry. I'm too good looking to go to prison. I'd get bummed!
BLUEMAN 69 says – I'll try and send you some books. And see about publicity. Someone MUST be interested in what happened to your village.

Aizat FIGHT THE POWER says – Thanks. Got to log off. Only 52 seconds left and no more money.
BLUEMAN 69 says – When will you be on MSN again?
Aizat FIGHT THE POWER says – Hard 2 say. But I try to get online once or twice a week when I've got the money. Web cafe shows football, so usually whenever Arsenal play.
BLUEMAN 69 says – Goodbye.

Your last message was not received. Aizat FIGHT THE POWER has been disconnected.

Kyle's brain started working as soon as he got the disconnection notice. He wondered when Aizat would be online again, he wondered where he'd put the piece of paper with Aizat's details on and he started trying to think of ways to help Aizat out.

Kyle began by typing a few search terms into Google. *Tsunami victims* was too vague, bringing up thousands of links to news stories about the disaster. *Tsunami forced evacuation* was no more helpful. Then he tried a different tack and typed in *Hotel developer land theft*.

The first few links on the results page were to construction companies and some news stories about American legal disputes between property developers. The fifth link seemed more useful, bringing up a PDF version of a report written by the United Nations entitled *Costs and Opportunities in Global Tourism*.

The report was 226 pages long and contained pages of graphs, statistics and densely written text. Kyle saved the document on his hard drive, but decided to try and find something more easily digestible on Google before attempting to read any of it.

However, as he was about to close the report he noticed *Appendix H – Non Governmental Organisations specialising in tourism issues*. The first listing was for a charity called *Guilt Trips – campaigns for sustainable tourism and indigenous populations threatened or undermined by tourist developments*. Below this were contact details and a web address.

Kyle opened a new tab in his browser, typed in the Guilt Trips address and arrived at a disappointingly crude website that looked as if it had been designed as a school homework assignment. But while the site wouldn't win any design awards, Kyle became fascinated as he clicked on a world map and read reports about the damage done by tourist developments around the world.

According to Guilt Trips, giant French hotel chains had deprived Indian farmers of water, Romany people had been thrown off land used to build a theme park, a Florida wildlife park led to the local extinction of several endangered species and dozens of other atrocities were committed in the name of global tourism.

The most relevant link was to an article in a Canadian newspaper about Thai fishermen who'd been kicked off their land after a cyclone three years earlier.

On another page he read an article written for the Guilt Trips website on the tsunami.

While the world mourns the deaths of more than half a million people, the Boxing Day tragedy represents a boon for construction companies, landowners and property developers who stand to make huge profits from redevelopment. Few of these plans represent the best interests of poor and desperate tsunami casualties and in many cases, land is being compulsorily purchased and parcelled out to government officials and their cronies at the expense of victims.

Kyle had hoped he'd be able to contact a group like Guilt Trips or a journalist and whip up a storm of outrage. But Aizat's fate seemed to be a common one for poor people all over the region. He was actually luckier than most because on Langkawi the government had been planning to evacuate the villagers before the tsunami and had pre-built somewhere for displaced people to go.

Kyle felt depressed, but he liked Aizat and didn't want to let him down before he'd at least tried a few more options.

Over the years Kyle had made money on a variety of scams, including selling pirate movies and video games on campus. The least he could do was use some of his ill-gotten gains to send Aizat the books he'd asked for, and maybe throw in a few quid from his savings to help him out.

*

Kyle had a maths class first thing the next morning. He avoided James, who was in an absolutely vile mood after the four-two defeat. Kyle had a free second period and while he didn't hold out much hope, he went to his room and called the number for Guilt Trips' London office.

The woman who picked up was called Helena Bayliss. She'd written several of the articles Kyle had read on the website the night before, and sounded much younger than he'd imagined her being.

He told Helena what had happened during and after the tsunami, though for the purposes of his explanation he said he'd been holidaying with a youth group rather than conducting a training exercise for a top secret organisation.

'There's nothing particularly unique about Aizat's situation, sadly,' Helena explained. 'There's not been much media coverage of the tsunami's effect on Malaysia, but obviously there isn't going to be when the damage in other places was so much greater.'

Kyle sighed. 'That's pretty much what I thought you were going to say.'

Helena laughed. 'Let me finish. The one thing that makes your case interesting to me is that you said your friend Aizat was willing to start some sort of local campaign and that yourself and perhaps some other members of your youth group might be willing to give him help and some financial support. Guilt Trips is a small charity with limited resources. We can't launch a major campaign on your behalf, but we'd certainly be willing to offer support and advice to any activists who want to start their own campaign.'

Kyle smiled. 'That does sound quite useful. I mean, I want to help and Aizat says he's got a group of friends together who want to try doing something on Langkawi. The trouble is, none of us have a clue how to go about it.'

'I think we should probably meet,' Helena said. 'I'd be willing for either myself or one of our volunteers to come and give a talk to your youth group. And I can get in touch with Aizat directly.'

Kyle smiled at the thought of Helena turning up on CHERUB campus.

'Your offices are in London,' he said. 'I'm down that way on Saturday. I was thinking I could meet up with you somewhere and we could talk about this. Sort out a strategy, both for here and some things we can do to help Aizat.'

'Let me check my diary,' Helena said. 'Yes, looks like I'm free any time up until 4 p.m. Will you be able to find your way to our offices? Or I could meet you at the station.'

'I'm only *slightly* stupid,' Kyle replied, with a laugh. 'I'm sure I'll find my way.'

18. JUNKET

Helena Bayliss was twenty-three years old. She had the tall slender figure of a fashion model but a beakish nose and squeamishness about having it doctored ensured that she'd never become one. She'd studied law at university, but found it boring and now lived an impoverished existence writing one-off articles on travel and environmental issues for newspapers while working part-time as a campaigner for Guilt Trips.

Shortly after meeting Kyle she'd called in a favour from a friend who worked on a national newspaper, securing herself an invite to the official opening of the Regency Plaza Hotel on Langkawi. The flight from London was on a luxury 737, accompanied by thirty journalists, golf pundits and travel industry professionals.

Helena's editor at the newspaper gave a simple brief: a thousand words on the newly opened resort, and she'd been enrolled in a beginner's golf package in order to give the story an interesting angle.

The newspaper travel supplement had just inked an advertising deal with Regency Plaza Hotels and Tourism Malaysia, so the piece had to be upbeat. She might be allowed a few jabs about towels in the room, or mediocre restaurants, but demolished villages and refugee camps wouldn't do at all.

*

The brochure Helena had been handed by a Tourism Malaysia official had promised year-round hot weather and the sun seemed to be delivering. The tarmac steamed in the aftermath of a tropical storm as she walked down the aircraft steps, behind the boss of Britain's biggest online travel website and a man of unknown origin who'd tried chatting her up three hours into the flight.

A VIP channel was opened through customs for the distinguished guests. Documents weren't checked and bags travelled unmolested from the aircraft hold to a luxury coach. Within an hour of touching down, Helena had showered and lay on a king-sized bed in a soft hotel robe.

Her room was huge, with a balcony overlooking the ocean. There were three gift baskets: one hamper of chocolates and champagne, a bigger one packed with Malaysian produce from whisky and luxury toiletries to native carvings, and a final basket holding a huge spread of flowers in a cut-glass vase. Slid underneath was a letter and a CD-ROM containing a press kit of information and photographs about Malaysia and the hotel.

Dear Miss Bayliss,

Regency Plaza Hotels and Tourism Malaysia would like to welcome you to our new Langkawi Golf Resort & Spa.

As a VIP guest, you are welcome to use any of the hotel's restaurants, spas, golf courses or other facilities. Mini bar and all other in-room facilities are also complimentary, including your Regency Spa robe.

You are also invited to our hotel's official spectacular opening dinner at 8 p.m. on Saturday. Our roster of special guests will include Langkawi governor Tan Abdullah, celebrity entertainment and a surprise appearance by one of the world's most distinguished golf professionals.

Our staff is available twenty-four hours a day, so please get in touch if you require any assistance, or would like us to put together an itinerary for you to explore Langkawi island.

We hope you enjoy your stay,

Michael Stephens

European Director for Tourism Malaysia

Helena brushed her face against the soft robe, and

thought it would make a great replacement for the scrappy towelling rag she had in her London flat. She also remembered how excited she'd been, aged ten, staying in her first ever hotel. Sharing a room with her older sister and getting yelled at by their dad because they'd drunk Sprites from the mini bar without realising they were $7.50 each.

This hotel was far more luxurious and a part of Helena wanted to spend her three days eating, boozing and indulging every whim, just like she'd wanted to do when she was ten. But the slogan at the bottom of the letter snapped her out of the fantasy: *Tourism Malaysia – forging onwards*.

The bland slogan was a subtle reminder that Malaysia was doing fine, while most rival destinations in the region were rebuilding after the tsunami.

Helena felt a surge of anger as she looked around her opulent room and thought about all the resources that had been used to put all this luxury in a remote corner of Langkawi island, just so that some rich people could sunbathe and play golf.

Steel and cement from China, carpets from India, towels made in Vietnam, flowers from Saudi Arabia, TV and surround sound system manufactured in the Philippines. On top of that were the enormous amounts of energy used to keep the vast hotel building lit and air-conditioned, huge quantities of water and sewage and jet fuel burned to fly tourists in and out.

Helena dreaded her golf lessons most of all. She'd always hated golf, but a golf outfit had been provided by the newspaper and a fashion photographer was travelling from the mainland to take her picture. Helena might not have been up to catwalk standard, but she wouldn't have got this assignment if she'd been short and dumpy.

The mix of awe and horror at her surroundings made Helena want to lob something breakable at the wall. She didn't because her mess would only create work for some underpaid chamber maid.

But Helen wasn't just here for a thousand words on the joys of massage and golf lessons in Malaysia's newest resort. She perked up as she took her mobile phone from a glass-topped desk, stepped out on to the balcony and dialled a stored number as she looked out to sea.

'*Hai.*'

'Aizat, hello!' Helena said cheerfully. 'I'm glad I could get through.'

Aizat laughed. 'The only good thing about the new hotel: mobile reception around here is great now. How are you? Was your flight OK?'

'Not too bad,' Helena said. 'Comfy plane, so I slept for most of the flight. I'm in my room and I've got a few hours free. I'd really like to meet up somewhere and chat. Are you busy?'

'Just a few things, but nothing I can't interrupt,' Aizat said.

'I'd also like to take some pictures for the Guilt Trips website,' Helena explained. 'Showing where your village used to be, and where you live now. We're putting together an educational resource pack on sustainable development. So if you wouldn't mind, I'd like to record a short video interview with you.'

'Make me famous if you like,' Aizat answered. 'How about I meet you where my village used to be. It's beyond the hotel, near the breakwater.'

Helena looked along the golden sand. 'I see it,' she said.

'After that I'll take you up to see the camp and you can meet the other members of our campaign. Does that sound good?'

'Perfect! When do you want to meet? I've got to unpack my camera and things and get dressed, but apart from that I'm free.'

'Five o'clock then,' Aizat suggested. 'Do you have a flash? It might be getting dark by the time we get back from the village.'

*

Helena had been on all-expenses-paid junkets like this before and knew that the people running the trips liked to keep a close eye on their pampered guests: a journalist getting mugged, or stumbling drunk into a storm drain doesn't make for good press coverage.

To deflect attention from her exit, Helena dressed in Lycra and running shoes, with just a water bottle and camera in the small pack on her back. She set off at a jog from the side entrance, unnoticed by hotel employees and Tourism Malaysia officials.

Aizat sat in the sand by the breakwater less than two hundred metres from the hotel. He was muscular, good looking and surprisingly well dressed, in counterfeit Nikes, cargo shorts and a linen shirt. It seemed like he'd put on his best clothes, which was disappointing. Helena could have done with someone more desperate in her photographs.

She unzipped her pack and took out a pen and a small notepad, then began confirming and jotting down basic facts.

'So you're sixteen?'

'Seventeen now,' Aizat corrected. 'Wati is still eight, and my grandma is seventy.'

'And do you go to school, or work, or . . . ?'

'Wati has a teacher who comes into the camp. I work, otherwise we'd be broke.'

'Kyle said you'd been doing some jobs for a carpenter.'

Aizat nodded. 'I have a boat now, as well. I run errands, take fish to the mainland, carry passengers.'

'Wasn't your boat destroyed?'

'We repaired it after the wave, but the thugs pissed off with it. It wasn't there when we went to get it. So now I have another boat.'

'How?' Helena asked, as she double-checked to make sure that her voice recorder was running.

'Some people clubbed together,' Aizat said vaguely. Then he changed the subject. 'So how is Kyle? Do you see him often?'

'I've met him twice since he contacted me at the beginning of last month,' Helena explained. 'Once at the Guilt Trips offices and once at a demonstration we held outside the Kenyan embassy. But he lives a fair way from London and seems to lead a busy life. Exams and things, I guess.'

'Kyle's a great guy,' Aizat said brightly. 'He even sent me an Arsenal shirt, and some old match programmes.'

'So you said you've got a new boat. Did you get a grant or anything to buy it?'

'Grant!' Aizat laughed. 'I like that, but I'd rather not talk about business on tape. Come along the beach, I'll show you where our huts used to be.'

Kyle had explained that Aizat had been a kind of leader in the village before it was destroyed, but Helena was surprised at the way he acted. He looked seventeen, but seemed far more grown-up than the pimple-faced teens she caught eyeing her up in London.

Aizat found a stick and burrowed into sand until he found a splintered wooden post. 'That's one of the huts that took the full brunt when the scaffolding came washing along the beach. There were two babies trapped inside. Kyle and his youth group helped to rescue them.'

Helena was disappointed. She'd hoped that there would be some trace of the abandoned huts that would be more photogenic than a broken stick poking out of the ground.

'What's this?' she asked, pointing to a greyish-brown layer uncovered by Aizat's stick.

'A lot of our beaches are still covered with silt,' Aizat explained. 'But with the hotel opening, they didn't bother cleaning up properly. They just shipped in container loads of sand and dumped it on top of the silt. If you take a boat along the coast, you'll see that the sand here and all around the hotel is yellowish, not white like you'll see everywhere else on the island.'

A strange voice came from the other side of the breakwater. It belonged to a fearsome looking man in a blue shirt with epaulettes marked *Regency Plaza Guest Security*.

'Is this gentleman bothering you?' the guard asked, as he glowered at Aizat through mirrored sunglasses.

Helena shook her head and smiled sweetly. 'We got chatting,' she said. 'Admiring the new hotel.'

'I'm afraid that this section of beach is for hotel guests only,' the guard explained.

Helena looked around. 'But there are no fences, or signs.'

'We don't need them,' the guard explained. 'There are only a few hundred people living on this part of the island. Most of them work in the hotel, and those that don't know where they can and can't go. Would you like me to escort you back to the hotel, madam?'

'Is the road public?' Helena asked. 'Am I OK to carry on my conversation up there?'

'I suppose,' the guard said reluctantly. 'You know, if you want to exercise there's a good gymnasium in the hotel. It's got all the latest equipment.'

Helena laughed and spread her arms out wide. 'Why on *earth* would I want to drip sweat on to a Stairmaster in some air-conditioned room when it's so beautiful out here?'

She then gave the guard an *I'll be fine* wave and started walking up towards the road, with Aizat close behind.

'He's the big boss, that one,' Aizat explained. 'He was beside the police chief the night they threw us out of our village. It probably wasn't a good idea to meet you this close to the hotel in daylight.'

'This is supposed to be a free country, isn't it?' Helena complained.

'Are you fit to walk?' Aizat asked. 'I'll take you up to the camp to meet everyone.'

19. EYES

The sun was dropping behind the treetops by the time Aizat and Helena reached the resettlement camp in the jungle. Although many people had left for the mainland immediately after the tsunami, those that remained had either chosen to stay or had no other option.

The sterile environment that Kyle had seen three months earlier had changed as the huts became homes. Kids had formed gangs, people had built screens for privacy and adapted their huts with ventilation holes, extra windows and even extra rooms built from scrap.

But the situation was far from ideal. In particular the drains had been poorly installed. The toilet blocks swarmed with flies and had a heave-inducing stench, while the paths through the camp weren't suited to heavy foot and cycle traffic and the tropical rains had turned them into a bog.

Helena's white running shoes sloshed in thick mud as Aizat led her towards his home. He'd found his family a pair of the best huts, far away from a toilet block and on high ground where the soil drained. To make extra space, he'd built a waterproof wood and polythene extension between the two structures.

Inside Aizat had filled the space with furniture rescued from his hut on the beach and some western-style items from the Starfish Hotel. Mrs Leung had given the hotel furniture to the displaced villagers after selling the property to Tan Abdullah and moving to the mainland.

As Helena stepped out of her trainers and entered the hut in sodden white socks, she noticed Aizat's collection of books piled against one wall. Beyond these were thousands of items that she recognised from her hotel room: towels, flannels, soap dishes, sheets, table lamps, matchbooks, glassware and light bulbs stacked all the way up to the ceiling.

'I'm a hustler,' Aizat confessed, as Helena admired the stash. 'Tan Abdullah steals our land, so we steal from his hotel. The workers pilfer and bring it to me. I take it back to the mainland, and sell it to the stallholders in the markets.'

Helena clapped her hands and howled with laughter. She also imagined the wonderful newspaper article she could write about stolen land, corrupt politicians building vast hotels and the poor refugees who end up stealing from them to survive. She badly wanted to take a picture of the stolen hotel goodies, but didn't because it would be bad for Aizat if it got published.

'Do you make much money?' Helena asked.

'I do OK,' Aizat shrugged. 'But I had to borrow to buy the new boat, and people who lend to the likes of me charge a steep rate of interest.'

As Aizat said this, a boy and girl came inside. They were a little older than Aizat and looked so alike that they were obviously brother and sister.

'Me, Abdul and Noor make up the campaign committee,' Aizat explained, as Helena shook their hands and smiled.

'So what sort of things have you been doing?' Helena asked.

'It's hard because we're stuck out here in the north-west,' Noor told her. 'But I spent some time in the south of the island giving out leaflets and trying to speak with as many influential people as possible. I also met with charity workers and non-government organisations.'

'What sort of response have you had?' Helena asked.

Noor shrugged. 'Lots of people are supportive when you speak with them, but there's a real sense of hopelessness.'

Helena nodded solemnly in agreement. 'Tourism is the biggest industry in the world. We're just tiny groups, fighting against companies with billions of dollars. It can be frustrating, but all you can do is keep chipping away at people's consciences.

'Right now fewer than one person in a thousand thinks about people like you being kicked off their land to build a hotel, or the damage that gets done to the environment when they go on holiday. But if we keep plugging away, maybe that will go up to one person in a hundred, or even one in ten. And when you get to that stage, companies and governments *have* to pay attention because it becomes too costly not to.'

Aizat, Noor and Abdul all nodded in agreement.

'It can be depressing because it takes so long,' Abdul said sincerely. 'But my ancestors lived in our village for hundreds of years. Now all that's left are stumps of wood.'

'So do you have any kind of campaign strategy?' Helena asked.

Aizat nodded. 'We're concentrating on Tan Abdullah. He's been governor of this island since before I was born. But rumour has it, he's up for a government minister's job in Kuala Lumpur and he wants his oldest son to replace him as governor back here.'

'Anything that makes Tan look bad right now could stop him getting the government job,' Noor explained. 'So we're trying to cause as much of a stink as possible, harassing him at public appearances and that sort of thing.'

'He's coming here on Saturday for the opening dinner,' Helena said.

Noor nodded enthusiastically. 'There are supposed to be celebrities, so we're expecting media coverage. We're working on a plan to cause some kind of disruption at the event.'

Helena smiled. 'Sounds good, but don't be too forceful. As soon as you try anything extreme, your enemies start branding you as terrorists and you lose all your popular support.'

'We know,' Aizat nodded. 'But it's not often that Tan Abdullah makes it out here and brings the press with him, so we've got to make the most of it.'

A lad of about twelve leaned in the doorway and said something to Aizat in Malay. Aizat thanked the boy, gave him some elaborate instructions and then explained in English for Helena's benefit.

'It looks like the big boss sent someone up from the hotel to follow us.'

'Damn,' Helena said nervously.

She'd called in a favour from one of her oldest friends to get the Regency Plaza assignment, and if word got back to the newspaper in London that she was spurning the luxury hotel and offending advertisers by speaking to local activists, her journalism career would be down the pan and her friend would be in trouble too.

'Let's go mess with the man,' Aizat said, as he stood up and walked barefoot into the mud. 'Come on, Helena.'

Helena sighed as she put on her almost-new Asics running shoes which were now flooded with muddy water. Aizat led her between the lines of huts towards a stocky man in a blue shirt and shorts, skulking around close to a stinking toilet block.

'Are you following us?' Aizat asked, sticking to English for Helena's benefit.

The man smiled dopily and shrugged. 'What are you talking about?'

'Some people have short memories,' Aizat said

accusingly. 'You worked for Mrs Leung at the Starfish, didn't you? You got kicked out of your village same as the rest of us, didn't you? And now you do their dirty work!'

The guard tutted and flicked his hand towards Aizat, as if he was swatting a fly.

'You're a stupid little kid,' he grunted. 'What do you know about anything? Mrs Leung told the people at Regency Plaza that I was a good man and they fixed me up with the job when she sold the Starfish. I've got five young kids and two old ladies to feed.'

Helena understood the guard's position, but Aizat stayed angry. 'You have no dignity,' he hissed. 'You could move to the mainland like everyone else. You don't have to work for Tan Abdullah.'

A car horn sounded a hundred metres away, just beyond the first row of huts. The guard spun around as the moonlight silhouetted the boy who'd spoken to Aizat, spattering through the mud at full pelt. This was followed by the sounds of a car freewheeling down the sloped road that led back to the beach. The guard swore violently in Malay, before charging after it.

Helena looked at Aizat. 'That sort of thing makes enemies for no good reason,' she warned.

'Nothing to do with me,' Aizat grinned. 'I was standing right here when it happened.'

The car was a small Suzuki four-wheel drive. The open rear had made it easy for the lad to climb inside, release the handbrake and then push it off down the hill with the help of a mate.

People emerged from their huts to see what the guard

was swearing about as his vehicle picked up speed. At the first bend, the little Suzuki clattered noisily off the road, crunching through tangled undergrowth before thudding against a tree trunk and finally rolling on to its side.

Dozens of kids and adults scrambled down the road to view the wreckage. The guard led the way, but when he stopped a couple of boys in their early teens grabbed rocks and threw them at him.

'Don't spy on us,' they shouted. 'Stay out of here or you're dead.'

But the resettlement camp's residents were divided. Some bore a grudge, but almost as many had swallowed their pride and now worked inside the Regency Plaza, or as construction workers on other Tan Abdullah projects along the coast.

Helena shuddered with fright as a ball of orange flame lit up the jungle. She couldn't tell if the little Suzuki's petrol tank had ignited accidentally or deliberately, but the crowd was getting nastier and she was scared that the police would arrive and start asking questions.

The journalist in Helena wanted to stick around and take photos, but a mix of fear and shock sent her storming rapidly downhill towards the beach.

'Where are you going?' Aizat asked, as he chased after her.

'I'm going back to my hotel,' she said nervously. 'I'll be fine.'

'You don't want to be out here after dark,' Aizat said. 'There's some dodgy people around since the hotel opened.'

Helena said no more as her long legs strode briskly, with Aizat behind struggling to keep up. It was pitch dark with the canopy of trees hanging over both sides of the narrow trail and she had to dive for cover when a Toyota swept past at high speed.

It was different at the bottom of the hill, where the trees ended and artificial light shone from the hotel windows and a floodlit driving range. Instead of going directly towards the hotel, Helena crossed the beach and stood in the surf, washing the mud off her trainers.

Aizat stopped behind her. 'Are you mad at me?' he asked.

Helena turned, with a stiff expression and her long arms folded. 'I don't see what good it does us. Wrecking cars just makes people mad.'

'Maybe,' Aizat shrugged, as he moved closer to the water and let the incoming wave wash up over his own trainers. 'Then again, if everyone who was angry like I am damaged something, or stole a few thousand dollars' worth of property, places like the Regency Plaza wouldn't exist. Why shouldn't I fill a truck up with petrol drums and drive the bastard straight into the Regency Plaza reception?'

'Because you'd either get burned to death or spend the rest of your life in prison,' Helena said bitterly. 'You'd probably take half a dozen low-paid hotel staff with you. The insurance company would pay to rebuild the reception and Tan Abdullah wouldn't miss a beat.'

'Probably,' Aizat said, before erupting in a dry laugh. 'But what good have all your articles and campaigns ever done? Have you ever actually achieved *anything*, sitting in your office typing words?'

Helena threw up her hands with frustration as Aizat stepped closer to her.

'What do I know?' she shouted. 'Bugger it, go and kill yourself. Not that you need my permission anyway. I just came out here to try and help with your campaign. Maybe get you some publicity, but if you don't want my help I'll go back to my hotel. I can use the spa, take my stupid bloody golf lessons while some perv photographer leers at my arse, write my thousand-word puff piece for the travel supplement and forget all about this crazy shit.'

'Has anyone ever told you that you look sexy when you're angry?' Aizat grinned.

This comment threw Helena completely off her train of thought. 'That is *such* an awful pick-up line,' she said, laughing.

'So what do you want to do?' Aizat asked. 'Are you going to help us or not? Isn't that the whole reason you scammed this free trip off the newspaper?'

Helena shrugged as she began strolling through the surf. 'To be honest Aizat, I feel out of my depth. I came here to help some seventeen-year-old kid to kick-start his campaign, but you're more sorted than I'll ever be, with your little thieving scam, and kids looking out for spies.'

'People have always said I'm mature,' Aizat noted. 'Didn't have a lot of choice really. No parents and a seventy-year-old granny who's a sweetheart, but also the kind of person who'll give her last scrap of food to a stray dog and forget that she's got two hungry kids coming home from school in an hour's time.'

'Actually,' Helena said resolutely. 'You asked me what I want to do. Well right now my head is spinning and the only thing I want to do is go back to my hotel room and get blitzed on all the free booze.'

20. THREATS

Helena opened one eye. She was hanging over the side of the king-sized bed with her legs tangled up in the duvet. Her head was pounding and her mouth tasted like sour milk.

Someone was banging on the door. 'Miss Bayliss?'

'What?' she shouted irritably. 'You've got the wrong room. I didn't order anything.'

She wondered if it was the photographer, or the golf instructor, but the clock said it was nine and she wouldn't have to endure that torture until noon.

'It's Michael Stephens, from Tourism Malaysia,' the man explained. His accent was English public school. 'Could I step into your room for a brief chat?'

'I'm just having a . . . Hold on, let me put a robe on.'

'No rush,' Michael said calmly.

Helena sat up in bed. The mirror on the wardrobe

caught her long hair, horribly tangled. Her soaked trainers had left a dark stain on the brand-new carpet. The shower was running and Aizat's clothes were strewn over the floor.

She kicked his trainers under the bed, picked up his shorts and shirt and ran into the bathroom. It was a large space, with a jetted tub at one end and two sinks. Aizat was blasting himself in the shower cubicle at the far end.

'Morning!' he said cheerfully as he opened the shower door. 'Are you coming in?'

He had the same triumphant morning-after expression as every other man Helena had ever slept with. She dumped his clothes on the slate floor, reached into the shower and shut off the water.

'What the hell?' Aizat protested, as streams of foam rolled down his chest.

'You need to be quiet,' she warned. 'It's a guy from Tourism Malaysia and he can't know you're here.'

She closed the bathroom door, hurriedly pulled on the hotel robe and rushed across the room to let Michael inside.

'Sorry,' she said, as she faked a yawn. 'Jetlag *and* I'm a heavy sleeper. Did I miss something?'

Michael was a smoothie, dressed in a tailored linen suit and mirror-shined shoes. 'I wanted a quick word,' he said, as he glanced disapprovingly at the clothes, beer cans and half-drunk wine bottles strewn across the room. 'Out on the balcony perhaps?'

'Of course,' Helena said.

She felt like a naughty little girl who was about to be told off as Michael settled into a chair on the balcony.

'Is everything OK?' Michael began.

'It's good,' Helena agreed. 'A really beautiful place.'

'You went up to the resettlement camp with one of the locals,' Michael said. 'The security office was concerned for your safety.'

Helena realised this was going to be one of those conversations where nobody said what they really meant. Michael knew that she'd met with local activists who'd then trashed a car belonging to the hotel spy.

'He seemed like a nice guy,' Helena said. 'I went out for a jog. We got chatting. He invited me up to his home. I suppose that's a risk for a girl on her own in a strange place, but–'

Michael took some folded papers from the pocket of his suit. They were printouts of articles she'd written for the Guilt Trips website.

'Are you the same Helena Bayliss who wrote these?' Michael asked. 'Because to be frank, Tourism Malaysia doesn't have a good relationship with this organisation.'

Helena combed her fingers through her hair and tried to laugh it off. 'I finished university less than a year ago. I'm trying to get a full-time job on a newspaper. A friend of mine recommended that I work for Guilt Trips as a way of adding to my CV. They pay for each article. Not a lot, but I've got rent and twenty grand of student debts. The big newspapers aren't exactly battering down my door, so I take whatever work I can get.'

'I see,' Michael said suspiciously. 'And it's travel journalism that you want to work in?'

'Oh yes,' Helena agreed.

Michael gave a patronising wag of his finger. 'It's a small field,' he warned. 'Everyone knows everyone else. Your article must have been commissioned by Jane Baverstock.'

'She's my editor on this piece,' Helena nodded.

'Great lady,' Michael smiled. 'Jane and I go a long way back. We worked together for the New Zealand tourist board for a number of years. She's a good contact to have if you want to get on as a travel journalist. You want to keep on the right side of her.'

Helena understood that Michael was making a veiled threat: if her article mentioned displaced villagers, his old pal Jane Baverstock wouldn't publish it.

'That's why I'm really excited about doing this piece on the Regency Plaza,' Helena said, as she pumped herself with false enthusiasm. 'Up to now I've done all serious stuff. But this article, with the golf lesson angle, gives me a chance to show that I write lighter things as well.'

To Helena's relief, Michael seemed to swallow this line and his tone became warmer. 'So you won't be writing about Langkawi for Guilt Trips?' he asked.

Helena laughed the suggestion off. 'I'll be sticking to my brief from the newspaper.'

'Sensible,' Michael said stiffly. 'And you know, there are a few whingers up in those jungle settlements, but most now earn good money working in the tourist industry and the Malaysian government has put a lot of money into their welfare. They've got clean water and electricity. Education, health programmes. None of that could happen without the money that tourism brings.'

Helena sighed with relief as Michael left the room. She wasn't sure if he'd believed everything she said, but she reckoned the wannabee journalist act had at least bought some breathing space.

As she settled on the bed, feeling sick and headachy, Aizat emerged naked from the bathroom.

'Did that dickhead say *health* programmes?' he spluttered angrily. 'My grandma nearly died up there. Half the kids in the resettlement camp had diarrhoea and vomiting. We've had no doctor and no plumber to look at our drains. In the end a group of relatives on the mainland clubbed together and paid a doctor to come out. I know because I brought him in my boat and picked up our medicines on the mainland when I brought him back.'

But Helena wasn't listening. The trip wasn't going the way she'd planned and she was in a state.

She'd imagined that she'd arrive, sneak off to meet Aizat and use her experience of campaigning for Guilt Trips to enthuse Aizat's followers and revitalise their campaign. She'd then take her golf lessons and further her newspaper career by writing her bland travel supplement article and head home having accomplished two major goals.

Instead, she'd been rumbled by hotel security within minutes of stepping outside and found that the local campaigners had their own radical ideas. To make everything completely perfect, she'd got hopelessly drunk and slept with a seventeen-year-old.

The only good thing was that she was a long way from home and hopefully nobody who mattered would ever get to hear about it.

21. SWING

Over the next two days Helena took three golf lessons, made some useful contacts while dining and drinking with fellow journalists and tried not to feel guilty as she indulged in spa treatments, whirlpool baths and a speedboat tour around the island.

Her relationship with Aizat was awkward. He was cute, but she wasn't going to sleep with him again. They exchanged a few texts and discussed meeting up one more time to talk about campaign strategies, but she didn't speak properly to Aizat until he called her mobile at half-six on Saturday evening.

She was in her room, hair wrapped in a towel and trying to pick an outfit for the official hotel opening.

'We need your help to get us into the hotel,' Aizat explained.

Helena was alarmed at the prospect after what she'd

seen happen to the Suzuki two nights earlier. 'What are you planning to do, exactly?' she asked. 'They've brought in extra guards for all the celebrities. This place is sealed up tighter than a bank vault.'

Aizat laughed. 'Have you ever watched *Star Wars*? You know, the plucky team of raiders going in to knock out the Death Star. That's me, Noor and the gang in about three hours' time.'

'You're not going to be violent, are you?' Helena asked.

'No violence,' Aizat said. 'But it'll be hard getting out of the hotel with all this security. So we were thinking that some of us could hide out in your room for a bit and leave the hotel when things die down.'

Helena was torn. She'd come out here to help Aizat, but wasn't sure how far he was prepared to go.

'I don't know,' she said warily.

'Words unmatched by deeds have no importance,' Aizat said fiercely.

'You're quoting Che Guevara at me?' Helena said. 'At least you read the books I sent you.'

'I think you're getting soft, sitting up there with your free mini bar and your double quilted bathrobe.'

Helena sat on the corner of her bed and bit her bottom lip. Aizat was intense, compelling and more or less right. She'd been charmed by her surroundings and the comfortable lifestyles of older journalists, with their kids at public school and holiday cottages in Sicily. But did she really want to spend her life taking golf lessons and writing about restaurants?

'Are you still there?' Aizat asked.

'Just thinking,' Helena said eventually, before sighing. 'OK, OK, of course I'll help you.'

*

Helena came out of the lift and stepped into the Regency Plaza's huge lobby. It was just after eight o'clock. The space was crowded and men in tuxedos walked their eyes up and down Helena's long legs and shoulderless ivory dress.

'You look stunning,' Michael Stephens said. 'Have you been enjoying your stay?'

'Very much, thank you,' Helena agreed. 'Though I feel outgunned, surrounded by all these big diamonds and designer outfits.'

A black Bentley pulled up in front of the lobby. Flashguns popped as a vaguely familiar face and his girlfriend stepped out on to red carpet.

'So who is he?' Helena asked.

'Not a golf fan, I take it,' Michael laughed. 'That's Joe Wright-Newman. Currently ranked third in the world, winner of two major titles. How have your lessons been going, by the way?'

'My shoulders are aching, but I've hit a few good drives. My teacher said I'm above average.'

Michael spotted someone across the lobby and broke into a big smile. 'If you'll excuse me Helena, duty calls.'

As Michael shook a fat man's hand, Helena turned left out of the lobby. She walked along twenty metres of marble flooring, with lush palms and trickling water on either side, then swept her room key through an electronic reader. A large door slid open and she stepped outside into the hotel's deserted pool complex.

She glanced at her watch, then strolled innocently along the poolside until she reached a women's rest room. Noor stood inside a cubicle, dressed in a set of the blue and orange overalls worn by hotel maintenance staff.

'That's my spare,' Helena explained, as she handed over a credit-card style key. 'Is there anything else you need?'

'Just this,' Noor said. 'Thank you.'

*

The opening ceremony required everyone to leave the hotel – which many of the guests had been staying in for the past three days – and line up behind a thick gold ribbon outside the hotel entrance. This ribbon was then cut simultaneously with five pairs of giant scissors held by Joe Wright-Newman, a famous opera singer, two Malaysian pop stars and governor Tan Abdullah.

After cheers and applause, four hundred guests filed into the hotel's main dining-hall. Tan Abdullah was a small man who limped about on a crumbling hip joint, and he sat at the head table, which ran horizontal to all the others.

The rest of the guests were arranged in order of importance. This left Helena in the last row, by a set of swinging doors leading to the kitchen.

The food was average, and cold by the time four hundred guests had been served. After three courses, there was dessert and coffee, and Tan Abdullah stood up and began making a speech in Malay. The island TV station loyally recorded their governor's triumph, while a small group of photographers knelt in front of the head table and snapped pictures of the celebrities.

As Tan Abdullah bowed graciously and sat down to take his applause, six masked figures dressed in hotel overalls burst from the kitchen doors at the back of the room. Four young men ran towards the head table while two women stayed at the back and began unfurling a banner with pictures of beachfront villages on it.

Diners gasped as the first two men sprayed fire extinguishers filled with sticky white liquid towards the head table. Tan Abdullah was the target, but golfer Joe Wright-Newman and the pop stars were also badly spattered.

Gasps and screams rippled across the hall as another masked activist ripped open a bin liner stuffed with bird feathers and threw them over the head table. His companion had a smaller bag filled with leaflets and he ran between the tables throwing them at the diners.

'We demand Tan Abdullah be prosecuted for illegal destruction of villages,' Aizat shouted.

One of his comrades jumped on to a dining-table and shouted a similar message in Malay, as teams of police and black-uniformed hotel security officers swarmed into the room. The masked men began running along and between the tables back towards the kitchen, pursued by hotel security and Tan Abdullah's police protection squad.

Aizat was the first to be caught, his short frame

brought down by a burly dinner guest. Within seconds he was surrounded by guards and fitted with handcuffs. The two woman activists were near the doors into the kitchens and stood the best chance of escaping.

Helena thrust her leg out as a police officer sprinted past her table, tripping him head first into the next table. Another officer was a few paces behind, but the women got through to the kitchens and friendly staff blocked the pursuing officers by wheeling a heavy serving trolley in front of the double doors.

Tan Abdullah raged as the feathers flying all around him stuck to his wet clothes and skin. Photographers snapped as he lunged towards the television cameraman and tried putting his hand over the lens.

Some diners' shock had turned to laughter, but Aizat and his colleagues had nothing to laugh about as police officers and hotel security guards frogmarched them out of the dining-room and on through the lobby.

Helena had her own problem as the officer she'd tripped up stumbled towards her in a daze.

'Who are you?' he demanded. 'You're under arrest.'

But a journalist called Jennie who'd been chatting to Helena throughout the meal shot to her feet and spoke fiercely.

'It was clearly an accident, don't be so preposterous.'

A couple of Malaysian guests sitting directly opposite also began berating the officer in Malay. A more senior officer strode across and told his colleague to calm down.

'Accidents happen,' the senior officer told Helena. 'I apologise on behalf of my colleague. He's overreacting, but he's just had a nasty bump on the head.'

'That's OK,' Helena said, as she dabbed sweat off her brow.

Jennie smiled as the officers walked away. 'I thought he was going to clap you in irons there, girl.'

'So did I,' Helena said shakily. She clutched her chest with one hand and downed her glass of red with the other.

The leaflets had all been thrown at the opposite end of the room, but they'd been passed along the tables and one was slid in front of Helena.

We congratulate Governor Tan Abdullah on destroying our homes, our environment and leaving us to rot in the jungle. Below this headline were three short paragraphs detailing what had happened to local villagers after the tsunami and a link to a website where you could find out more.

'Looks interesting,' Jennie noted. 'Everyone says Abdullah's a bloody crook. But in this business, who isn't?'

'You really think he's corrupt?' Helena asked, as the blood returned to her face.

A waiter had spotted her empty wine glass and moved to refill it, but Helena covered the glass with her hand. 'No I've had quite enough, thank you.'

A chill shot down her spine as she turned back towards the table. Michael Stephens stood three tables across. He was speaking to a hotel security guard while looking straight at her.

22. CELL

'Strip, you piece of shit!' the police officer shouted, unlocking Aizat's handcuffs.

The police cell was open to the elements, with a rusted mesh roof, a floor sprouting mildew and a drain hole in the corner crusted with spatters of shit. Aizat had known his chances of capture were high, but that didn't make the reality of the police compound any less frightening.

'And your shorts,' the officer ordered, as he swung his baton hard against Aizat's back. 'Your scrawny ass is really in the shit. Messing with Tan Abdullah on this island isn't good for your health.'

The officer belted Aizat again, knocking him against the back wall. He then grabbed him by the shoulders and kneed him in the stomach. Rage flashed across Aizat's face.

'Wanna hit back?' the officer laughed. 'Come on, I dare you. See what you get.'

He then kicked Aizat's clothes through the barred cell gate before slamming it shut behind him.

Aizat slumped with his back against the wall. The open-air cells were built around four sides of a rectangular exercise yard. He listened as men shouted, and cell doors opened and closed. He recognised the voices of Abdul and his other two male comrades.

'Did they catch the girls?' he shouted.

A man across the dark courtyard shouted back that he didn't know, but within seconds a huge guard loomed in front of Aizat and rattled his barred cell door.

'One more word and we'll gag your mouths,' he threatened. 'Prisoners may not communicate.'

'Up yours!' a prisoner yelled.

'Oh, you think you're clever?' the guard shouted back.

Two more police guards came across. 'Cell six,' one said.

A cell door clanked open, but the sound came from Aizat's side of the block. He tried to see through the bars as the three guards dragged a man into the middle of the courtyard.

'What?' the man complained. 'I was sleeping.'

'If someone speaks, someone gets hurt,' an officer shouted.

The naked prisoner was thrown to the ground and belted several times with clubs, then booted brutally in the stomach.

'On haunches,' another officer screamed.

The prisoner had previous experience and knew what this meant. He spread his feet wide apart, squatted down with his bare bum hovering a few centimetres above the ground and placed his hands on his head. This stress position required constant alertness to stay upright and could cause agonising cramps in less than twenty minutes.

'He stays like that until morning,' an officer announced. 'Any more noise and the rest of you join him.'

Aizat shuddered as his hands gripped the bars of his cell. He'd read a lot of philosophy and books about guerrillas and freedom fighters who'd spent time in prison. It seemed heroic on the page, but right now he was bruised, naked and completely terrified.

*

It would look suspicious if Helena left the banquet in a rush, so she stuck around in the dining-room, trying to hide her nerves. There was a light-hearted consensus among the journalists that the goo and feathers had enlivened a dull meal and possibly saved them from sitting through further speeches.

The campaign leaflet didn't have much impact and Helena asked Jennie about it.

'The locals bang the same drum wherever tourist facilities are developed,' Jennie said. 'You feel for these people, but development has to happen. Some fat cat like Abdullah will make a packet, a few locals will get screwed over.'

'There *must* be a way of developing tourism without

ripping off the locals,' Helena said, as she turned the leaflet over in her hand.

'I'm sure there is, sweetheart,' Jennie said, giving Helena a patronising tap on her bare shoulder. 'But I spent three years reporting on war in the Balkans. I ate shit food, had dirt in my underwear and my heart in the right place. But all my words didn't change a goddamned thing and when you land a cushy number like this my advice is to write the copy your editor wants, steal the towels and don't rock the boat.'

Helena didn't like Jennie's cynical attitude, but understood it after her frustrations over the past two days.

An elderly male journalist who'd chatted to Helena a couple of times bid her goodnight. His departure made it seem reasonable for her to leave too. She entered her room anxiously, half expecting to find a cop ready to arrest her or a pair of female activists cowering in the bathroom.

Everything seemed fine when she flipped the light switch. As she moved deeper into the room, she saw that her spare room key had been placed in front of the television and a short message scrawled on a piece of notepaper next to it:

Borrowed a few bits. Thx!

Helena saw that her suitcase had been rummaged. Two pairs of jeans, a lightweight coat and her black pumps were gone. It made her feel slightly violated. She was pleased that the activists had got away, but she didn't have much money and one pair of jeans were expensive

Diesels she'd had to save up for.

At least they'd taken their overalls and hadn't left masks or any other evidence for her to dispose of. The balcony doors were open and Helena realised it would have been easy for Noor and her companion to dangle off her first-floor balcony and drop down to the beach. The only thing was, a modern hotel like the Regency Plaza must have some CCTV cameras. She suspected that a replay of the footage would show them entering her room.

After the way Michael Stephens had stared at her downstairs, she wondered if it might be best to pack up and leave. But this remote corner of Langkawi wasn't the kind of place where you could call a taxi and she'd just seen the only person she knew with a boat get dragged off by the police.

And what would happen if she was arrested? What was the procedure? Would the other journalists help her when they found out? How would she get a lawyer? Was she even entitled to a lawyer in Malaysia? Would the British embassy come and rescue her?

Helena had a law degree, but it hadn't taught her anything useful. She wished she had a laptop and an internet connection so that she could do some searches, but a laptop was beyond her means and she'd planned to tap out her article on the ancient PC in her flat when she got home.

She thought about calling her parents and telling them that she was in trouble – or at least might be in trouble. But she was far from home, there wasn't much they could do and she could imagine her mum crying helplessly.

Helena crashed on to her bed and heard her heart drumming in her chest. She could hardly believe that she'd been naive enough to get herself tangled up in this sort of thing. She imagined everyone laughing at the stupid English girl who'd got herself involved with a group of crazy locals who burned cars and tarred and feathered politicians and celebrity golfers.

'I'm so dumb,' Helena told herself angrily, before rolling up against the pillows at the top of her bed and bursting into tears.

*

It was 3 a.m. but Aizat was wide awake when an officer rattled his door. His feet squelched in the mildew on the cell floor as he pushed his hands through the serving slot in the bars to have his handcuffs fitted. The prisoner squatting in the centre of the courtyard moaned in pain as Aizat was frogmarched past.

The interrogation room was inside the police building, two floors up. Two cops handled him roughly, shoving him hard against walls and using his head to open a set of doors. They wanted him to fight back, giving them an excuse to use the clubs and pepper sprays swinging off their belts.

The interrogation room was brightly lit with a table, two chairs and a stocky female officer leaning against the wall. Aizat's books were stacked high on the table. Karl Marx, Che Guevara and all the other communists had been placed at the top of piles, along with books on urban warfare and terrorist tactics.

'Sit down Aizat,' the woman said firmly, as she dismissed his two escorts. 'There's no need to act shy, you're not the first suspect I've seen naked.'

'Just another way to humiliate me,' Aizat spat.

The interrogator shrugged. 'I've worked with the governor's security detail for the past ten years. My job is to deal ruthlessly with anyone who crosses him.'

Aizat looked at the arrangement of books. 'So let me guess, I'm a communist and a terrorist. A major threat to state security. You want to lock me up and throw away the key.'

The woman laughed. 'You've got to be a dumb shit to mess with Governor Abdullah on his own island. The only thing you can do to make things easier is sign a full confession. Admit that you're a terrorist. Implicate everyone else involved in your organisation and throw yourself on the mercy of a judge. You're only seventeen. You might only get five years and remission if you behave.'

Aizat shook his head. 'I threw paint and feathers at the governor and handed out leaflets. I'll confess to that, but not this crock of lies.'

'Think it through,' the interrogator smiled. 'If you want to be a tough guy, we'll get other witnesses to cut deals and write statements saying that you're a terrorist who planned to buy explosives and make bombs. You'll get thirty years. They'll walk free.'

Aizat pointed at his books. 'None of this is proof of anything except intellectual curiosity. There are as many books written by right-wing politicians on that table as there are books about communism. There's three books about Gandhi – he was a pacifist for god's sake.'

The interrogator dramatically swept some of the books off the table top and drummed a finger against her temple. 'Get this into your head, Aizat. This has *nothing* to do with the truth. This is about Governor Abdullah. You humiliated him in front of hundreds of people, the press and a TV crew.

'Do you think he's going to let this police department take you to court on charges of throwing paint and walk out with a thirty-day sentence? He wants a clear message sent to anyone who messes with him. That message will be that insignificant little worms like you get chewed up and spat out.'

'I'll confess to what I did,' Aizat repeated. 'And I'm not saying another word until I get a lawyer.'

The interrogator picked up a long black baton. She flipped a switch in its base, which set sparks crackling between two electrodes at the far end. She swung the baton, touching the end against Aizat's kneecap. His body shot into spasm and his chin banged painfully against the table top as he crashed forward out of his chair and lay convulsing on the floor for several seconds.

'It's called a stinger,' the interrogator said pleasantly. 'And now you can see why.'

One of Aizat's escorts burst back into the room after hearing the crash. 'Is everything all right?' he asked.

'I'm doing fine,' the interrogator laughed. 'But I'm not so sure about him.'

She jabbed the electrodes between Aizat's shoulder blades. He screamed in agony and rolled into a foetal position facing the wall.

'Are you sure you don't want to confess your sins, Aizat?'

Aizat scowled defiantly. 'Sod you, you old witch.'

He expected another shock, but instead the interrogator looked across and spoke to her colleague. 'Cuff his wrists and ankles to the table top. Then shock the soles of his feet every three minutes until I come back.'

Aizat had read somewhere that getting whipped on the soles of your feet is excruciatingly painful, so he didn't want to even imagine what the stinger baton would feel like. He wanted to be strong, but his fear felt like a block of ice in his stomach.

'Maybe I can sign something,' he suggested urgently as the two guards moved in to lift him off the floor.

The interrogator stepped closer to Aizat and faked a yawn. 'You've had your chance, Aizat. I need my rest. I'll be back eventually. Remember officers, every three minutes.'

'Evil bitch!' Aizat shouted, as the interrogator headed out and the two cops tipped his books off the table before slapping his body face down against its shiny top. They each strapped one of his wrists to a table top with plastic cuffs.

'I don't think it's gonna be your night, mate,' one of the officers said, as he used all his strength to tighten the cuff strapping Aizat's right ankle to the table top.

Aizat screamed in agony as the stinger hit the bottom of his foot. 'Come back,' he begged, as tears ran up his brow and hit the floor. But he couldn't say any more because one of the officers ripped his head backwards and crammed a piece of filthy rag into his mouth.

23. TV

Helena couldn't sleep. The hotel room's powerful shower was no consolation and when she stepped out her nerves sent most of the four-course banquet spewing into the toilet bowl. She tried to calm down by closing her eyes, imagining herself checking out of the hotel and arriving safely at the private jet terminal at Biggin Hill.

She looked up the number for Langkawi airport, concocted a story about a sick grandfather and asked when the next flight to London left. There was a plane to Singapore the next morning, with a connecting flight to London. But at £1,460 the last-minute fare was beyond the limit on her credit card.

Helena was a good runner and the island was small. She thought about abandoning her luggage and running along the coast road to the south of the island. From there she could pick from any of a hundred small boats to the mainland.

But how would that really help? It might buy time, but the police could still pick her up when she tried to leave the country and suspicious behaviour wouldn't exactly help with any claims of innocence.

As Helena's brain spun, she kept expecting her door to burst open. But it didn't happen and by 3 a.m. she was starting to think that it might not. She'd tripped up an officer and met with Aizat, but what other evidence did they have?

Shortly afterwards, she gave up any hope of sleep and switched on the giant LCD mounted on the wall beyond her bed. As she flipped channels she came to a Malaysian news channel and saw the names Tan Abdullah and Joe Wright-Newman on the ticker scrolling across the bottom of the screen.

It wasn't in English, so she couldn't understand anything apart from the names. She sat on the end of the bed and watched the screen until Tan Abdullah's picture appeared in a rectangle over the newsreader's shoulder.

Seconds afterwards, the screen cut away and showed the attack with paint and feathers. The footage was much clearer than what Helena had seen from her seat at the far end of the room and the horror on the faces of Tan Abdullah and his highly paid celebrity guests was priceless.

The American golfer and the opera singer got spattered with almost as much paint as the governor, and Helena realised this would guarantee the footage airtime on news bulletins all around the world.

Some of those news channels might even discuss the reasons behind the protest. Helena swelled with admiration as she realised just how clever Aizat had been. The seventeen-year-old had devised and executed a scheme that used the power of celebrity to bring his campaign to prominence.

But Aizat must have known that he'd be caught by police thugs who were in Tan Abdullah's pocket. For the first time since the attack, Helena thought about someone other than herself and hoped that Aizat and his comrades were OK.

*

'Oh you *messy* pup!' the female interrogator jeered, as she stepped into the interview room and ripped the gag out of Aizat's mouth.

His soles had been shocked every three minutes for the past two and a half hours. During the involuntary spasms he'd pissed and shat himself several times and then writhed about in the resulting mess. The room stank, but the interrogator was hardened to it in the same way that a pig farmer can handle the smell of manure.

'Ready to confess?' she asked.

Aizat thought about the heroes in his books who'd heroically resisted torture. He felt pathetic as tears streamed down his face.

'Anything you want,' he sobbed. 'Just stop hurting me.'

'You're a lucky little bastard,' the interrogator hissed, before addressing the two guards. 'Take him out of here. Hose him off with disinfectant, get him clean clothes and put him in one of the air-conditioned cells downstairs.'

The two officers looked stunned.

'But he's completely broken,' one of them gasped. 'He'll confess to killing his own granny if you stick the paperwork in front of him.'

'His little publicity stunt is all over the news,' the interrogator explained. 'Star TV, BBC, CNN. So no dodgy confession, no quick sentencing before a local judge. The eyes of the world are on us and the governor says that everything has to be done by the book with this one.'

'Looks like your lucky day, Aizat,' one of the officers said, as he cut open the plastic cuffs. 'On your feet, boy.'

Aizat's burned soles seared with pain as he put them down in the puddle of urine surrounding the table. Only the officer grabbing his arms saved him from collapsing on to his face as he took his first step forward, but Aizat couldn't help smiling.

It was all worth it if the world found out what Tan Abdullah had done to his village.

*

Helena watched the story in Malay, before switching to CNN and seeing it in English. *World number three Joe Wright-Newman was tarred and feathered during a protest at the opening of a new luxury golf resort on the Malaysian island of Langkawi.*'

There was no mention of the reason behind the protest, but Helena being involved in a global news story at least made her feel a lot less isolated than when it had just been herself and a few local activists pitched against the island governor and his loyal police force.

Just after six the phone beside her bed rang. The call came from the reception desk, saying that a courier was waiting for her with a package in the basement lobby and was insisting that she come down and present some identification to collect it.

This seemed vaguely suspicious, but Helena figured that if the police wanted her they'd just come to her room and arrest her. She dressed rapidly in shorts, trainers and one of her golf shirts. The ground-floor receptionist directed her down a set of stairs into a valet parking area beneath the hotel.

The courier wore the smart uniform of an international delivery company and held a large rectangular package. After inspecting Helena's passport, he handed her a clipboard with a form attached to it.

'What is this?' she asked, speaking slowly in the hope that the courier would understand.

'Customs declaration,' he replied. 'For import.'

Helena nodded and began filling in the form. Full name, passport number, home address in UK, signature acknowledging receipt of package in good condition. After filling the form, she had to repeat her signature on the grey screen of a handheld electronic pad.

Finally, the courier handed her the mysterious box that had been standing on the ground between his feet.

'Have a good day,' he said, before walking off.

The package was light and didn't seem to be particularly well sealed. Helena balanced it on top of a concrete bollard nearby and ripped open the flap. Her jaw dropped as she saw her black pumps and Diesel jeans, now muddy and with a tear in the seat.

She looked around the deserted parking garage in a state of panic. It reminded her of the scene from a hundred movies, where a hit man emerges from behind a concrete post, or a van squeals down a ramp and runs you down at ninety miles an hour.

But nothing happened as Helena hurried nervously towards a row of elevators. Instead she found the door of her room open and realised that the package was just a ruse to enter her room with minimal fuss. A hotel maid was packing up her things, and Michael Stephens stood by the end of her bed.

Helena found a surprising burst of courage. 'Those are private things,' she said indignantly. 'You have no right!'

'Miss Bayliss,' Michael said, as smooth as ever as his hand pointed out towards the balcony. 'This is Mr Singh from the Malaysian immigration service.'

Mr Singh flicked a cigarette away as he stepped inside. He was a slim, effeminate looking man with a shiny plastic briefcase.

'Sit at the desk please,' Singh said.

Helena sat warily across from Singh at the narrow hotel desk. An anglepoise lamp hung awkwardly between them.

'Is this your handwriting?' he asked, as he slid a piece of paper in front of her.

It was a photocopy of a hand-addressed package of

books that she'd sent to Aizat a few weeks after she'd first contacted him.

Helena nodded. 'Yes it's my handwriting. Is it illegal to send a package of books to Malaysia?'

'No,' Singh said. 'Unless the books are banned or pornographic. We have no proof of what was in the package. But you did sign a declaration when you filled in your application to visit Malaysia stating that you intended to work as a travel journalist. Did you mention that you knew this Mr Aizat Rakyat? Or that you intended to contact him whilst in Malaysia and discuss his political campaign?'

Helena sat up a little straighter. 'Isn't asking questions a journalist's job?'

Singh shook his head. 'Your entry visa is not valid for political journalism. Therefore I am cancelling your visa. You will be escorted to the airport and placed on the first aeroplane leaving for the United Kingdom. May I please have your passport?'

Helena had spent the whole night wanting to escape the island, but felt angry and humiliated now that she was actually being kicked out.

'Do I have a right of appeal?' she demanded.

Singh nodded. 'If you do, you will be taken to the immigration detention centre in Kuala Lumpur. Your case will be heard in six to ten weeks.'

'It's not as nice as the Regency Plaza,' Michael added, with a sneer. 'And if you choose not to leave us quietly, I have some *fascinating* CCTV footage that I could show to the police.'

Helena reluctantly handed over her passport. Singh pulled a large stamp and a red inkpad out of his briefcase. The stamp matched the size of a passport page and comprised a huge X and the words VISA VIOLATION EXPELLED MALAYSIA. ABSOLUTELY NO RETURN.

Singh enjoyed playing with his big stamp, so rather than just doing it once he went through the passport inking the message on to every alternate page. This meant that Helena would have to pretend that she'd lost her passport and apply for a replacement, unless she wanted to answer detailed questions on why she'd been expelled from Malaysia every time she arrived in a foreign country.

'Your flight is at ten,' Singh said, as he took a quick glance at his watch. 'Mr Stephens will arrange your transport to the airport. If you do not board the flight, you will not be able to board another without first passing through the immigration detention centre in Kuala Lumpur. Understand?'

'Yes,' she nodded.

Singh handed back the passport and smiled. 'Have a safe journey home, Miss Bayliss.'

Helena sighed as Mr Singh left the room.

Michael looked down his nose at her and shuddered with contempt. 'I'll make sure you never work in travel journalism again. You *silly* little girl.'

May 2009 (again)

24. SLEEP

'I had no idea about any of this,' James said, as he sat at his desk and opened up YouTube on his laptop. 'Why didn't you tell me about it?'

'I had to keep it quiet,' Kyle explained. 'I screwed up my mission in the Caribbean, I got caught for smoking spliff on our drugs mission. If anyone here on campus had found out that I'd contacted Guilt Trips to try and help Aizat out, I would have been kicked out of CHERUB for good.'

James was slightly put out. 'But you could have trusted *me*.'

Kyle burst out laughing. 'Bull crap! Nobody ever keeps a secret on campus. Look at you when you shagged that Lois bird down in Luton. Bruce and Dana were the only ones who were supposed to know, but within three weeks your bath-time bonk was the hottest topic on campus.'

'I guess,' James admitted. 'But nobody ever grassed me. None of the staff know, even now. Anyway, what should I be typing here?'

Kyle looked at the laptop screen and shrugged. 'Try *Wright, Newman, Feather*.'

YouTube found the CNN clip and James watched Aizat throwing paint and feathers over Tan Abdullah, followed by his take-down by the cops. The video had been viewed more than a quarter of a million times and there were pages of comments typed beneath:

Free Aizat and Abdul
Aizat rocks!
Good feathering. Tan Abdullah is a dick.
Visit the Guilt Trips website and sign online petition TODAY

But not all the comments were in Aizat's favour.

Tan brought jobs and money to Langkawi and his son continues the legacy. The island had NOTHING *before he came!*
Aizat is a whiny knob and should be hung
These boys are so gay. Would have done better with a Glock 9!!!!!

'So what happened after Helena was deported and Aizat got busted?' James asked.

'Even with the press attention, Aizat was still in deep shit,' Kyle explained. 'But he got a lawyer, and he agreed to plead guilty to the paint and feathers deal. The police dropped terrorist allegations. In return Aizat's lawyer didn't lodge any official complaints about being tortured. He got five years in prison. Abdul and the other men got three years and Noor and the other woman eighteen months suspended.'

'So they must all be out except for Aizat?'

'Yeah,' Kyle agreed. 'And Aizat's due out soon.'

'What about Tan and the villagers?'

'There was a bit of a scandal. Tan became National Tourism Minister and passed legislation protecting any remaining villages. That made him look good, but he'd already demolished every village on Langkawi island, so it was actually to his advantage because it stopped rival hotel operators developing the beachfront in other parts of Malaysia.'

'Sly bastard,' James said, shaking his head.

'Now he's been promoted to Defence Minister and it looks like your job is to play nice with his wife and kids while he buys lots of shiny new guns and tanks.'

'And Helena?'

Kyle tapped Joe Wright-Newman's face on the laptop screen. 'Joe turned out to be a pretty stand-up guy. His people looked into the situation with the villages. He donated three hundred grand to Guilt Trips, so they could move into a decent office. He also helped them set up in America. He raises shitloads more through charity golf tournaments, and runs his own campaign on sustainable golf development.'

'What's that?' James asked.

'Every time you build a golf course, you have to clear a bunch of land, then you dump tons of fertiliser on it and have to use huge amounts of water to keep all that pretty grass growing. So Joe's charity builds golf courses, but they do it on brown field land. Like, they built one on the site of an old coal mine and another on the site of a car factory. They only use rainwater on the greens, there has to be public transport and membership is open to underprivileged kids and stuff like that. Though they'd probably still draw the line at scum like you playing there.'

'You're a funny man,' James said, before giving Kyle the finger.

'Helena's done really well. She's in charge of Guilt Trips' global operations, and they've gone from a tiny office over a shop in Camden Town to quite a big set-up. She also writes newspaper articles and lectures at universities and stuff. Oh, and Aizat slipped one past the goalkeeper: she's got a three-year-old son, Aizat Jr, who's also my godson.'

'Godson,' James spluttered, before he burst out laughing. 'You're such a sly one, Kyle. We've been mates for five years now, but you've still got all these secrets coming out. And you've got to admire Aizat: he's smart, he impregnates hot older women *and* he supports Arsenal.'

'James,' Kerry moaned from the bathroom.

'What?' James asked as he popped his head around his bathroom door and laughed at Kerry, still lying in his bathtub with the shower running. 'You're all shrivelled up. You look like a raisin!'

Kerry was feeling sorry for herself and spoke in a whiny voice. 'Don't be mean. Can you get a towel and robe from my room?'

James pointed at his towel rack. 'There's towels up there.'

'You never wash them,' she complained. 'The last time I showered in here I towelled off, looked in the mirror and found about twenty of your pubes stuck on my face.'

Kyle overheard this and started howling with laughter. 'Don't worry Kerry, I'll go fetch them.'

Kerry's room was only two doors down the hall and Kyle was still laughing when he came back and threw the stuff at James in the bathroom. 'I got your furry slippers as well.'

'Huggles!' Kerry shouted back.

'That's great,' James moaned, giving Kerry an arm up. 'He gets huggles, I have to hoist your fat drunken arse out of the bathtub.'

'I'm not fat,' Kerry moaned, as she giggled and slapped James on the back.

He tried making her stand up so that he could help her towel off, but she couldn't even stand up straight, so he grabbed her around the waist and threw her over his shoulder.

'Kyle, lift up my duvet.'

After ducking down so that Kerry's head didn't bang on the door frame, James stepped into his room and threw Kerry across his bed. Kyle threw James' duvet back over Kerry and she burrowed under James' pillows.

'I feel so ill,' she moaned. 'I'm never drinking again.'

James grabbed the wastepaper basket from under his desk and stood it on his bedside table. 'Don't you dare puke on my sheets. If you throw up again, aim for that.'

Kerry didn't respond, so James leaned across and studied her face.

'Spark out,' James told Kyle, and shook his head. 'And I'm such a gentleman that I'm not even *slightly* tempted to take embarrassing pictures while she's unconscious.'

Kyle fingered James' mission briefing. 'This is kind of awkward, but would you mind if I mentioned this to Helena? They probably know that Tan Abdullah is coming, but they won't have the full itinerary like you've got here.'

'Go ahead,' James said. 'I'm not doing a mission to protect this scumbag. I'll tell Lauren about it and I'm sure she'll drop out as well.'

'It might be the last mission you're offered,' Kyle warned. 'I wouldn't hold doing the mission against you, as long as you let me copy his schedule down.'

James shook his head. 'I know there are always going to be grey areas, but cherubs are supposed to be the good guys. I didn't train my guts out to protect a shithead like Tan Abdullah. Hell, I'm almost tempted to come along with you and join the protest.'

25. LEAVING

Meryl Spencer's recent promotion to chief handler meant she now had a full-time assistant and an office on the ground floor of the main building, two rooms along from the Chairwoman. It was Monday morning and James had a ten o'clock appointment.

'You're moving up in the world,' James grinned, as he looked around the spacious office at a trendy plywood desk, chrome coffee pod machine and orange swivel chairs. 'It certainly beats that pokey dive you had up on the sixth floor.'

Meryl smiled. 'Even better, I can't hear you lunatic kids running up and down the corridor and yelling between rooms when I'm trying to work.'

James moved to sit at the desk, but Meryl aimed her arm towards a sofa and coffee table, on which sat a mound of fat university prospectuses.

'You only sit at the desk when you're in trouble,' she said. 'Take a comfy seat. Would you like a tea or coffee?'

'I'm fine,' James said. Meryl grabbed a chunky ring binder with a label on the front marked *James Adams – Exit and Resettlement Plan.*

'With your Brigands mission running longer than expected, we're quite behind on your leaving arrangements,' Meryl began. 'It's nothing to worry about, but I called you in for this meeting today because we need to start making decisions about your future.'

'Right,' James agreed. 'So if I wanted to start university this October it's not too late to apply or anything?'

'Some people – like Kyle for instance – are very organised. He knew he wanted to study law, he knew where he wanted to study it. So we amalgamated his qualifications and put in a standard university application.'

'Amalgamated?' James asked curiously.

'Sorry,' Meryl said. 'I thought you understood. Over the past few years, you've passed GCSEs and A-levels as and when you had the ability to pass them. Exam certificates were issued under the name James Adams. When you leave, you'll take on a new identity. We'll reissue your qualifications under your new name, and give them new dates so that it looks like you took all your exams in the same year, like a normal school kid would have done.'

'Gotcha,' James nodded. 'I don't suppose there's any chance you can add a few extras to the list?'

'You're about the hundredth person to ask that,'

Meryl sighed. 'And the answer's no. We'd get no schoolwork out of anyone on campus if we just gave you a bunch of made-up qualifications when you left. And you don't have to worry with that maths brain of yours. What A-levels have you got?'

'B in Spanish and As in Russian, maths, physics, further maths and statistics.'

'Five As and a B,' Meryl smiled. 'Imagine what you could have got if you'd actually applied yourself.'

James laughed. 'What can I say. I'm a genius.'

Meryl grunted. 'And if your head gets any bigger you won't get out of the door. So the first question on my agenda: have you thought about your identity?'

James nodded. 'I thought I'd go back to my mum's name, Choke. And then I'll switch my first two names around. So I'll be Robert James Choke.'

'Sounds reasonable,' Meryl said, as she jotted it down. 'The next question is regarding your father. Have you thought any more about whether you'd like to meet with him?'

'That one's been doing my head in a bit,' James said, sounding stressed as he ran a hand through his hair. 'I read the letter my dad sent to my old flat. He sounds like a nice guy. But–'

'You don't have to decide right now,' Meryl interrupted. 'But when we create your post-CHERUB identity we have to consider the fact that your father is alive, and take this into account if you want to make contact with him at any point in the future. If you'd like I can arrange for you to talk your feelings through with one of the counsellors.'

'I think I'm OK,' James said. 'I've spoken to Lauren and Kerry about seeing my dad. I think at some point in my life I'll want to delve into my past and go see him. Maybe that's in a couple of years, or maybe it's in twenty when my own kid asks about his granddad.

'But leaving CHERUB is a really big deal and I've got to start this whole new life. I don't think I want the extra complication of a dad I've never met, and a stepmum and a baby sister. And what if the guy starts trying to act like a dad, telling me what to do and stuff?'

Meryl smiled. 'I see your point. I think you're being really sensible, keeping your options open for the future, while not rushing in to anything.

'The third thing we need to talk about is money. Your mother left quite a large estate. She owned your flat in Tufnell Park and rented out another that belonged to your grandmother. The mortgages on both were paid off by life insurance policies when she died. There were also large sums in bank accounts overseas, plus jewellery and cash in three safety deposit boxes.

'Your mother's money was invested in bonds and now stands at six hundred and eighty thousand pounds. Split equally with Lauren that will leave you with three hundred and forty thousand pounds each.'

'Not bad,' James grinned.

'In addition, you'll receive mission pay. That's equivalent to the basic wage of the most junior employee of the intelligence service, from the time you passed basic training until your eighteenth birthday. It works out at eighteen thousand six hundred a year from January 2004 to October 2009.'

Meryl reached behind for a calculator. 'Seventy months at one thousand five hundred and fifty a month.'

'A hundred and eight thousand five hundred,' James interrupted.

Meryl laughed. 'I do like the way you can do that. So in total you'll receive about four hundred and fifty thousand pounds.'

'Great,' James grinned. 'I'll buy a couple of Ferraris and blow the rest on birds and cocaine.'

Meryl cleared her throat. 'The money is yours on your eighteenth birthday and there's nothing I can do to stop you from buying Ferraris, but I *will* arrange for you to meet with a financial advisor. She can set your money up in an investment portfolio so that you get a decent income as you go through university. Then when you're older you can use the money to buy a property, or start your own business.

'If you're sensible with this amount of money it will give you financial security for the rest of your life. Half a million pounds may sound like a lot, but once it's gone you'll have nothing to fall back on.'

James nodded seriously. 'I might buy a motorbike, but that's gonna be my only extravagance.'

'Great,' Meryl said. 'I was worried when I set up this meeting with you. I'm relieved that you're being so sensible about this.'

James grinned guiltily. 'To be honest, it's not down to me. Kerry, Kyle and Lauren have all been nagging me for months, telling me that I've got to take things seriously.'

'Good for them,' Meryl said, as she placed her palm on the pile of university prospectuses. 'So we've covered your identity, the issue with your father and your finances. Now the trickiest bit, have you decided where and when you want to study?'

'Stanford University in California,' James said. 'Nice and sunny. I spent over an hour on the telephone discussing my options with that curriculum advisor guy in Chicago. It's supposed to be the fourth best college in America, the mathematics department is one of the best in the world and ninety-eight per cent of students live on the campus so I won't have to worry about being lonely, or not making friends.'

'And you're quite sure that you want to study in America?'

James nodded. 'Yeah. I think it would be really cool to live over there for a few years. And after being undercover with the Brigands for the best part of a year, John Jones says it's a good idea to stay out of the UK, just in case some Vengeful Bastard recognises me and comes at me with a hatchet.'

'I spoke to John about the safety issue,' Meryl said. 'You associated with a large number of bikers over a long period, so you could be in some danger, especially while there's a gang war going on. And besides, American colleges are the best in the world and Stanford is among the best of the best. The only thing that worries me is that it will be very academic. We can pull strings to get you through the door, but there's nothing we can do to keep you there if you fail your exams.'

James nodded. 'As long as it's maths or physics, I think I'll be fine. It's only when it comes to reading books and writing long essays that my brain turns to sludge.'

Meryl stepped up to the computer on her desk. She crouched over her screen and spent a few seconds studying a spreadsheet.

'Two other CHERUB agents have gone to Stanford in the last ten years,' she said, as she read from the screen. 'Both previous Stanford admissions have been handled for us by the CIA's relocation department at short notice and without any problems. And because of the security angle with the Brigands, CHERUB will pay all of your tuition fees and living expenses whilst you remain in full-time education.'

'The advisor said I should ask about American citizenship too,' James said.

Meryl nodded. 'I'd suggest setting you up as a British citizen. If you want to change that later, we'll be able to fix you up with an American passport.'

'Sounds good,' James said.

'The other obvious problem with going to America is that you can't pop home and visit Lauren on campus, or go see Kyle for the weekend,' Meryl warned. 'And I thought you were still in a serious relationship with Kerry.'

'American courses are modular,' James explained. 'So I can do my first and take a year off. So when Kerry leaves CHERUB this time next year, she can either start college with me, or we can take a year off and go travelling. And the beautiful thing is that there are other good colleges near Stanford. So Kerry could study at Berkeley, or USC and we'll still be near to each other.'

'I take it you want to fly out and actually visit the Stanford campus before making a final decision?' Meryl asked. 'You'll have to do it fairly soon because even our CIA relocation contacts need time to process your application and arrange your student visa.'

James nodded. 'The advisor suggested that I go and take a look. He said he can arrange college tours, with proper guides and everything.'

'I'll book you a flight,' Meryl said. 'It'll probably be the week after next if that's OK with you? And Kerry really needs to come along too if she's a serious part of your plans.'

James liked the idea of a trip to California with Kerry and broke into a big smile.

'There's one other thing,' Meryl said. 'I almost hate to ask the question, but I feel that I have to. How confident are you that your relationship with Kerry will stand up to at least one year of living apart?'

James shrugged and looked awkward for a couple of seconds. 'We've been separated on missions and stuff. But, I'm a realist, I guess . . . I mean, we're both young. We've broken up before. I *really* hope it works out with Kerry and that we end up studying in California together. But shit happens, you know?'

Meryl laughed as she walked back from her desk.

'Lots of shit happens!' she agreed. 'Stand up James. Give me a hug.'

James was startled. Meryl was always friendly, but not to the extent that she usually went around hugging people.

'Get your hairy butt over here,' she ordered, and held out her muscular arms.

Meryl pulled James into a tight hug and slapped him hard on the back. The six-foot three-inch retired Olympic sprinter was one of the few women big enough to mother a stocky seventeen-year-old like James.

'I've been tough on you at times, but only because I had to be,' Meryl said, as she let James go. 'But I'm *really* proud of the way you've thought your future through. You're a great lad, and I'm gonna miss the hell out of you when you're gone.'

James felt a tear well up in his eye. 'I never knew you cared that much,' he said, as he stifled a sob.

'Of course I care you daft boy,' Meryl said incredulously. 'You're all little sods at times, but you're all my babies. Well, with the *possible* exception of Jake Parker.'

26. SHOPS

James was humming *Going to California* by Led Zeppelin as he walked into the campus dining-room. It was morning break and there were crowds of younger kids queuing to get hot drinks and bacon rolls. He couldn't be arsed to wait in line, so he headed directly to a table by the window and joined his sister Lauren and her boyfriend Rat.

'You look cheerful,' Lauren noted. 'Did Kerry buy some kinky underwear or something?'

'Oh aren't you hilarious,' James said dryly. 'Where'd you disappear to yesterday?'

'Long walk with a bunch of wedding guests. It was really nice. The sun was out, we ate lunch in this country pub.'

'I got blisters,' Rat complained.

Lauren swivelled her head and glared at him. 'You

said you enjoyed it.'

'It was OK,' he shrugged.

James laughed. 'You two have been together *too* long. You're starting to peck at each other like you're married or something. So anyway, I had my meeting with Meryl.'

'Take it from the humming that it went well?' Lauren asked.

'Trip to California being planned to check out Stanford University. She did the financial figures as well. I get about four hundred and fifty grand. You'll get even more when you leave, because you passed basic training when you were ten.'

Rat looked down and blew casually on his fingertips. 'That's not much,' he sneered. 'ASIS found that some of my dad's paintings were registered in my name. I think the Picasso was sold for five and a half, then there was a Pollock, and a couple of Warhols. It came to about eight and a half million at auction as I remember . . .'

'Rich bastard,' James grinned.

Lauren nodded. 'I'm only really his girlfriend because of all the money he'll get when he turns eighteen. I'm gonna marry him and then totally screw him for a massive divorce settlement.'

'Well I'm no millionaire,' James said. 'But there's enough in the kitty that I won't have to worry about student loans or saving up for a car.'

'I feel bad for people like Bruce and Kyle,' Lauren noted. 'Their parents didn't leave them anything.'

'Kyle did OK though,' James said. 'Because his parents were povs, he gets an extra allowance from the

CHERUB trust fund. We're lucky that we're so well looked after. I remember when I was staying at the Zoo in Luton. The kids there got a council flat, dole money and a two-hundred-quid furniture grant when they turned seventeen.'

'They have to look after us after we leave,' Rat said. 'If they didn't, some desperate sod would write a book about CHERUB, or try sneaking out photos of campus and selling them to a newspaper.'

'So speaking of Kyle,' James said, as he gave Lauren a serious look. 'Did you read the e-mail he sent you about Tan Abdullah?'

Lauren looked a little awkward. 'I saw it quickly when I got back from the walk last night.'

'But you got the gist?' James asked, and Lauren nodded. 'I'm going to see Ewart Asker about the mission after break. I think we should go together and tell him that we're not doing it. I might speak to Kevin as well if I see him around.'

'I think I'm doing the mission,' Lauren said.

James gasped. 'You what?'

'You're in a different position,' Lauren explained. 'You're about to leave. If you quit, it makes no difference. But if I drop out of a mission less than a week before it's due to start there's going to be a black mark against me.'

James shook his head. 'No there won't. Your record on missions is one of the best on campus. If they need someone for an important mission and you fit the bill, they won't not send you just because you withdrew from this half-arsed bodyguard detail.'

Rat put a hand up to his mouth and spoke in a whisper, pretending like Lauren wouldn't be able to hear. 'She wants to go shopping.'

'What does shopping have to do with anything?' James asked, as Lauren gave Rat a dig in the ribs.

'She's been going on about this for ages,' Rat explained. 'Tan Abdullah is a billionaire. His latest wife is a top model and they have a reputation for spending big in the shops.'

'Ahh,' James said, as the pieces clicked into place.

Lauren had never been a girlie girl when it came to make-up, dressing up and that sort of thing. But the stereotype that girls were obsessed with shopping fitted Lauren perfectly.

'Tan Abdullah's wife is called June Ling,' Lauren explained, half excited, half apologetic. 'I've read about her in magazines. She's a shopping fiend. She goes into Harvey Nichols and spends sixty grand on dresses. I found this article that said when Tan's kids were little she took them into Hamleys and spent eighteen grand on toys in one pop.'

As James shook his head, Rat's best mate Andy Lagan came towards the table holding a tray with two bacon rolls and a mug of hot chocolate with marshmallows floating in it. He nodded to James, then shook his head.

'You're not going on about that shopping trip *again*, are you?' Andy sighed. 'I got stuck on a table with Lauren, Bethany and Tiffany in maths yesterday. It was all they kept talking about.'

'They're *so* jealous,' Lauren cooed.

James pounded his hand on the table top and pushed back in his seat. 'I can't believe you, Lauren,' he blurted. 'You're usually the moral one. The one who's a veggie. The one who wants me to shell out on some "adopt an endangered bunny" scheme for your birthday present. But apparently people getting tortured and thrown out of their homes doesn't matter, as long as you get to hang around some posh shops with a Chinese model.'

'James, me going shopping isn't going to knock down any villages.'

'Well do it for Kyle then,' James suggested. 'He put his whole CHERUB career on the line for you when Mr Large threatened you.'

'I'm chumming up with a couple of kids, going shopping and staying overnight in a posh hotel,' Lauren said. 'If Kyle has a problem with that, I'll find some other way to make it up to him.'

'You're never gonna persuade her, James,' Rat explained. 'She's had her heart set on this for weeks.'

Lauren stood up from the table. 'I've got to get over to the pool block for swim training,' she announced, before looking accusingly at Rat. 'And *you* should be more supportive.'

James shrugged at Rat while Lauren pulled on a big pack filled with her swimming kit and started walking towards the doors.

'Sorry mate,' James said. 'I didn't mean to cause trouble for you.'

'Forget it,' Rat said.

James noticed that Andy was picking at his bacon roll. 'You gonna eat that?' he asked.

'Take it,' Andy said, sounding like he had the weight of the whole world on his shoulders.

'You OK?' James asked.

Andy gave a nod, but Rat explained. 'He's been like this ever since Bethany came back from her mission with Bruce and dumped him. I think she's at it with Bruce as well – I walked past Bethany's room and you could hear them. We were talking about putting a surveillance camera in their room and posting the result on YouTube.'

James laughed at this thought as he bit a chunk out of Andy's bacon roll. But as much as he hated Bethany, Bruce was still one of his best friends. 'You're not serious though, are you? I mean, they'd both get expelled.'

'Of *course* I'm not serious,' Rat laughed. 'Imagine if Bruce found out. Your life expectancy would be about four-point-seven milliseconds.'

*

James was determined to try and stop CHERUB getting involved with Tan Abdullah, even if it meant pissing off Lauren. The mission control building was one of the newest on campus, but the hi-tech steel and glass roof had also sprouted leaks over the winter, leaving stains and mildew patches on walls and a smell like a musty cellar clinging to the air.

Senior mission controller Ewart Asker looked frazzled as James stepped through the door of his office. He had paperwork mounded on his desk and was crawling around the back of his computer, jiggling a lead.

'Nothing works,' Ewart complained violently as he stood up. 'What can I do for you, James?'

James looked up at a metal column streaked with rust. 'They still haven't fixed this place up?' he asked.

'Nightmare,' Ewart explained. He slumped in his chair. 'There are several companies that can fix this type of roof, but do you know how many of them have the security clearance required to work on CHERUB campus?'

'None,' James guessed.

'Got it in one.'

'What about the company that built the building?' James asked.

'Bankrupt,' Ewart said. 'And on top of that, my fellow senior mission controller, Dennis King, is in hospital having his prostate removed, my sodding computer isn't working and I've been waiting for an IT engineer for thirty-five minutes.'

James thought about saying it wasn't important and coming back later, but decided to start speaking. 'This mission that you've set up for me,' James said. 'I looked up Tan Abdullah. He's a scumbag, to put it mildly.'

'You mean the arrests last summer?' Ewart asked.

'Arrests?' James asked.

'Opposition politicians, arrested by the army on terrorist charges? Isn't that what you're talking about?'

'I only saw about tossing villagers out of their homes on Langkawi island,' James said.

Ewart shrugged. 'I hadn't heard that one. But Tan

Abdullah is a nasty little crook, no doubt about it.'

'So why are we helping him?' James demanded.

Ewart shrugged again. 'Abdullah is coming to Britain to ink a five-billion-pound defence deal, for everything from sidearms to trainer jets to gas turbines for new Malaysian frigates.'

James sounded a little cross. 'So we turn a blind eye to torture and violence, as long as there's a bit of money coming our way?'

'Oh, come off your high horse James,' Ewart said, sounding slightly irritated. 'You've been on too many missions to be that naive. Not many people get into high ranking positions in politics, business or most other fields without being ruthless. I'm not proud of the fact that we welcome someone like Tan Abdullah into our country, but if we didn't pocket the five billion the Americans, French or Russians would.'

James appreciated Ewart's argument, but still didn't want to take part in the mission out of loyalty to Kyle.

'I'd just rather not be involved in this one,' James said.

James didn't mention Kyle as a reason because he was no longer an active CHERUB agent and discussing the mission with him was a serious breach of the rules.

Ewart looked put out and sighed. 'Will I be getting a visit from Lauren too?'

'No, she's fine with it,' James admitted. 'She wants to go shopping with a billionaire's wife. And I didn't even speak to Kevin about it. He's a sweet kid. I didn't want to make his life complicated.'

'OK,' Ewart said, putting his hands together and nodding. 'You're off the mission, no problem. We can get away with two kids anyway.'

'Oh,' James said, disappointed that his moral stand had apparently made no difference whatsoever.

'So am I right in thinking that your academic programmes have all finished?' Ewart asked.

James nodded. 'I'll restart training in the dojo and lifting some weights once my legs have healed, but I think I've written my last essay on campus, thank god.'

'I'm a bit short-handed and getting rather stressed out, as you might have noticed,' Ewart said. 'Is there any chance you'd be able to give us a hand over here for two or three hours a day?'

James wasn't hugely keen on the idea, but he could see that Ewart was desperate and having experience working in mission control would put him at an advantage if he ever wanted to come back to campus for a summer job.

'Why not?' James said. 'It might even be interesting to see how missions work from this end.'

27. EARLY

One week later

It was half-four in the morning and James' mobile was blasting the theme tune from *The Godfather*. Kerry's room was dark and James had been sleeping alongside her with his face almost touching the back of her neck. They rarely shared a bed because Kerry was a fidget and James hogged the duvet, but they'd snuggled up after watching a movie and fallen asleep.

James backed hurriedly out of bed. Kerry's DVD player had gone into screensaver mode and the blue Sony logo drifting across the screen produced enough light for James to see his jeans strewn across the floor.

'Who rings at this time?' Kerry moaned, as she propped herself on her elbows and gave a long yawn.

'Don't worry about it,' James said, but as he rolled

over and reached to grab his mobile out of his jeans a plastic dish of corn chip crumbs and half eaten dips plummeted off the bed. 'Balls!'

'Aww, you tit!' Kerry moaned.

As Kerry flipped on a bedside lamp and dived across her bed to rescue the carpet from salsa and guacamole, James slid his Nokia open.

'Kyle, mate,' James said quietly.

'This is your early-morning alarm call!' Kyle said cheerfully. 'You fit? You ready to help us kick Tan Abdullah's arse? You're not gonna roll over and fall back to sleep?'

'I'm good. But I fell asleep in Kerry's room. I'll call when I get to the car and let you know everything's on track.'

'Sweet,' Kyle said. 'Talk later.'

James ended the call and started stepping into his jeans, as Kerry squatted on her carpet using the clear plastic lid of the nacho tray to scoop green guck off her carpet.

'Sorry about that,' James said. 'Phone startled me. I had no idea there was food lying on the bed.'

'Accidents happen. What did Kyle want at this ungodly hour?'

This was an awkward moment. James had told Kerry and everyone else on campus that he was going to visit a couple of UK universities, to check them out in case he didn't like Stanford when he flew to California a week later. He'd planned to be gone before everyone woke up and Kyle's alarm call would have caused no problems if he'd been in his own bed.

'I told you I was meeting up with him, didn't I?'

Kerry looked up at James suspiciously. 'No you didn't. And Kyle lives in Cambridge, so why is he going to meet you at Birmingham University?'

'I've gotta dash,' James said weakly. 'I asked Kyle to come along. He's at university, so I thought he could help me out. Pass an expert eye over things, you know?'

Kerry shook her head in disbelief. 'James, it's half-four in the bloody morning. Birmingham isn't that far away.'

'Rush-hour traffic though,' James explained. 'Want to get an early start.'

Kerry sprung up from her crouching position and faced James off. 'I don't like being lied to,' she said stiffly.

Kerry was only wearing a pair of tartan pyjama bottoms and James looked down at her chest and gave a smile. 'You really turn me on when you're angry.'

Kerry grabbed a fold of flesh around James' stomach and gave it a hard twist. 'Don't try and talk me around,' she warned, as James' face contorted with pain. 'Now speak.'

'Owww,' James protested. Kerry twisted harder. 'Your nails are like razors! OK, I've got this thing that's to do with Kyle and the babysitting mission that I pulled out of. I didn't mention it to you because I didn't want you to worry and I can't live with that pissy look you give me when you don't approve of something I'm doing.'

'What pissy look?' Kerry asked.

'The one you're giving me right now,' James smiled.

'Kerry, you're beautiful, sexy and I love you, but you have to trust me. I'll explain everything when I get home. Now will you *please* stop clawing me.'

Kerry pulled her nails out of James' stomach and gave him a little two-handed push. 'You'd better have a good explanation when you get back,' she said. 'And the next time you pull the wool over my eyes it won't be your belly that gets twisted hard.'

James grabbed his polo shirt and a denim jacket off Kerry's sofa, then gave her a quick kiss. 'You'll understand, I promise.'

The lights in the hallway were dimmed at night as part of a campus-wide scheme to save water and energy. James pulled his shirt over his head as he strode through the gloom and entered his room. He opened the drawer in his desk and pulled out a Micro SD memory card in a clear plastic case.

After sliding his bare feet into the nearest pair of trainers, James grabbed a mud-stiffened gym sock from his laundry basket, then hurried back out into the corridor and raced stealthily up four flights of stairs to Lauren's room on the eighth floor.

There was no way for James to ensure that Lauren was asleep when he entered her room. If she wasn't he'd pretend that he was planning a prank by sticking the crusty sock over her face while she slept.

But he needn't have worried. Lauren hadn't locked her door and her snore sent James down memory lane: he hadn't shared a room with his sister for years, but she was making the exact whistling sound that she'd made since she was about three years old.

Because James was leaving CHERUB soon he hadn't been upgraded to the latest handset, but Lauren's state-of-the-art smart phone stood in a charging dock on her desk. The handset bleeped as he picked up, but luckily not loud enough to disturb Lauren.

James slid the Micro SD card out of the plastic case and slotted it into the side of Lauren's phone. He then slid the handset open, and shuddered as he saw that Lauren had set her wallpaper to a picture of herself and Bethany draped in tinsel and poking their tongues out at a Christmas party.

The memory card contained a small hacking program designed by the intelligence service. It used the smart phone's built-in GPS receiver, logging the exact coordinates of the handset and sending them as a text message at regular intervals without the phone's owner knowing anything about it.

The software took an agonising minute and a half to install, before presenting James with a list of options. He set the interval at which Lauren's phone would send the text message containing its location to five minutes, then had to enter the number to which the regular text messages would be sent. Rather than risk his own phone being tracked, James had borrowed a battered handset from the campus storeroom.

As James typed in the number, Lauren missed a snore. He backed up towards the window and stood like a statue as Lauren's duvet shifted in the dark. Her arm moved out from under her duvet and she rubbed the back of her hand against her forehead, as if she had some kind of itch. But she settled without fully waking up, and James was relieved as the familiar snore whistled through the darkness again.

He finished entering the number, and selected OK. All trace of the hack program disappeared and the screen went back to the picture of Lauren and Bethany with their tongues out. The phone made a final bleep as James replaced it in the charging dock. He then crept out of the room.

James now had an hour to spare. He'd only asked Kyle to call at four-thirty because Lauren was most likely to be asleep at this time, but he did want to leave campus before lots of people got up and started asking questions about his business and in particular before there was a member of staff on the front desk keeping an eye on anyone checking out the pool cars.

The dining-room downstairs wouldn't open until six, but there was a storeroom on the sixth floor opposite the handler's office which contained hot and cold drinks machines, dry snacks like fruit and chocolate bars, as well as a fridge with sandwiches and microwave meals so that cherubs could feed themselves when they had to leave early, or arrived home from a mission at two in the morning.

James put a pod into the coffee machine and smiled as he noticed a hand drawn sign that had been stuck on the wall above the chocolate bars: *Eat Healthy! A chocolate bar and a can of fizz contain up to six hundred calories. That's more than an average thirteen-year-old burns in two hours running on a treadmill. For a healthier alternative, try carrot sticks dipped in cottage cheese or a low fat sandwich filling!*

He opened the fridge and was pleased to see a fresh supply of microwavable pancakes, which he could zap in his room. He put the pancakes on a plastic tray, then grabbed three small oranges and two sachets of Nutella, plus cutlery and a plate. As he turned around to take his coffee, Bruce Norris strolled in, dressed in shorts and trainers, with damp T-shirt and a whiff of sweat about him.

James did a double-take. 'Have you been out running?'

'Couldn't bloody sleep,' Bruce explained breathlessly. 'Tossing and turning, walls closing in on me. Thought I'd run a few Ks and try to knacker myself.'

'Something the matter?'

'Bethany dumped me,' Bruce said matter-of-factly.

'Oh,' James said. 'Sorry about that.'

'No you're not,' Bruce laughed. 'You hate her guts.'

'I'd be lying if I said I was her biggest fan,' James admitted. 'But I'm still sorry – because you're a mate and your feelings are hurt.'

Bruce shrugged. 'It's not even Bethany that's keeping me awake,' he explained. 'When I broke up with Kerry it hurt. I mean, physically hurt like some big dude had smacked me around. It's different with Bethany. It was fun but I always knew she'd move on to someone else.'

James felt awkward knowing how his friend felt about Kerry. He took a sip of his coffee before answering carefully. 'You'll find your Kerry some day,' he said, smiling slightly. 'I'm glad you had the sense not to let Bethany hurt you. How'd you get off with her, anyway?'

'When we were on that mission,' Bruce explained. 'She waltzed into my room in the middle of the night, climbed under my duvet, moaned that she was bored. So I goes, *What about Andy?* And she's like, *Andy who? And by the way I'm on the pill.*'

'Great story,' James laughed. 'What a classy little lady.'

'It was what it was,' Bruce said. 'And it's not like any guy is gonna say no to that, is he?'

'So if you expected Bethany to break it off, why are you running around campus at three in the morning?'

'If I pour my heart out, do you promise not to call me a wuss?'

'You can always kick my head in if I do,' James said. 'But nah, course I won't.'

'When I was with Kerry I was in love, but I don't really think she was. Even though you were going out with Dana, it always felt like I had Kerry on loan until you and her got your shit back together. With Bethany it was pure randiness. But I've never had that thing where you feel perfect with someone. You know how some people are *completely* comfortable with each other? You know the way your sister is with Rat? Or the way Michael and Gabrielle used to be? Or you with Kerry.'

'You're only sixteen,' James said. 'It'll happen someday. It might even be better that you don't meet Miss Right until you're older. Do you know how awkward it's gonna be with me going off to university and Kerry being an agent for another year? I want to be with her for the rest of my life, but we're seventeen. If I'm totally honest with myself, the odds of us still being together ten years from now are pretty remote.'

'So why are you up so early?' Bruce asked.

James lowered his voice. 'The thing I mentioned, with Kyle.'

'Oh, that's *today*?' Bruce said, as his face brightened up. 'Good luck with that. When are you heading off?'

James pointed to his pancakes. 'Soon as I've zapped these and eaten 'em. I'll check out a car. I've told them I'm going to visit Birmingham University. You can come along if you want. It might take your mind off things.'

Bruce glanced at his running watch and seemed to be considering it. 'I've got lessons though. I'll get punishment laps.'

James shook his head. 'Meryl's been promoted and Joe is the softest handler on campus. I'll go in with you and say that you were upset after your break-up with Bethany and that I took you out to take your mind off it. You'll get twenty or thirty laps and if you glaze over and say that you want to speak to a counsellor you might even get off scot free.'

Bruce was tempted, but still not convinced. 'Knowing my luck they'd throw the book at me. And I've got previous with Joe. Remember when I dangled Ronan Walsh off my balcony after he kept tormenting those red-shirt girls?'

'The protest against Tan Abdullah could easily turn violent,' James noted casually.

Mentioning violence to Bruce was like mentioning chocolate sauce to a six-year-old.

'Do you think?' Bruce said, as his eyes lit up. 'I suppose I could bunk a day's lessons. I mean, what's a hundred punishment laps between friends?'

'Exactly,' James agreed. 'So go shower off that stink, grab some brekky and I'll see you downstairs by the pool cars in about half an hour.'

28. SALES

The Royal Suite at London's Heathrow airport was a separate mini terminal with two aircraft gates, a customs post and a luxurious lounge where white-coated waiters served drinks at your seat. Lauren Adams and twelve-year-old Kevin Sumner had flown down from campus by helicopter and now sat in huge leather armchairs overlooking planes landing on the south runway.

Lauren wore a striped dress, lemon cardigan and white pumps that she wouldn't normally be seen dead in. Kevin wore chinos, striped Ralph Lauren shirt and had a cable knit sweater tied around his waist. The idea was for them to look like the well-heeled children of the smartly dressed man sitting alongside them.

David Secombe was balding and slightly overweight, while his chunky, diamond-encrusted watch looked like it cost more than a family car. Secombe had a reputation as a man with connections at the highest levels in British government. When defence contracts worth billions were being negotiated, Secombe was the man who could get your weapons for the right price and secure the export licences needed to get them out of the UK without awkward questions being asked.

Tan Abdullah didn't know that this was a sham. David Secombe was really an officer of the secret intelligence service. His identity was false and his company a front for the British government. This served a dual purpose: giving customers a sense that they were getting a special deal from a well connected insider, while the British government could pass blame along to Secombe's company when things went wrong.

If a human rights group ever started asking questions about why Britain was selling leg cuffs to South American dictators, or anti-personnel mines to African guerrillas, a vigorous government investigation would unveil an immaculately constructed chain of paperwork showing that Secombe's company had provided false information. Secombe would vanish into thin air, the politicians would keep their jobs and the intelligence service would set up a new front company to pull the same ruse all over again.

Secombe's standard background story was that he had three kids, and a wife who'd passed away. The dead wife was a perfect salesman's pitch, because it won you sympathy but also meant you could hang around in seedy bars with clients and not look like a total sleazeball.

Knowledge about CHERUB is kept on a need-to-know basis even at the highest levels of government and the intelligence services. Secombe had panicked when Tan Abdullah appeared keen to bring his family to London and meet his non-existent children, but strings had been pulled and Zara Asker had agreed to provide as many kids as Secombe needed if it helped to secure a five-billion defence contract and the twelve thousand British jobs that went with it.

Lauren looked around as pointed heels click-clacked across the marble. Their owner sat down next to her. Her name – at least as far as Lauren and Kevin knew – was Melissa. The twenty-eight-year-old intelligence officer was stick thin and would play the role of their stepmother during Tan's visit.

'Looks like our birdy,' Kevin said, pointing through the glass as a long-range executive jet thudded down, sending up plumes of tyre smoke. 'Not exactly the smoothest landing I've ever seen.'

The twenty-four-seater had to wait for a Qantas A380 to take off before it was allowed to cut back across the runway and taxi up to the Royal Suite's second gate. As the plane closed in, Kevin read *Abdullah Construction & Leisure* painted on the fuselage, with the words repeated below in Arabic script.

David Secombe left his armchair as the aircraft steps swung down towards the tarmac. 'Let's move, family,' he ordered.

Down on the tarmac, Tan Abdullah formally shook hands with the deputy British defence minister, an RAF helicopter pilot and the Malaysian ambassador. His face lit up when he saw the big man standing behind them.

'Secombe, you old goose!' Tan roared cheerfully.

Tan Abdullah was tiny and his feet lifted off the ground as David Secombe hoisted him into a tight hug. Standing directly behind, Lauren and Kevin leaned over to see kids following their father and stepmother down the aircraft steps.

Lauren hated her summer dress and cardigan more than ever as she eyed Tan's fourteen-year-old daughter Suzie. She was a chubby Asian Goth, wearing battered Converse, striped tights with ladders all the way up and a furry purple sweater that engulfed her torso and went down to her knees. Lauren was annoyed because being dressed like a little princess would make it more difficult for her to get along with Suzie than the jeans and sweatshirts she'd have worn normally.

Kevin had less to worry about. Tan Jr, known as TJ, was eleven years old and had apparently come dressed to shoot a rap video. He wore Nikes, baggy tracksuit bottoms, a Phoenix Suns basketball vest and the inevitable backwards baseball cap.

'You must be Kevin!' TJ shouted enthusiastically over the whirring jet engines. 'Wassup, dog?'

His bad English and with a Malaysian accent made the homeboy act sound hilarious, but Kevin kept a straight face and gave TJ a high five.

David Secombe was chatting to Tan and Melissa was complimenting Tan's model wife June Ling on her leopard-print dress. As the others paired off as planned,

Lauren smiled at Suzie.

'Hello, I'm Lauren.'

Suzie looked down her nose and made a big choking noise like she was trying to hack a dead sparrow out of her windpipe. 'Do English girls still dress like *that*?' she sneered.

'Only when their idiot dads buy something that they think will look nice,' Lauren said. She meant it to sound sarcastic, but English wasn't Suzie's first language so she didn't pick that up and just thought that Lauren was a daddy's girl and even wetter than the summer dress and cardigan had led her to believe.

Suzie raised a middle finger, painted with chipped purple nail varnish. 'If my daddy ever told me what to wear, I'd tell him to go screw himself.'

Lauren was saved from further embarrassment because the Royal Suite's manager was trying to herd everyone inside.

'Would any of our guests like to eat, or use our shower facilities before continuing their onward journeys?'

As huge trunks filled with luggage were unloaded from the jet, the RAF pilot led David, Tan and the other politicians towards a waiting helicopter, which would take them to a missile demonstration at a defence contractor's factory in the Midlands.

The women and kids headed upstairs into the Royal Suite.

Tan Abdullah yelled back at his wife. 'Try not to spend *all* my money in Harrods! *Forbes* magazine says I'm down to my last four-point-seven billion.'

*

The spare phone in James' pocket bleeped and the onscreen map showed that Lauren was heading east on the M4 towards London. He was passing through the main door of a central London church, which was being used as the assembly point for a planned demonstration by Guilt Trips activists.

An olive-skinned toddler belted out from between the pews and raced towards Kyle.

'Superman!' he shouted, proudly holding an action figure up for Kyle to see.

'Very cool,' Kyle said, as he picked the boy up. Then he looked back at James and Bruce. 'This is little Aizat,' he explained. The boy turned shy and burrowed under Kyle's arm.

Helena Bayliss walked briskly down from the altar. She wore a smart business suit and looked confident as she kissed Kyle on the cheek.

'These are my good mates, James and Bruce,' Kyle explained. 'What's the turn-out looking like?'

'Great, especially for a weekday,' Helena said. 'I've tried to round up as many people as possible. Tan Abdullah's unpopular with the anti-defence industry mob and June Ling is notorious for wearing and modelling fur, so we've got a bunch of animal rights activists coming along to give her some stick too.'

Kyle smiled. 'Three protests for the price of one. I had no idea there was an animal rights angle on this.'

'We need a lot of bodies if we're going to make an impact,' Helena said. 'And you can always rely on the animal rights mob to make plenty of noise.'

'I've got information from my source,' Kyle said. 'Tan's jet touched down on time. Looks like the shopping party is on the way to London.'

Helena smiled. 'Ahh, your mysterious source. How often can we expect location updates?'

'As often as we need them,' Kyle said, as Spiderman's head went into his ear. 'Aizat, don't be silly.'

'The TV people are off in a side room. Would your friends excuse us while I introduce you?'

But Kyle shook his head. 'They can come with us, I trust them completely.'

Helena looked uncertain. 'No offence to your friends, Kyle, but the more people who know about our plans, the greater the risks of a leak.'

'These are my guys,' Kyle said firmly. 'Have I ever let you down?'

'Well, if you're completely sure,' Helena said, as a little stress came into her voice. 'But you're the one who told me to always keep the numbers as small as possible.'

'I'll play later,' Kyle said, as he put a grumpy looking Aizat down on the church tiles.

Kyle, James and Bruce followed Helena past a group of activists using staple guns to nail campaign posters to wooden posts. They ducked through a low door below a staircase that led up towards the rows of organ pipes and walked down an uneven-floored passageway into a large vestry. The sunlight coming through a circle of stained glass projected spectacular colours on to the rough stone walls.

Three people stood around a metal-legged table. All in their twenties or thirties, they examined a small video camera like a surgical team around an operating table.

'Problem?' Helena asked.

'Clip's broken on the battery pack,' a tall Frenchman with curly hair explained. 'Insulating tape should fix it. It's no biggie.'

'It's only the small camera that we use for side angles,' a woman added.

Beyond the table sat an elderly man. He wore a padded storm vest with rows of small pockets, and looked over the top of half-rimmed glasses at *The Times* crossword. James instantly recognised the face from hundreds of news reports but didn't know his name.

'I'm sure you boys know Hugh Verhoeven,' Helena said brightly.

Kyle looked starstruck as he shook Hugh's hand. 'We're really grateful that you're able to cover our story, Mr Verhoeven,' he said. 'I remember watching your reports from Kosovo when I was about eight or nine. They were really moving.'

The elderly reporter smiled warmly. 'Call me Hugh,' he said. 'Helena has told me how helpful you've been with the Guilt Trips campaign. You're a very impressive young man, by the sound of things.'

As Kyle smiled at the compliment, Helena introduced Bruce. James shook Verhoeven's hand and wanted to say something intelligent like Kyle.

'I watched that video of you getting shot on YouTube. It's had over a million hits.'

Verhoeven raised one eyebrow and reared up in his chair. 'I'm glad you found it entertaining,' he barked. 'Would you like me to unbutton my shirt and show you the exit wound?'

James realised he'd pissed Verhoeven off. Helena and Kyle both glowered at him.

'I didn't mean it like that,' James said, and then saved himself by thinking up a question that was intelligent. 'Kyle said you were semi-retired. Why the sudden interest in Tan Abdullah?'

'He's my great white whale,' Verhoeven roared enthusiastically. 'A couple of years ago, I had the slimy bugger bang to rights. The Malaysian government cut a deal with the French to buy a batch of Mirage fighter aircraft on the cheap. I did an investigation and uncovered a whole web of corruption. Kickbacks, bribes and at the heart of it all was Tan Abdullah, greasing the palms of a dozen people, taking a huge commission on the deal and getting himself promoted to Defence Minister into the bargain.'

'So what happened?' Kyle asked.

'My story died a sudden and unnatural death,' Verhoeven said. 'I woke up with a bad headache and a ransacked hotel room. My Malaysian researcher and camerawoman both disappeared, along with all our tapes and interview notes. People stopped picking up the phone when I called and a couple of days later my Malaysian press accreditation was withdrawn. I had to jump on the fast ferry to Thailand before they deported me.'

Kyle smiled. 'But we'll set that right today.'

'Oh yes,' Verhoeven said as he pounded his fist into his palm. 'Today's the day we make Abdullah pay!'

29. HARASSED

Three black S-Class Mercedes with diplomatic plates roared down a bus lane, heading towards the posh end of London's Oxford Street. TJ and Kevin had acres of room in the back, while up front sat Lauren and a statuesque driver/bodyguard from the Malaysian embassy.

TJ had showered before they'd left the Royal Suite. His highlighted black hair was still wet and he'd put on a retro-style Adidas tracksuit for Britain's colder climate. Kevin thought TJ was OK, but he acted younger than eleven.

In particular, TJ carried a cloth bag filled with dried lentils. He dropped one into a plastic straw, put the straw in his mouth and then shot it at the back of Lauren's neck.

By the fifth time this happened Lauren was getting mad. 'Stop it you dick.'

TJ and Kevin both laughed at the furious expression on Lauren's face.

'What you looking at?' TJ grinned, looking over his shoulder as he buried the straw in his tracksuit pocket. 'Did something hit you? I don't know *where* it came from. Some of it hit me as well.'

Kevin was trying to stay neutral, but couldn't help smirking when he saw TJ's look of mock innocence. He seemed to relish Kevin's approval and dropped another lentil into the straw.

Lauren was frustrated. If one of the younger lads on campus shot her with a lentil she'd have made him sorry, but she couldn't go around thumping the Malaysian guests.

TJ passed the straw across to Kevin. 'Wanna take a shot? Try getting it in her ear, then she'll really go nuts.'

Kevin wouldn't have dared, but TJ holding out the straw was an opportunity for Lauren to make a grab.

'Too slow!' TJ teased obnoxiously, before quickly firing off another lentil.

It was only tiny, but moved fast enough to sting when it hit Lauren's neck, just below the earlobe. She didn't like the idea of ending up in casualty having a lentil tweezered out of her ear, so she glowered at Kevin.

'Stop him now,' she ordered. 'Or I'm blaming you.'

Kevin's face straightened up when he saw the fury in Lauren's eyes.

'Game's getting old, mate,' Kevin said, as he sneaked his hand under the armrest and snatched the bag of lentils.

TJ made a grab, but only managed to tilt the bag. Lentils spewed over the leather seats and across the car's thick carpets. The bodyguard was used to obnoxious passengers, but drew the line at people making a mess that he'd have to clear up.

'Pack it in,' he shouted, in a forceful voice that made TJ jump.

But after the initial shock TJ was determined to act like a brat. 'Don't speak to me that way,' he said sniffily. 'Do you know who my dad is? He could have you sacked like that.'

TJ snapped his fingers, but this only seemed to irritate the bodyguard, who waited to negotiate a roundabout before responding.

'I don't care if your dad is the King of China,' he shouted. 'Pick that up, then sit still and shut your mouth. If you don't like my rules you can get out and bloody well walk.'

Kevin watched TJ's face. His expression mixed defiance with shock and for a couple of seconds it looked like TJ was going to erupt into a full tantrum. But the bodyguard resembled a heavyweight boxer and TJ decided against tangling with him.

Kevin helped scoop lentils off the seat and back into the bag as TJ undid his seatbelt and crawled around the spacious foot well picking them out of the carpet. Lauren gave the bodyguard an appreciative smile.

There were still a few lentils floating around as the black Mercedes convoy stopped at a side entrance of the exclusive Elbridge department store. A doorman helped the drivers and bodyguards open car doors and a man in a suit who seemed prepared for their arrival rushed out to greet June Ling, who looked pissed off as he kissed her on the cheek.

TJ was one of the few people in the world who didn't defer to June Ling's supermodel status and he unceremoniously grabbed her arm.

'You'll be hours looking at dresses,' TJ said sourly. 'Give me a bodyguard so we can look at boy stuff.'

Lauren felt slightly depressed as she headed off behind June Ling, Suzie and Melissa. Kevin looked more cheerful as he charged off through a large perfume department with a pair of oversized bodyguards close behind.

'Do you always have bodyguards?' Kevin asked.

'Everywhere,' TJ nodded. 'My oldest sister was kidnapped once. They wanted a million dollars, so my dad told them to keep her.'

'Not Suzie?'

'No, one of my half-sisters from my dad's first marriage. They're all ancient, like thirty or something.'

TJ seemed to be an expert in Elbridge's layout and by this time they'd raced down an escalator and reached the sportswear department.

Kevin occasionally shopped with his mates, but cherubs weren't given huge allowances so they mostly just looked around. TJ lived in a different world. He walked up to the trainer wall, picked off six pairs and told a disbelieving sales assistant to get his size in all of them. He then attacked the rails of football shirts.

'Who do you like?' Kevin asked.

But before he got an answer, TJ had pulled Chelsea home and away shirts from the rails and held them out towards one of the bodyguards.

'Actually, I'd better get two of each,' TJ explained. 'One to collect, one to wear.'

'You're a teensy bit spoiled, aren't you?' Kevin grinned.

The assistant had come back with the four pairs of trainers that were in stock in TJ's size. He tried one on and furiously berated the assistant as he pulled balled-up brown paper out of the toe.

'Why leave this in?' he shouted, as he threw it across the store. Then he turned to Kevin. 'Who's your team?'

'I'm not a big football fan,' Kevin said. 'But if I have to pick I'd go for Arsenal.'

'Dog shit,' TJ grinned, then he looked at the bodyguard. 'Get him an Arsenal shirt.'

'I can't,' Kevin said modestly.

But Kevin smiled as the bodyguard came back and held up an Arsenal home shirt. As Kevin slid off his jumper and pulled on the shirt to check the size, TJ grabbed a couple of Nike footballs and two tracksuit tops and added them to his pile of purchases before staring at a signed Gridiron helmet in a display case.

'How much is this?' TJ demanded, then looked disappointed as the assistant told him it wasn't for sale.

'Do you have a spending limit?' Kevin asked, as one of the bodyguards told the sales assistant to charge all the stuff to Tan Abdullah's account and bring it down to the parked Mercedes.

'This is nothing,' TJ explained. 'All this lot is like five hundred pounds. My stepmom will spend ten times that on one dress. Where next?'

'I've only been here once but the video games department is pretty cool. And it's a school day, so you'll be able to play on all the consoles.'

But TJ shook his head. 'I get every single video game that comes out.'

Kevin thought this was just a boast, but TJ explained how it worked.

'My dad owns more than fifty hotels and some have games consoles in the rooms. So the big companies send all their games and new consoles as samples. I never even bother to open most of the games. The clothes here are OK. Wanna go look?'

Kevin shrugged. 'You're the guest.'

TJ staged a repeat performance in the kids' designer wear, dropping nearly three thousand pounds on all the best labels. Kevin was playing the role of the son of a rich arms dealer and had a two-hundred-pound allowance. The only thing he really liked was a leather jacket, but it was five hundred quid.

'Try it on,' TJ urged.

Kevin fingered the soft black leather. The coat was fixed to the rail with a security lock that ran down the sleeve, but as soon as the assistant saw that Kevin was with TJ he bolted over to unlock it.

'I can't really afford it,' Kevin said apologetically.

'Your dad's tight,' TJ said. 'Two hundred pounds is a shitty allowance.'

'We're not poor,' Kevin explained. 'But we're two houses and nice cars rich, not private jets and fifty room mansions rich like your mob.'

'If my dad ever says no I go crazy ape and start smashing stuff,' TJ explained. 'One time I smashed an ash tray. My dad freaked out because it was in some famous movie and he'd paid like, seventy thousand dollars in an auction.'

Kevin wasn't sure if TJ was making stuff up to sound cool. The shop assistant was holding out the leather jacket and it seemed plain rude not to slip his arms inside and take a look in the mirror. The fit was good, and Kevin could just see himself striding around campus in it, making Jake and the rest of his mates wildly jealous.

CHERUB had a rule that kids weren't allowed to keep expensive items or any money that they made during a mission, but it wasn't like anyone kept a log of what clothes he owned, so Kevin reckoned he'd easily get away with it.

TJ told the assistant to unlock an almost identical jacket, but his one had snakeskin trim and cost twice as much. Then he lined up beside Kevin in front of the mirror.

'We look so awesome!' TJ said. 'I'll get them both.'

Kevin shook his head. 'The football shirt was enough, mate. I can't take *this* as a gift.'

But the matter didn't seem to be up for debate. TJ had decided and was looking Kevin up and down.

'I know I'm sexy, but it's rude to stare,' Kevin told him.

TJ gave him the finger. 'I'm not a queer! But I like your shoes, and the chinos. Where can I get those?'

Kevin's shoes were Timberland, and the assistant directed them towards the store's Timberland concession on the next floor up. TJ found shoes and trousers like Kevin's and he insisted on putting them straight on, along with the leather jackets.

'Now I'm hungry,' TJ said. 'You hungry? The diner on this floor does massive burgers.'

*

Lauren hadn't hit it off with Suzie straight away, but their relationship warmed up when they split off from Melissa and June. The two teenagers headed away from three-thousand-pound dresses designed for women shaped like pencils and sauntered around the patronisingly named *Young Miss* section on the next floor down, with a bodyguard keeping a discreet distance.

If TJ was the personification of a spoiled brat, Suzie was making a good stab at the stereotypical surly teenager. She walked between the rails, picking things up and announcing that they were rubbish, or that all London shops were crap compared to Tokyo or Paris. Lauren was no flag-waving patriot, but found herself grinding her teeth as the Malaysian girl slagged off her birthplace.

'Camden Market would be better,' Lauren said. 'More our kind of stuff.'

'Camden's OK,' Suzie admitted, which in her world was the equivalent of a twenty-one-gun salute. 'Do you know any bars near here? I feel like eating sushi and drinking vodka and Cokes 'til everything goes wobbly.'

'I'm sure there's lots of bars, but they wouldn't serve us,' Lauren said. 'And my heroin dealer's skiing in the south of France this week.'

Suzie took a couple of seconds to realise that Lauren was joking, but when she did she laughed noisily.

'Fourteen is the worst age,' Suzie moaned. 'Want everything, but can't do shit.'

'My dad's a pain in the rear,' Lauren agreed. 'I never should have let him persuade me to wear these clothes. I feel like such a dork.'

'You should buy something outrageous and let him see you in that,' Suzie suggested. 'PVC trousers, or a leather hat with swastikas.'

Lauren nodded. 'Or a T-shirt with some really buff naked guy showing his willy.'

Suzie howled with laughter. 'Oh, if only they had those,' she beamed. 'My dad would *completely* chuck the shits.'

As the girls rounded a shop-within-a-shop selling a bizarre range of day-glow Lycra gear they saw a tacky looking fifties diner. Kevin and TJ were below the partition separating the dining area from the rest of the store, but the slab-like heads of two bodyguards loomed above it.

'Wanna go piss our little brothers off?' Suzie asked. 'TJ is such a prick. He's eleven, but he acts more like he's eight.'

The diner was almost empty and the two boys sat opposite each other in a booth designed for four. Their bodyguards sat a couple of tables across, demolishing triple cheeseburgers.

'They're eating the entire cow,' Lauren grinned, as they approached the boys' table.

'Budge up,' Suzie ordered, giving TJ a powerful sideways shove as she sat on the padded bench.

Kevin moved aside more willingly for Lauren, who looked at his jacket. She examined the distinctive pock marks in the soft leather, checked the label and gave him a very hard stare.

'That's ostrich leather,' Lauren said disapprovingly.

'Don't care if it's panda,' Kevin said, with burger crammed into his cheeks. 'It's the awesomest jacket I have *ever* owned.'

TJ held up his slightly more elaborate jacket. 'This one's got snakeskin trim as well.'

Suzie shook her head as she looked at TJ's chinos. 'You copied Kevin's look. Have you *ever* had an original thought in your life?'

'Kiss my arse,' TJ snapped back.

'You know the funniest thing about TJ,' Suzie said to Lauren as she pushed her middle finger deep into her mouth. 'He's got a phobia about saliva.'

To prove her point, Suzie wedged TJ against the side of the booth and shoved her spit-glistening finger in his ear.

TJ yelled, wriggled and started freaking out at the top of his voice. 'Get off me . . . Suzie you bitch! Jesus, you're disgusting.'

The waitresses and passing shoppers looked horrified,

but the bodyguards had clearly seen worse and kept chewing like nothing was happening.

After a brief struggle, TJ stood up on his seat and flopped over the partition into the shopping area. Kevin was surprised to see that TJ was practically crying. He ran off, shouting that he had to find a toilet and wash out his ear.

'What the hell was that?' Kevin gawped, as one of the bodyguards chased him across the store.

'Saliva phobic,' Suzie explained. She waggled her finger experimentally in front of Kevin in case it had a similar effect. 'It'll be interesting when he gets his first girlfriend.'

Kevin blew off the threat by flicking his tongue out and cheekily raising an eyebrow. 'I like Goth birds. I'll exchange saliva with you any day.'

Kevin was quite cute, but he was only twelve so Suzie acted like she was repulsed. Lauren put one arm around Kevin's neck and rubbed her knuckles against the top of his head. 'Isn't my baby brother sweet?' she said. 'The little ostrich-wearing pervert.'

TJ came back a few minutes later. His ear and the side of his face were bright red where he'd scoured them with soap and hot water. He wanted to leave the girls and go off with Kevin again, but June Ling had called and wanted to meet up by the cars.

When they got downstairs one of June Ling's three bodyguards was throttling a woman who'd snapped the moderately famous model on her camera phone.

'Delete the shot, or I'll delete you!' he ordered,

then loomed over her as she erased her picture with trembling hands.

Outside, the three identical Mercedes had been driven up from the store's underground car park and shop staff crammed the trunks with dozens of distinctive purple carrier bags. The boys headed out first and didn't notice anything odd as they got back into the last car, but all hell broke loose as June Ling and Melissa stepped on to the pavement.

A dozen scruffy looking animal rights protestors charged towards the Mercedes and blocked the doors. 'Fur is murder!' one of them shouted, as another ran behind June Ling and blasted her back with a squeezy ketchup bottle.

Several paparazzi photographers had been tipped off and flashguns popped as June Ling tussled with a woman dressed in a scruffy parka with an orange scarf wrapped over her face.

'Where's my security?' June Ling shouted.

Her answer came as a huge bodyguard dragged the protestor away from June Ling and flung her with such force that her head cracked noisily against Elbridge's plate-glass display window.

Lauren would always support anti-fur protestors over a bitchy model, but became a victim of guilt by association as her route to the car was blocked by a man holding a placard with an horrific photograph of a freshly skinned mink.

'Fur is murder,' he spat. 'Rich little princess.'

'Get out of my way,' Lauren screamed, as Suzie broke

away from her and ran towards the front car. 'I'm vegetarian, so what do you know?'

As the man processed this, a female protestor grabbed Lauren around the waist and started trying to drag her backwards. Lauren tried using minimal force, by hooking her white pump around the woman's leg and tripping her up, but this move is tricky when you're being dragged backwards and she was forced to use her elbow.

The blow connected with the woman's jaw, sending her crashing backwards on to the pavement minus two front teeth. As Lauren looked up, ready to deal with the male protestor still blocking her path to the car, one of the huge bodyguards grabbed him by the scruff of his jacket and sunk a knee into his stomach.

Someone inside the Mercedes flung the door open and Lauren jumped inside.

'Thanks Melissa,' Lauren said, as she pulled up the door and looked outside where two of the bodyguards were dealing brutally with the largest and most persistent of the protestors.

Inside the car, June Ling was screaming her head off to the man in the driver's seat. 'Why am I getting ambushed by this unwashed scum? Where is my protective screen? Kidnappers could have plucked me off the pavement before you useless turds even noticed.'

Melissa was calmer, but wore a puzzled expression. 'How could they possibly know we're here?'

Another bodyguard got in the front passenger seat and the car started moving rapidly away from the store.

'Maybe someone in the shop tipped them off,' Lauren suggested.

'Possible,' Melissa agreed. 'But it was well organised. A dozen protestors, all with banners, and the press were clearly tipped off too.'

'We have a traitor in our midst,' June Ling insisted. 'I only made my mind up what shop to visit when we first got in the car. Only people inside these cars could have known where we went.'

'Do you want to visit any more stores?' the driver asked.

June Ling practically bit his head off.

'What do you think?' she shouted. 'Why are you a total dipshit? Do you think I'm going to walk around London with this red shit stuck all over my back? Take us to the hotel.'

As Lauren looked out of the car at the posh shops, feeling guilty about thumping an animal rights protestor and wondering if there really was a mole passing information to a protest group, the phone in her pocket sent a text message to James, indicating that they were back on the move.

30. FLOWERS

'Cheers for the warning, James,' Kyle said. 'I'll get right on it.'

Kyle sat in the cab of a Japanese micro van, wearing jeans and a green polo shirt with the logo of Mayfair's top flower delivery company embroidered over his nipple. After pocketing his phone, he started the engine and got honked by a black cab driver as he pulled out.

'Sorry, mate,' Kyle said, as he made an apologetic wave out of the window.

The one-litre engine and high body didn't make it easy to drive fast and then Kyle got trapped behind a dustcart on the last hundred-metre stretch. The Leith was a recently opened boutique hotel, with a gaudy pink and yellow reception and a surreal sculpture made from brass instruments sprouting from the ceiling.

A doorman in pinstripes trotted towards Kyle as he

stopped the van in the hotel driveway.

'We have guests arriving imminently,' the doorman warned. 'You can't stop here, poppet.'

'The Tan Abdullah party?' Kyle asked.

He hopped out of the van and noticed a small gathering on the opposite side of the narrow one-way street. Hopefully there would be twenty or thirty more by the time the three Mercedes arrived.

'You really *can't* stop here now,' the doorman repeated, his voice becoming shrill.

'I have June Ling's flowers,' Kyle said. 'We just got a call to say she was arriving early. These *have* to be in her room when she arrives or she'll throw a fit.'

'Oh goodness, we wouldn't want that, would we?' the doorman said, shuddering at the thought. 'Well you'd better pass the flowers over, we'll take them up to the room.'

Kyle shook his head and looked offended. 'This is a floral display. Only I can set them up in the room.'

The doorman pranced inside and called out for Carlo, who duly arrived with a baggage trolley. Kyle loaded three huge displays of flowers on to the trolley, as the driver took the van into an alleyway at the side of the hotel.

A glass lift had been constructed in the hotel courtyard, and Carlo had to swipe a card to bring the lift up to the luxury suites on the top floor. Tan Abdullah and June Ling each had a personal assistant, who had travelled directly from the jet to the hotel so that the billionaire couple would arrive to find bags unpacked, beds made the way they liked and any other special requests fulfilled.

Carlo knocked and double doors swung open, admitting Kyle into the lounge of a spectacular hotel suite, centred around a circular leather couch with strips of pink neon running between the cushions. June Ling's chunky-legged assistant looked horrified when she saw the flowers.

'What is this?' she said urgently. 'Mrs Ling will be here *very* soon. She's not in a good mood. You must *not* be in here.'

Carlo looked alarmed, but Kyle stayed cool as he glimpsed a huge marble bathroom where a tub was being filled ready for June Ling's arrival.

'These flowers were sent to Mr and Mrs Abdullah by the French ambassador,' Kyle lied smoothly. 'Would you like us to pass any message back to the embassy on why you refused them?'

Tan's personal assistant was hovering in the background, but as soon he heard the word *embassy* he came rushing over. 'From the embassy?' he smiled. 'Of course we shall accept the flowers. Would you like to display them on the dining-table?'

Kyle contemplated the table for a couple of seconds, before nodding. 'I think the light coming through the skylight will illuminate them beautifully in that position. There's also a message for Mr Tan Abdullah.'

Kyle passed over an envelope, embossed with the crest of the French embassy in London.

'I'll make sure Mr Abdullah is aware of the message as

soon as he arrives,' the assistant said.

Carlo had already pushed the trolley stacked with flower vases towards the dining-table and Kyle began standing the pots on the table and fiddling with the stems, using the limited knowledge of flower arranging he'd picked up in a North London florist's shop a few hours earlier. As Kyle fiddled, Tan's assistant waved an electronic wand over the pots to make sure none had been fitted with listening devices.

'I just got a text from the driver,' June Ling's assistant shouted. 'They'll be here in two minutes. I need *everyone* out of this room.'

*

Following the attack outside Elbridge's, a marked police car had picked up the convoy of Mercedes. But even an occasional siren blast wasn't much help and the two miles between Oxford Street and the Mayfair hotel took twenty-five minutes.

The Leith was situated on a narrow lane, with upmarket boutiques opposite and a coffee shop on the corner. As the final black Mercedes clipped the kerb, half a dozen latte drinkers stormed out behind waving placards.

Kevin looked back and was confused by a long banner with an anti-arms trade slogan, placards bearing the Guilt Trips logo and others holding up the picture of a skinned mink he'd already seen outside Elbridge's.

He jumped as an egg pelted the back windscreen.

'Full reverse,' TJ demanded. 'Run the bastards over!'

'Quiet,' the bodyguard at the wheel said firmly. He

was trained in advanced combat-driving techniques, but no amount of skill could counteract being stuck in a long car on a narrow street. The way ahead was blocked, so he put the car in reverse and began edging back while making regular blasts on the horn.

The protestors didn't appreciate this aggressive gesture. They surrounded the car on all sides and pounded on the windows and the boot lid. TJ got rather excited with his hand pressed against the window giving them the finger.

'Don't provoke them,' the driver said irritably, as he continued crawling backwards.

Up ahead the middle Mercedes was half in the road and half on the driveway of the Leith Hotel. There were a couple of dozen protestors stopping them from going any further.

'Why are the police just sitting in their car?' June Ling complained.

'Waiting for backup I expect,' the bodyguard in the front passenger seat explained. 'Get out in front of a mob that size and they'll just make fools of themselves.'

'Well I'm not anyone's prisoner,' June Ling shrieked, with such violence that Lauren put a hand over her left ear in case of a reprise. 'I'm getting out of here. You're my bodyguard, now guard me!'

The crowd surged as June Ling threw open the passenger door. She'd left her high heels in the foot-well, and a couple of cameras flashed as she scrambled barefoot across ten metres of concrete and into the hotel lobby.

The jostling crowd reacted furiously because their prime target had got away. But they were better prepared by the time the bodyguard flung his door open. The protestors threw eggs through the open doors, one of which cracked on the seat beside Melissa and spattered her leg. She turned quickly towards Lauren.

'Wanna make a run for it?'

'Sod it,' Lauren nodded. 'We could be stuck in this car for ages.'

The police officers grabbed a protestor as Melissa and the bodyguard in the front passenger seat made the dash towards the hotel.

Lauren flipped her cardigan up over her head and ran through the gap in the protestors cleared by the huge bodyguard. A hotel doorman stepped out bravely, shielding the three runners with a large umbrella. Lauren almost made it, but took simultaneous egg hits as she passed through the doorway. One hit her back, the second spattered noisily against the cardigan over her head.

'You OK, sweetie?' Melissa asked, as Lauren peeled off the cardigan.

Outside, one of the protestors was yanking at the glass door, while a doorman pulled in the other direction. June Ling stood with folded arms, breathing fire as she waited for the lift.

'I'm really sorry about this,' Melissa said.

'Not your fault. You're not security,' June Ling snapped, as she turned angrily towards the bodyguard. 'This is the biggest shambles I've ever seen. These people know every step we make.'

The lift doors made a dinging sound and in her rush to get upstairs to her room, June Ling knocked into a young man dressed in a green polo shirt who was trying to step out. Lauren's mouth dropped open as Kyle emerged from the lift and brushed silently past her.

31. CALL

The Leith wasn't a large hotel and the entire top floor had been booked out by the Malaysian government and David Secombe. Lauren had a two-bedroom suite which she was supposed to be sharing with Kevin, but he was off with TJ as she padded out of her bathroom in her robe and slippers. She picked up her mobile, slid a glass door and stepped out on to a balcony.

She dialled Kyle, then peered down into the street below, and saw that the protestors had been cleared into a pocket on the opposite side of the street. There was a police van parked on the hotel driveway and armed officers standing by the main entrance.

'Kyle, what the hell is going on?' Lauren asked, sounding angry but keeping her voice low in case someone was out on another balcony.

'Oh, hi,' Kyle answered awkwardly.

'You went through James' mission briefing before he pulled out, didn't you?' Lauren asked accusingly. 'That's how the protestors knew what hotel we were staying at.'

'I might have glanced at it,' Kyle admitted.

Lauren shook her head. 'If security finds out, you'll never be allowed on campus again. They'll cut you off financially and throw the book at you in court if you give them an excuse. And the last thing you need is a criminal record when you want to become a lawyer.'

'That's why I didn't tell you,' Kyle said. 'But I'm not an idiot, Lauren. I'm working with good people.'

'They know there's a leak,' Lauren said. 'So you'd *better* have covered your tracks. And what about James, is he involved?'

Kyle had to think before answering. He didn't want to lie, but it was more important that he didn't drop James in it.

'I have no idea where your brother is,' Kyle said.

'Is there anything I should know?' Lauren asked. 'What are you planning exactly with your flower delivery?'

'It's better if you don't know,' Kyle said firmly. 'You'll probably encounter a few more protestors when you're out and about, but the element of surprise is gone. The cops will follow every step you make from now on.'

'Just be careful, OK?'

'I will,' Kyle said. 'Are you pissed off that I didn't tell you?'

'Slightly,' Lauren admitted. She heard the boys coming into her room. 'I've gotta go, bye.'

'What do you want?' Lauren said aggressively as she

stepped back into her bedroom.

'They've taken the booze out of the mini bars and locked out porn on our TV,' Kevin explained. 'We're bored.'

TJ inspected the eggy cardigan balled up on the floor. 'They got you good,' he grinned. 'Should have stayed in your car for five minutes. We had about twenty cops escorting us.'

There was a knock at the door. Kevin opened up and Suzie strolled down towards Lauren.

'The bodyguards say there's no way we can go out until dinner this evening,' Suzie explained. 'So how about we get down to the spa and have ourselves massaged by a couple of hunks?'

'Oooh, I *like* the sound of that,' Lauren agreed.

*

While the protestors chased June Ling and her family across London, the elderly journalist Hugh Verhoeven held court in the church vestry. James, Bruce, Helena Bayliss and a hastily assembled volunteer camera crew hung on every word as Verhoeven told stories from fifty years as a reporter.

He'd gone undercover to join the Ku Klux Klan in the sixties and narrowly escaped death when his identity as a British TV journalist was unearthed. He'd been in Dallas when JFK was shot, interviewed Clint Eastwood and Marilyn Monroe, seen the Berlin Wall come down and been in Baghdad at the beginning of both Gulf Wars.

Verhoeven had led a remarkable life and James was

disappointed when Helena handed over fifty quid and told him to go and buy lunch for everyone at the nearest Prêt à Manger.

Kyle arrived back at the church as James was distributing chicken wraps, fruit smoothies and boxed salads.

'All good,' Kyle announced, before taking James aside and warning him about the situation with Lauren.

The final piece of Verhoeven's plan to bring down Tan Abdullah arrived a few minutes later. He was a fat man, who wore a beautifully cut navy suit and rimless glasses that gave him the air of a professor. He had an expensive briefcase and a *Financial Times* tucked under his arm.

'This is Dion Frei,' Verhoeven announced. 'For twenty years a leading salesman for a Franco-Swiss turbine and missile manufacturer, recently made redundant. He helped a friend of mine in Geneva write a *terrific* whistle-blower piece on the Swiss armaments industry and now he's going to help us nail Tan Abdullah.'

'Twenty-*six* years,' Dion corrected, with a hint of bitterness. 'A lot of men got rich off deals I made. I got redundancy and a letter saying that the company pension was a crock.'

Verhoeven laughed, and looked at Bruce, who'd been wrapped up in all his stories and was conspicuously the youngest person in the room. 'You see, young man, some of us are motivated by the greater good and others by the sting of a meagre redundancy cheque.'

Bruce nodded. 'So how does it work exactly?'

Verhoeven opened up into a smile that made it look like he'd been waiting his whole life to unveil his clever scheme.

*

Tan Abdullah and David Secombe arrived at the Leith to find the women in the spa, the bodyguards playing poker for matchsticks and the two boys charging around Tan's suite, battling with cushions and hurling Minstrels and M&Ms taken from the mini bar.

TJ gave his father a quick hug as Tan's assistant, Max, came across the room holding the envelope that had been attached to the flowers.

'I thought you'd want to see this straight away,' Max explained. 'I couldn't risk it on the phone.'

Tan opened the envelope. His eyebrows shot up as he pulled out an aerial photograph of an island in the Pacific.

Tan looked around at David Secombe, who'd decided to act fatherly by grabbing a bag of Minstrels from Kevin and eating them.

'You're scoffing all my ammo!' Kevin protested.

'David, I have family business to attend to,' Tan said smoothly. 'Would you excuse me for a few moments?'

Tan followed Max into his luxuriously appointed bedroom and closed the door.

'Is this genuine?' Tan asked.

Max nodded. 'The envelope is from the French embassy. The number given for Dion Frei is a genuine French embassy number. What's the significance of the island?'

Tan grabbed the remote for a large plasma TV. He switched it on, turned up the sound and then stood near the speakers.

'Can't be too careful,' Tan explained. 'The British government have had weeks to bug this place if they'd wanted to.'

'I swept thoroughly,' Max said, sounding a little offended.

'You can't detect the really good ones,' Tan said, before lowering his voice even further. 'The island is in the Pacific. It's part of a chain on the edge of the zone where the French used to test their nuclear weapons. Quite unspoiled, beautiful wildlife and ideal for diving and island hopping. If you developed it the right way for tourism you could generate sixty to eighty million dollars per year.'

'So what's the significance to you?'

Tan raised an eyebrow, indicating that he thought Max was being thick. 'I tried to develop this island years back, but the French government won't sell. Now, the day before I sign a deal to buy turbines for our new frigates from the Brits, they're dangling it under my nose.'

'They're offering a bribe?' Max asked.

'Never use that word!' Tan said urgently, then jumped as the door swung open.

TJ burst in as Kevin lobbed a cushion after him.

'Out!' Tan roared furiously. 'You want a smack up the side of the head?'

TJ froze in shock before grabbing the cushion and bolting back out.

'Do you trust Dion Frei?' Max asked after a moment.

'He's rock solid. A company man,' Tan said. 'First met him fifteen years ago, when we were buying marine engines for boats to service an island resort. His company tendered for the frigate engine contract, but they couldn't meet our delivery schedule.'

'So what do we do?' Max asked. 'Set up a meeting?'

'Yes,' Tan nodded. 'David Secombe can't know I'm meeting with a rival and there are cops everywhere.'

'The embassy?' Max suggested.

'Too many people sticking their noses in there. Speak *discreetly* to the hotel concierge. See if they have a room, or a meeting space on one of the lower floors where I can sneak off for an hour. Then call Dion Frei. Tell him that I'm very interested in his photograph, but I'll only meet him face-to-face and just him. I want *nobody* else in the room.'

'When?'

'Soon as possible,' Tan said. 'I'm supposed to be signing a deal tomorrow so if this has legs we need to move fast. You call Dion now. I'd better go back outside before Secombe thinks we're talking about him.'

*

Over the years, Dion Frei had done billions of euros' worth of business at the London arms fair and as a result knew everyone who mattered at the French embassy. Getting an embassy telephone number re-routed to his mobile phone hadn't been a problem.

He shushed the crowd in the vestry as his mobile phone rang.

'Max?' Dion said curiously. 'Oh you must be new, what happened to Lucy? Oh that's a pity, she was a lovely girl . . . Of course I'd be happy to meet Mr Abdullah today. I've got a short meeting right now, but I can be with you in about an hour and a half . . . OK . . . OK, I'll see you there, Max. Good talking to you.'

'And?' Verhoeven asked, the instant Dion shut his telephone.

'He's organised a private dining-room on the sixth floor,' Dion said.

Across the room, Helena grabbed a floor plan of the Leith Hotel and unfurled it on the table. There were several private rooms, but they were all close together.

Verhoeven tapped on the hotel floor plan and traced a line out of the sixth-floor restaurant. 'He could go this way, down in the lift, through the front of the restaurant. But it'll be half past two and it's a popular spot so he'd get seen. It's much more likely that Tan will come out of his suite, go down the back stairs and enter the dining-room through the kitchen.'

'Agreed,' Kyle nodded. 'Especially as they're glass-sided lifts.'

'How do we know that Dion won't be padded down and searched for a wire?' James asked.

'We don't *know*,' Verhoeven said. 'This kind of thing is a calculated risk. There's a chance that Dion will be padded down. There's also a chance that at some point between now and two-thirty, Tan Abdullah will discover that Dion is no longer a hard-working and loyal salesman for a Franco-Swiss jet turbine manufacturer.'

'They won't pad me down,' Dion said certainly. 'I've been to literally thousands of meetings over the years. I've never been searched. It just isn't done.'

'OK,' Verhoeven said, as he focused everyone's attention back on the map. 'We carry our equipment into the hotel in suitcases. Nobody will bat an eyelid. We hang around at the bar while the meeting takes place and use toilet cubicles to discreetly unpack our equipment. When Tan Abdullah leaves the meeting, we ambush him here on the staircase as he heads back up to the eighth floor.

'The major threat is to our recordings. When Tan finds out what's going on, he's going to send his bodyguards after us to grab tapes and memory cards.'

'Will they have guns?' one of the assistants asked.

'No,' Kyle said. 'At least not unless they're carrying them illegally. But they're bloody *enormous*, so I wouldn't tangle with them.'

James noticed a look of gleeful expectation on Bruce's face.

'The important thing is that whoever is carrying our recorded material gets out of the building as quickly as possible. I'm a doddery old fart, so *don't* wait for me. Just get out of the building, run or jump in the first black cab you see and we all meet up back here.'

32. STING

Kyle pulled a cap down over his eyes as he stepped into the Leith Hotel holding an elaborately wrapped gift box. James and Bruce walked ahead as a policewoman standing by the lifts politely asked what they were doing in the hotel.

James wasn't fazed. 'We're having a birthday lunch with our grandfather. We're supposed to be meeting in a bar on the sixth floor. Has something happened?'

'Heightened security for some VIPs staying upstairs,' the officer explained. 'No need to worry. You lads have an enjoyable lunch.'

'We'll try our best,' James smiled, as Kyle thumbed the lift button.

Kyle warned Bruce as they cruised up to the sixth. 'I'm out of CHERUB and James is counting the days, but you're younger. Your career still has legs. You could get kicked out if anyone on campus finds out about this.'

'You should stay in the background,' James agreed.

But Bruce wasn't having any of that. 'Yeah *right*. I've come this far, you think I'm gonna back away from a punch-up?'

The bar and restaurant were as pimped up as the rest of the hotel. The floor was made from silver and gold mosaic tiles and the curved bar was glass so you could see the flickering legs of the black-uniformed barmaids standing behind it.

Hugh Verhoeven had put on a tweed jacket and carried a flat cap and a cane. He sat at a table near the bar, drinking a gin and tonic.

'Happy birthday, Granddad,' Kyle said, as he passed over the gift.

Verhoeven raised one eyebrow and smiled. 'Why thank you grandson, whatever *could* it be?'

A waitress came to the table. Kyle ordered a bottle of Peroni, James and Bruce had to stick with Cokes.

'This place reminds me of a whorehouse I visited during the Vietnam war,' Verhoeven noted. 'Though I expect the drinks are pricier up here.'

James grinned. 'Is it me, or do a lot of your stories seem to involve brothels?'

Verhoeven's pompous veneer had worn off as he'd got used to the boys and he roared with laughter. 'I was always a gentleman,' he said, wagging his finger. 'But if you want to know the truth, you're more likely to get it in a bar full of drunks than at a press conference inside the Hilton.'

Bruce seemed to have really taken to Verhoeven. 'Journalism sounds pretty interesting. I could quite see myself as a war correspondent or something.'

As the waitress put drinks and a fresh bowl of nuts on the table, James looked around discreetly and noticed the three-strong camera team sitting in a booth a few tables away. Once the waitress was out of sight, Verhoeven opened his present.

The stiff-sided box contained a foam-topped wireless microphone, of the kind news reporters stick in people's faces, and a short-range receiver that would pick up the audio signal from a bug under Dion Frei's lapel.

Kyle glanced at his watch. 'Shouldn't be long now.'

*

Tan Abdullah slipped downstairs with a pair of bodyguards and would have got into the private dining-room unnoticed, but for the fact that people in the restaurant were specifically looking for him.

As well as the transmitting microphone in his lapel Dion Frei had a pinhead video camera recoding on to a memory card in the briefcase laid out on the large oval dining-table in front of him. He'd been in thousands of meetings like this, dozens with Tan Abdullah. He felt calm, but waiting around for twenty minutes is long enough for anyone to think dark thoughts and it was a relief to see his guest.

'Good to see you, Dion,' Tan said, as their handshake became a brief hug. 'That's a *beautiful* suit. You always manage to look younger than me.'

'No wife and kids to stress me out and a good tailor,'

Dion laughed. 'I gave my tailor's card to your previous assistant when we met in Geneva. You should give them a call, I'm sure they'd send someone to the hotel. You're five minutes from their place in Savile Row.'

'I just might,' Tan said. 'June is not happy. There's a bunch of protestors on to us. She got egged outside Elbridge's and we think there's a security leak so she can't do any more shopping.'

'Oh boy!' Dion said jovially. 'I'm glad I wasn't within shrieking distance of that.'

Tan beamed with laughter. 'Luckily I wasn't either. I flew out with David Secombe. The army demonstrated a K61.'

'Sweet missile!' Dion said. 'I heard they brought a bunch of USAF out to see it and it blew up in the launcher.'

'I asked about that,' Tan agreed. 'They all went *very* quiet! So how are things at TSMF? I heard a lot of people got laid off, one of the production lines has been shuttered.'

Dion felt tense as he wondered if Tan had made some calls and found out that he'd been made redundant.

'It was a bloodbath,' Dion admitted. 'Lost a lot of close colleagues when the French government bailed the company out. But I've been with TSMF twenty-seven years. Part of the furniture, I guess.'

'Must have been hard,' Tan said. 'So why am I here anyway? Why are you tempting me with pictures of islands?'

'Just a *little* something from the people of France, to

tide you over when you retire from politics and go back to making real money.'

'It won't be long now,' Tan nodded. 'Our prime minister is currently about as popular as a turd in a bowl of punch.'

'Fancy stealing his job as party leader?'

'Too old, too ugly and too much dirt on my hands,' Tan admitted. 'I'll retire from politics when he gets his arse kicked in September.'

'Good to take it easy,' Dion agreed, as he realised the value of having Tan slagging off his prime minister on tape and decided to fish for some more dirt. 'So you don't think he'll win a third term in office?'

'He's lost all momentum,' Tan explained. 'Got no spine. Spends all his time looking at polls, but a leader should lead, not try to work out what the public wants. My oldest son is the governor of Langkawi now. In another ten years he could be Prime Minister.'

'Good for business,' Dion laughed, before he began spinning his elaborate lie. 'As you know, TSMF couldn't bid on the turbine contract for your eight new frigates because our large turbine production plant was working at full pelt making engines for states in the Gulf.'

Tan nodded. 'There's a real naval build-up around there. South-East Asia is the same. We're all shit scared and want sabres to rattle at the Chinese.'

'But the Saudis are having trouble getting their boats built on time,' Dion continued. 'They ordered engines for 2013 delivery, but now they don't need them until three years after that. That leaves a hole in our production schedule big enough to build turbines for your frigates. We'll price it three per cent below the British, and in consideration for your personal inconvenience, the French government is willing to let you have a ninety-nine-year lease on your favourite Pacific island for ten million euros.'

Tan smiled. 'Ten is a good price!'

'The lease is worth forty, at least,' Dion said. 'You could sell it on and make thirty million with no risk, or develop the island and make ten times that over the long term.'

'But this is *awful* timing,' Tan said. 'The deal with London is ready to sign. I'm shaking hands and having my picture taken at Buckingham Palace tomorrow morning. The newspapers will be there. Five billion and twelve thousand British jobs.'

Dion shrugged. 'You just need to throw a little spanner in the works. Be creative: some paperwork goes missing, one of your admirals gets cold feet, or get a lawyer to throw up some obscure query on the turbine contract. It's only nine hundred million out of five and a half billion.

'You can still get your picture taken with the Prince tomorrow, subject to a two-line get-out clause on the turbine contract. Then in a few weeks, you announce that there's a rival bid from the French. You sign a deal with us for eight hundred and seventy million, and get your hands on that little island you've been hankering after for pennies.'

Tan sat back in his chair and thought things over for

twenty seconds, before smiling. 'I'll need to move fast in order to pull this off, but you've certainly done your homework, Dion.'

'So do we have a deal?' Dion asked, as he stood up and offered his hand across the table.

Tan nodded slowly as he grabbed the hand. 'Very much so, Mr Frei. I think we have an excellent deal.'

33. BOTHER

Hugh Verhoeven listened discreetly through an earpiece as Tan Abdullah and Dion Frei discussed the fictitious deal. He'd hoped to get a recording of Tan agreeing to accept a bribe, but to the experienced journalist the comments about the Malaysian prime minister were even more valuable.

Not only would the criticisms ensure that the story got huge media coverage in Malaysia, they also guaranteed that the most powerful man in the country would be going against his defence minister, rather than trying to cover his back.

But although the trickiest part of the sting operation had gone smoothly, they weren't home and dry.

'Take this,' Hugh told James urgently, as he passed over the tape recorder. 'Get in the lift and get it out of here. Kyle, meet Dion and run down the fire stairs with the briefcase. The audio recording isn't great, so we need the recording in that briefcase if our story is going to be credible.'

'What about me?' Bruce asked.

'You reckon you want to be a journalist,' Hugh said. 'So I guess you'd better stay here and see how it plays out.'

Dion and Tan were all smiles as they stepped out of the private dining-room. Hugh waited until Dion had taken a few steps into the restaurant before whipping out his microphone, and giving a hand signal.

The camera trio rose as one from the table: the curly-haired Frenchman with a large video camera and two female assistants. One carried a powerful video light, while the other held a small backup camera.

'Mr Abdullah,' Verhoeven shouted, as the short Malaysian headed towards the kitchen. 'Would you mind if I asked a few questions?'

Tan flinched as the bright light shone in his eyes. The bodyguards were ready to pounce, but Tan was a politician and had to behave when a camera got pointed at him.

'No interviews,' he said politely. 'Speak to my assistant. He'll try to fit you into my schedule.'

Verhoeven ignored the brush-off. 'Mr Abdullah, why did you accept the offer of a bribe from Dion Frei?'

Tan's expression wilted momentarily, before he adopted an aggressive posture. 'Who says that? This is ridiculous.'

'Mr Abdullah,' Verhoeven said politely. 'Dion Frei

was made redundant by TSMF eleven months ago. Your meeting was recorded. Would you care to elaborate on your comment that the Malaysian prime minister is *about as popular as a turd in a bowl of punch?*'

Tan realised he'd been had and turned anxiously towards his bodyguards. 'Get their equipment,' he shouted. 'What you're doing is illegal. You can't record me. I have diplomatic status!'

Kyle had run down two storeys, but still heard the chaos as the bodyguards lunged towards Hugh Verhoeven and his camera.

'Hope Verhoeven is OK,' Dion told Kyle, already short of breath. 'He's a few decades past his prime.'

It was only at this point that Kyle realised something was missing. 'Where's your briefcase?' he blurted.

Dion stopped dead and looked down, unable to believe that it wasn't in either hand. '*Merde!*'

'You leave,' Kyle said firmly. 'They haven't seen me. I'll sneak back and try getting it out of the dining-room.'

Upstairs Bruce cracked a smile as the two bodyguards lunged at the cameraman. They were the kind of large, slow-moving opponents that he loved to fight, but as he sprang forward to wedge himself between the camera crew and the two bodyguards, he tripped on a slightly raised section of floor and fell flat on his face.

As Kyle ran back on to the sixth floor he could hear more of Tan's heavyweight bodyguards running down from the floor above.

Tan had retreated to his suite, but one of his bodyguards had grabbed the camera and was wrestling the cameraman and two female assistants. The other one had Hugh Verhoeven pinned against the wall and was screaming in his face.

'Who put you up to this? Who the hell are you?'

Kyle couldn't see Bruce amongst the jostling bodies. This was a surprise, but he gave it no thought because his priority was the briefcase. The doorway into the private dining-room was clear and he headed inside and felt some relief to see that it remained on the table where Dion had left it.

He thought about taking the briefcase outside into the restaurant, but with more of Tan's bodyguards running down the stairs he didn't want to be seen with it. Kyle grabbed the case and was relieved to find that the spring-loaded catches weren't locked. He'd not seen this particular case, but it was a standard design and he'd encountered more advanced versions during CHERUB training.

After throwing out Dion's *Financial Times* and a collection of classical music magazines, Kyle felt around the lining of the case until he discovered a hidden flap. This contained a slide-out panel with buttons to switch the camera on and off and more importantly an SD memory card slot.

Kyle popped out the card and tucked it into his jeans. As he closed the case, two of Tan's huge bodyguards burst into the room.

'What are you doing here?' one of them demanded, as they each walked around one side of the oval dining-table. 'What's in that case?'

'Have it,' Kyle said, and slid the case across the table top.

He'd hoped that this would be enough, but he'd not had time to hide the control panel. The bodyguard took one look and realised what had happened.

'The card,' the bodyguard roared. He pounded on the table. 'Play games with me and I'll break your head.'

Kyle waited until the men got close before using a dining chair as a step up on to the table top. The bodyguards tried grabbing his legs, but Kyle sprinted the length of the table, leapt off and burst out through the door back into the restaurant.

The first thing Kyle saw was Bruce, standing three metres ahead of him. He had a cut on his forehead and looked dazed.

'You OK mate?' Kyle asked, in a state of alarm as he tried to imagine the magnitude of the bodyguard who'd apparently floored Bruce.

'I tripped,' Bruce said incredulously. He dabbed his middle finger against the blood running down his face. 'Uneven floor! I should sue.'

Kyle rapidly appraised the situation. One bodyguard still had Hugh Verhoeven pinned to the wall, two had wrestled the cameraman to the ground and two more would be coming out of the dining-room behind him at any second.

Bruce had noticed that the condiments and olive oil on each table rested in slots carved into narrow slate plinths. He swept the condiments away from the nearest table and picked up the slate baton as the two bodyguards burst out behind Kyle.

As Kyle launched a backwards kick, connecting with the lead bodyguard's stomach, Bruce cracked the piece of slate over his head, knocking him cold. The second bodyguard stumbled over the legs of the first and hit the floor, making it easy for Bruce to snatch his wrist. He twisted the wrist until the bodyguard's arm was tight then launched an almighty kick, which came with a sickening crunch sound effect.

'I've got the memory card with the video on it,' Kyle said. He looked down the corridor towards the kitchen and saw no sign of any more bodyguards. 'We need to get it out of here.'

'You go downstairs,' Bruce said decisively. 'I can handle this bit of bother.'

As Kyle ran back to the fire stairs, passing a couple of startled waitresses, Bruce grabbed a dining chair and ran towards the bodyguard who was holding on to Verhoeven.

'You should respect the elderly,' Bruce announced.

The bodyguard turned away from Verhoeven as he launched a kick at Bruce. Bruce easily dodged and the chair disintegrated as it hit the bodyguard over the back.

'Stay down,' Bruce ordered. 'Or I'll make you stay down.'

Not that the bodyguard was in any state to get up, with cracked ribs and the fingers of the hand he'd held out to defend himself pointing in directions they weren't supposed to.

'Bruce Norris, eh?' Verhoeven said, looking a little

winded. 'I take it that name's no coincidence?'

'Get the lift,' Bruce ordered, as he looked at the two bodyguards who now had the cameraman pinned to the floor. 'These bodyguards are rubbish. I'll just deal with those two and then we can all ride down together.'

*

Kyle made it down to the fifth floor before seeing that the next landing was blocked by two burly policemen, who seemed to be waiting for backup before approaching the restaurant. He thought about trying to bluff his way past, but he suspected they'd arrest him first and ask questions later.

Not only did he not want the hassle of an arrest and the possibility of a criminal record, he also suspected that the intelligence service wouldn't publicise the contents of the memory card if they got hold of it. Most likely they'd use it to blackmail Tan Abdullah.

So Kyle turned and headed back upstairs for a second time. Verhoeven and the others seemed to have caught the lift, because the sixth floor was quiet apart from scared looking waitresses and groaning bodyguards.

He thought about taking the lift, but he suspected that the cops in the lobby would have been reinforced. He might have got out of the building with the elderly Verhoeven and the camera crew for company, but he didn't fancy his chances as a young man on his own.

This meant going up was Kyle's only option. He stopped on the seventh-floor landing, hoping to find an escape route, but when he opened the door on to the floor itself, all he saw was a metal gantry overlooking the double-height bar and restaurant.

The eighth floor was Tan's and would be guarded. Kyle considered the roof, but didn't fancy a potentially fatal chase across rooftops. And that's when he remembered that Lauren was in the building. She was the last call he'd received, so he only had to press one button on his phone to call her back.

It rang five times. 'Have you any idea what's going on?' Lauren asked anxiously. 'I shouldn't even speak to you. If they find out we've been talking, they'll want to know why and I'll have a shitload of explaining to do.'

'I'm on the back stairs,' Kyle said, as he thought he heard footsteps coming up towards him.

'What stairs?' Lauren asked. 'It's pandemonium up here. Tan is screaming and yelling at his assistant. David Secombe is freaking out because Tan kicked us all out of his suite and won't say what's going on.'

'Lauren, I didn't want you to get tangled up in this,' Kyle said. 'But I've got a memory card. If the cops bust me, I might not get it back.'

'What card?' Lauren said. 'What's on it?'

'Lauren, I don't have time to explain,' Kyle said pleadingly. 'But you know I'm a good guy, right? Are there guards at the end of your floor? Can I get up to your room?'

'It's a nuthouse,' Lauren explained. 'Most of Tan's bodyguards rushed downstairs, but there's a policeman at each end of our hallway.'

'What room are you in?' Kyle asked.

'Kyle, I could get kicked out of CHERUB. You told

me it was *just* a few protestors. I have to know what's going on.'

Kyle didn't hear what Lauren said next. He'd taken the phone away from his ear because the feet on the stairs were getting louder.

'Lauren the cops are coming,' Kyle said urgently. 'What room are you in? I'm gonna try and get through to you, OK? Just take this memory card and give it to James.'

'802,' Lauren said reluctantly. 'It's right down by the lift. Zara put me on a final warning, Kyle. I can't get into trouble.'

'Lauren, please!' Kyle begged, and started running towards the eighth floor.

The boots pounding up the stairwell were getting louder as Kyle rounded the eighth-floor landing. He peered through a slot window and saw a police officer on a stall by the door looking bored.

Kyle blasted through the door with all his strength, knocking the officer flying. He then sprinted at full pelt down the corridor between hotel rooms, trying to find 802.

'Stop or I'll shoot,' the officer shouted.

Kyle knew this was a bluff: a British police officer will only shoot when someone is under immediate threat, so he kept moving. Up ahead, he saw Lauren's head bob out into the corridor. At the same moment, a huge man sprang through an open door and rugby-tackled him. Kyle smashed hard against the corridor wall and struggled for air as a huge knee crushed his chest.

Kyle flipped over and forced the huge bodyguard off with a double-footed kick, but he soon had the cop behind him ready to swing his baton and another officer coming down the hall towards him. Even Bruce would have struggled with those odds and Kyle raised his hands in meek surrender.

Lauren felt awful as the bodyguard stood with his shoe pressed against Kyle's back, while the officer locked handcuffs around his wrists.

Kevin stepped out of the room behind Lauren and looked shocked. 'Isn't that Kyle Blueman?' he gasped. 'Is he working with us?'

'Just stay quiet,' Lauren said impatiently.

Kyle was hitched to his feet, by which time the officers who'd stormed up the stairs now cluttered up the corridor.

'I was just in the restaurant with my granddad,' Kyle explained. 'It all started kicking off. I panicked and ran. I'm really sorry officer, I didn't see you when I ran through the door.'

Kyle was putting on a good act and sounded like he was close to tears. But at the same time he was making a signal, pointing downwards with two fingers.

'He just dropped a balled-up tissue down by his feet,' Kevin whispered. 'What's he up to?'

'Kevin, I don't know,' Lauren snapped, as Kyle kicked the tissue ball up against the skirting board. 'I'll pick it up. You get back in the room and don't speak to anyone.'

Lauren stepped out into the hallway and began

walking towards Kyle and the officers. When she got close, Lauren pulled a tissue out of her jeans and pretended to blow her nose.

'Excuse me,' Lauren said politely. 'I have to get something from my dad's room.'

'No problem,' one of the officers said, and backed up the wall.

As Lauren passed Kyle she dropped her balled-up tissue and bobbed down to pick it up. At the same time, she snatched the tissue that Kyle had kicked away.

Lauren kept imagining that she was about to get called back as she squeezed Kyle's tissue and felt the hard rectangular shape of the SD card wrapped inside it.

She wondered what was on the card and what she'd do when she found out.

34. INNOCENCE

Melissa opened the door of her suite and let Lauren inside.

'What's going on?' Lauren asked, trying to sound less flustered than she felt. 'Is David here?'

'All I know is that some media got into the hotel and cornered Tan,' Melissa explained, as Lauren followed her into the suite. 'David's trying to work out what happened. Tan wouldn't speak to him so he's gone downstairs to try and get some sense out of the police.'

The two-bedroom suite was identical to the one Lauren was sharing with Kevin down the hall. Melissa had a black silk evening dress draped over the back of a sofa, and Lauren swept her hand across the soft fabric.

'Wish I could afford clothes like that in real life,' Melissa smiled. 'Not that I get invited to anywhere I'd be able to wear them.'

Lauren looked out towards the balcony and saw a laptop standing on the desk. 'Mind if I use that?' she asked. 'I wouldn't mind checking my e-mails.'

'Go for it,' Melissa said. 'It's all logged in. Just make sure you save my expenses spreadsheet before you shut Excel.'

'I enjoyed the spa,' Lauren said, trying to make innocent conversation with the MI5 agent as she sat at the desk. To her relief, the chunky laptop had a row of memory-card slots along one side.

'You hit the jackpot,' Melissa laughed. 'That Scandinavian masseur you had was a peach.'

'Wasn't bad, was he?' Lauren agreed, but her mind was focused on the laptop and finding out what was on the memory card.

Windows recognised the card when she inserted it, but the laptop's media player refused to open the file. It gave her the option to search the internet to try downloading the correct video codec and Lauren clicked OK.

'Got a boyfriend on CHERUB campus?' Melissa asked.

This question momentarily startled Lauren. She wasn't used to being asked about CHERUB by outsiders, but Melissa was a senior MI5 officer.

'I do,' Lauren said. 'But even though you know about CHERUB, I'm still not supposed to talk about any details unless you have a good reason to know. No offence, it's just the rules.'

'None taken,' Melissa said. 'Careless talk costs lives.'

Green download bars blipped across the laptop screen

and finally the message *Codec Ready* flashed up in a dialogue box. Lauren had no idea what she was about to see, so she checked that the laptop's volume was set to one bar above mute.

Her phone rang before she could hit play and Kevin's name flashed on the screen. 'They just dragged Kyle off,' Kevin said, audibly panicked. 'What's going on? I thought he was retired.'

Lauren was irritated, but she had to calm Kevin down. 'Nobody knows what's going on,' she said, measuring her words carefully because Melissa was within earshot. 'Stay in our room with TJ.'

'TJ left with one of the bodyguards,' Kevin explained. 'Tan says it's not secure here. They're all packing up and leaving for the Malaysian embassy.'

Lauren saw the video waiting to be played on the screen. She was acutely aware of the urgency and of Melissa hovering a few paces away. 'Kevin, you'll know what's going on when I do. Speak later.'

She shut her phone and pressed play. The video showed what looked like an office, with a big table and a man in glasses and a blue suit. The view out of the window and the loud decor made her sure that it was somewhere inside the Leith Hotel.

The timeline running along at the bottom of the playback window showed that the recording lasted forty-four minutes. She clipped forward ten minutes, then twenty, and caught the moment when Tan Abdullah entered the dining-room.

Melissa had stepped into her bedroom. Lauren put

the volume up another notch so that she heard some dialogue through the speaker. She didn't have time to listen to the whole conversation, but didn't need to watch much to work out Tan was being offered a huge bribe and accepting it enthusiastically.

Kyle hadn't specifically said that the memory card held the only copy, but his desperation made it pretty obvious and David Secombe's entry into the suite confirmed it.

'Everything's going down the pan,' Secombe shouted, as Melissa came out of her bedroom to see what was going on.

Lauren couldn't risk watching more with the two adults in the room. She closed the media player and clicked an icon for the video file. She wanted to send a backup copy to her own e-mail address, but the forty-four-minute video file was over three gigabytes, which would take hours to upload, even on a fast internet connection.

'So what happened down there?' Melissa asked David.

'Tan Abdullah got caught out being a greedy little boy,' David said furiously. 'I've been working on this deal for eight bastard months.'

He lashed out with his foot, sending leather sofa cushions flying up into the air.

'I don't understand,' Melissa said.

'They've arrested some teenager,' Secombe explained. 'We think he was carrying a video of Tan being offered a bribe. If we can get that recording, we might be able to get the deal back on track by using it to blackmail Tan.

But if it gets into the media, Tan loses all credibility. He'll be a sacked from his job and the whole deal will be delayed for months, maybe even dead in the water.'

'Have they searched the one who got arrested?' Lauren asked, slipping the memory card into her jeans.

'There's no sign of the card on him,' David explained. 'He might have swallowed it, or tried sticking it up his butt. Or he might have hidden it somewhere in the building. I've ordered in all available backup and told the cops to stop at nothing in order to find it. Right now, that card is worth five billion to the British economy.'

'What a mess,' Lauren said, trying to hide her nerves as she stood up from the desk. 'I'd better head back to my room and let Kevin know what's going on.'

She kept her clammy fingers on the memory card in her pocket as she walked out of the suite and along the hallway to room 802. Tan's assistant and the bodyguards were trying to get a trunk in the lift, but the police were insisting that nobody could leave until everyone had been properly interviewed. June Ling could be heard screaming at the top of her voice from inside her suite.

In the section of hallway where Kyle had been captured the carpet had been torn up by officers trying to see if he'd managed to push the card into the gap between the thick carpet and the wall. Lauren shuddered. Before too long someone would ask questions about the girl who'd walked past and dropped her tissue moments after the arrest.

'It was definitely Kyle,' Kevin blurted, as Lauren stepped back into her suite. 'What's going on?'

Lauren shoved past Kevin, heading for her bedroom. 'Trust me, you don't want to know *anything* about this. We could get in a lot of trouble.'

Lauren shut the door in Kevin's face and sat on the edge of her bed trying to think.

'I'm not just a kid, you know,' Kevin shouted bitterly from the living-room.

Lauren didn't know what to do. If she was caught with the memory card in her pocket, everyone would assume she was in cahoots with Kyle and the protestors. She'd be expelled from CHERUB in two seconds flat.

Her options were to either hide the card, dispose of it by flushing it down the toilet, or find some way to get it back to the protestors.

Flushing would be the easiest option, but she thought about Kyle being arrested. Not only was Kyle a good friend, he'd put his CHERUB career on the line two years earlier when she'd been blackmailed by Norman Large. On top of that, Tan didn't deserve to get off.

She was torn over the five billion weapons deal, but only slightly: maybe a lot of British people would lose their jobs if the deal fell through, but she'd joined CHERUB to make the world a better place, not to boost the defence industry with dodgy arms deals.

Lauren couldn't call Kyle while he was under arrest. So she called her brother instead.

'James,' Lauren said anxiously. 'I need you to listen carefully. Kyle's been nicked. Do you have contact numbers for Helena Bayliss, or anyone else who's involved with Guilt Trips?'

'Shit,' James gasped. 'We've been hoping he'd turn up here. Do you know if Kyle had a memory card on him when he was arrested?'

Lauren was confused. 'How do *you* know about the card?'

'I'm at our rendezvous point, in a church about half a mile from where you are.'

'What rendezvous point?' Lauren shouted, angry that Kyle had lied when he said that James wasn't involved. 'I thought you were visiting some university.'

'Just a cover story,' James said. 'I didn't want you or Kevin dragged into this.'

'Kyle's a lying son of a whore,' Lauren said bitterly, stamping on the thick bedroom carpet. 'What else haven't you been telling me? Is it you lot that have been tracking us somehow?'

James didn't think it was the right moment to tell Lauren that he'd installed tracking software on her phone.

'Never mind all that,' he said nervously. 'Do you know *anything* about a memory card? Is there any way you could possibly get hold of it, or even just make us a copy?'

'The card is in my pocket,' Lauren said.

James gasped with relief and said something to Bruce who stood in the vestry beside him. Lauren overheard Bruce saying, 'Thank bloody god.'

'Lauren, we *badly* need that card. Can you meet me somewhere?'

'It might be hard to get out of the hotel,' Lauren said.

'There's a lot of cops around.'

Lauren jolted as she heard a voice behind her.

'I'll take it,' Kevin said.

Lauren hadn't heard him sneak into the room. She turned around and pointed at the door. 'I told you to stay out of this,' she roared. 'Get out of my room before I kick the shit out of you.'

Then she put her mouth back to the phone. 'I'll find a way. Where do we meet?'

'There's a coffee bar on the corner,' James said. 'That's about as close to the hotel as we can get at the moment with all the security. If I run I can be there in five minutes.'

'Right,' Lauren said. 'And you'd better get someone from Guilt Trips to call a lawyer for Kyle. David Secombe is desperate to get that card and it'll be fingers-up-the-bum time before he knows it.'

Lauren shut her phone and was furious to see Kevin still standing behind her. 'What part of *stay the hell out of this* don't you understand?' she shouted.

'I'm not a kid,' Kevin repeated indignantly. 'What's going on?'

Lauren realised she'd need Kevin to cover for her while she was gone. She sighed and rubbed her forehead before quickly explaining the basics about Kyle, the blackmail attempt and the contents of the memory card in her pocket.

'I trust you not to grass me and James up,' Lauren said finally. 'But if anyone asks, you don't know anything about this, OK? This is a nasty little mess. I might get kicked out of CHERUB, but there's no point you getting sucked into it too.'

Kevin nodded and looked miffed. 'I can't believe James didn't tell me why he really pulled out.'

'I'll be fifteen, twenty minutes maximum,' Lauren said as she put on a hoodie and headed towards the door. 'Turn the water on in my room and if anyone comes in, you thought I was in the shower.'

Lauren opened her door. She was confident she'd be able to bluff her way past the police, but was surprised to find that they'd been replaced by swarms of men dressed in dark suits. The nearest one was less than two metres from the door.

'Back in the room, little lady,' he said abruptly.

Lauren looked indignant. 'Who says?'

The big man was full of his own importance. 'Security service,' he said firmly. 'I need you back in your room. *Nobody* gets on or off this floor until we've searched everything and everybody.'

Lauren's heart sped up as she backed into the suite. Kevin had a curious look on his face as he came out of Lauren's bedroom.

'I tried turning your shower on,' he explained. 'But none of the taps work.'

'Oh shit,' Lauren gasped. 'They've done what the drug squad does: turned off the plumbing so you can't flush anything. And you can bet they'll have an interceptor in the sewage pipe to catch anything that does get flushed.'

Kevin nodded. 'They got here so fast that they must

have been on standby. They already suspected someone on the inside was passing information to the protestors.'

Lauren took the card out of her pocket and held it up. 'Do you think this will show up on an X-ray if I swallow it?'

'Definitely,' Kevin nodded, as he snatched the card from Lauren's fingertips. 'Give it here. I'll take it down to the coffee shop.'

Lauren shook her head. 'Your cute face won't get you past that lot. And now the card's got your DNA on it. I'm trying to keep you out of trouble and you just incriminated yourself.'

'Who says I'm going out *that* way?' Kevin smiled, as he turned and started walking towards the balcony. 'If anyone asks, just say you think I left with TJ about half an hour ago.'

Lauren grabbed Kevin as he slid the glass door on to the balcony. 'You can't climb down eight floors,' she said. 'I'll hold on to the card. You don't have to take any of the blame.'

Kevin surprised Lauren with his strength as he pushed her away and stepped briskly on to the balcony.

Before Lauren got her balance back, the twelve-year-old had pocketed the memory card and balanced himself on the metal railing, eight storeys above the narrow street. Lauren felt queasy with fright as Kevin pirouetted so that he faced the building and then leapt forward athletically, gripping the masonry half a metre above the sliding glass doors.

Lauren thought about grabbing Kevin's ankles as they

dangled in front of her, but she wasn't sure that she was strong enough to catch him if he fell awkwardly. Within seconds he'd grabbed the gutter running along the edge of the building's gently sloped roof.

Once he was out of Lauren's reach, Kevin leaned over the edge of the roof and smiled cheekily. 'If I fall to my death, tell James and Bruce that they overdid it when they taught me how to get over my fear of heights.'

'You be bloody careful,' Lauren warned. Part of her was impressed with Kevin's bravery, but mostly she felt sick with worry. 'Call me as soon as you're safe.'

Kevin rolled over on to his belly, then jumped as a pair of angry wood pigeons shot into the air directly in front of his face. He gave himself a few seconds to recover from the fright before standing up straight.

The height didn't concern him, and the roof made a much safer platform than the campus height obstacle on a windy day. The problem was he had no idea where to go next.

He kept low as he walked along the rooftop, eventually meeting a line of chimney pots where the Leith Hotel met a flat-roofed office building. The chimney stack was a nightmare, surrounded by air conditioning units, cables, satellite dishes and a mobile phone mast.

After negotiating this lot, it was a relief to peer between giant chimney pots and see a two-and-a-half-metre drop on to the flat roof of an office building. He collapsed sideways on landing in the exact way that CHERUB had shown him and began striding briskly across the roofing felt.

There was a grey painted fire door, but it only opened from the inside so he crossed to the back of the roof and made a huge metallic boom as he vaulted on to a set of fire stairs. He moved down quickly, keeping low as he passed windows with bored looking office drones inside.

When he got to the second floor, he found a group of men having a smoke on the landing directly below. Kevin waited as they discussed a boss called Jody who none of them liked and a new girl in accounts with a *cracking pair of hooters*.

Two men finished their smokes and went inside, but the others were joined by a woman who came out with a Starbucks cup and lit up a king-sized Marlboro. The longer Kevin waited, the greater the chance that the MI5 security team would be on his tail, so he took a calculated risk and put on a little boy lost act as he walked down in front of the smokers.

'Where'd you come from?' one asked curiously.

'It's bring-your-kid-to-work day,' Kevin explained. 'I was up on the sixth floor. Came out of the loo, went through the fire door and it shut behind me before I could get back inside.'

The woman laughed. 'You poor sausage!' she grinned, as she dropped her half-smoked cigarette into her coffee. 'I'll take you back to the lift.'

So Kevin got escorted through the shabby offices of a legal publishing company. The kindly smoker pressed the up button to call the lift, so he had to ride up to the sixth floor before riding back to the ground floor and stepping into a sunny May afternoon.

Kevin's smart chinos were now filthy, he had bird crap on his hands and a grazed elbow. He walked quickly towards the café, nervously passing the police officers guarding the Leith Hotel across the street.

James Adams sat at a table inside, drinking a can of Coke.

'Nice one mate,' James smiled, as Kevin passed over the memory card. 'I've gotta jump in a cab and take this straight up to a production studio in Soho. My reporter friend reckons he can get it in tomorrow's papers.'

35. TRAILS

Tan Abdullah's plane sat on the tarmac at Heathrow airport. The luxurious jet had backed up from the gate, but a storm was causing air traffic delays and the pilot had announced a forty-minute wait for a takeoff slot.

Tan would face bribery charges in Malaysia, and after being taped insulting the prime minister it was likely he'd face immediate arrest and imprisonment. His short-term solution to this problem was to file a flight plan to New York. June Ling was an American citizen, so he could stay there indefinitely.

TJ had a seat at the rear of the jet. He'd changed into pyjamas and fully reclined his seat. There was always some drama going on with his father and stepmother, but while nobody had taken the time to explain exactly what had happened at the Leith Hotel, he knew it was serious.

He couldn't concentrate on playing his PSP and sat with his cheek touching the aircraft window, looking into the dark at the flashing lamps on aircraft wingtips and the illuminated glass face of the terminal building on the opposite side of the main runway.

TJ was momentarily distracted as his father opened the overhead locker directly above him.

'Maybe we can see an NBA game in New York,' Tan suggested, as he took something from the case and slipped it into his suit.

'That would be really cool,' TJ smiled. 'There's an NBA shop in Times Square. They have every NBA shirt, and tons of other stuff.'

Tan shut the locker, then moved down towards the plane's tail and stepped into the toilet cubicle. TJ looked across the aisle and saw that Suzie had pulled her duvet up over her head and seemed to be asleep. He thought about lobbing his trainer at her, but Suzie was bigger than him and the pleasure of waking her up would be outweighed by the fact that she'd jump out of her seat and beat the crap out of him.

The steward approached with a mug of hot chocolate. 'I know you usually have it after takeoff,' she explained, as she passed the mug over to TJ. 'But seeing as we're stuck here on the tarmac for a while . . .'

TJ flipped out a tray and saw that the steaming mug had whipped cream and little marshmallows with jam inside, just how he liked. He took the mug and let the steam rise up to his face. He felt cosy, with his duvet up around his neck and a fresh blast of rain pelting the outside of his window.

Then he heard a bang.

It made TJ jolt and he swore as the cream and milk spewed down the side of the mug, burning his hand. Suzie sat up, looking startled. An alarm sounded in the cockpit, causing the pilot to flick a row of switches above his head.

The cabin lights and ventilation went off briefly, before the emergency battery kicked in. The co-pilot began walking down from the cockpit as the stewardess banged on the door of the toilet.

'Mr Abdullah, is everything OK in there?'

There was no answer. TJ and Suzie almost clunked heads as they leaned into the aisle and looked down towards the tail. The stewardess screamed as she saw dark liquid running under the toilet door and heading for her shoe.

'It's blood,' she shouted.

The co-pilot pushed between Suzie and TJ's heads and reached up to grab a T-shaped key built into a slot beside the toilet door. This fitted into a hole beneath the door handle, overriding the lock inside.

The co-pilot slid the door and backed off. The stewardess looked and screamed as she saw the gun lying in the blood pooled around Tan Abdullah's flight slippers and the huge spray of blood and a hole torn in the fuselage directly behind him.

*

It was pitch dark by the time James drove Bruce through the main gates of CHERUB campus in a black Mini. The boys parked in front of the main building and headed inside to reception.

'I'm starved,' Bruce said as James hooked the car keys on a rack behind the main reception desk. 'You wanna go straight to dinner?'

'I'll just do the paperwork and I'll come join you,' James agreed.

When you returned one of the campus pool cars, you had to fill in a short form, detailing the number of miles the car had driven and giving a declaration that the car wasn't damaged. Chairwoman Zara Asker crept up behind as James slid the completed form into a tray.

'Evening boys,' she said, in a tone James found difficult to read. 'Can we have a quick word in my office?'

The office was familiar. Any trouble on campus usually ended up with a sit-down in the chairwoman's office and James had been through this more times than he cared to count. When he'd first joined CHERUB, Mac had been chairman and you could rely on firm but consistent punishments. Zara had a softer manner, but made James more nervous because you could never predict what she was going to do.

'How was your university trip?' Zara began, as the boys sat down at her desk.

'Good,' James said, hoping that they'd only been called in because Bruce had left campus without permission.

'Couldn't find any record of you asking to leave,' Zara told Bruce, before turning to James. 'And it's the wrong time of year for university open days, isn't it?'

James and Bruce spoke at the same time.

'It wasn't an open day, we just went for a look,' James said.

'I didn't find out where James was going until the last minute,' Bruce said. 'I tried speaking to my handler, but it was early in the morning and nobody was around.'

Zara smiled, and pulled a folder across the desk. 'I had a call from CHERUB security. Apparently your friend Kyle got arrested this afternoon,' she said, as she opened the file and slid out some papers.

Shit, James thought to himself. He wasn't worried about himself, but Bruce, Lauren and Kevin had CHERUB careers ahead of them.

'Some *very* interesting reports,' Zara continued. 'There was a fight in a hotel restaurant shortly before Kyle's arrest. I wondered what you two might make of this statement, given by a waitress?

'A boy no older than sixteen who looked like he needed a haircut started attacking huge dudes the size of nightclub bouncers. I've never seen anything like it. This kid whizzed about like a tornado and absolutely slayed the bodyguards. It was like something out of a kung-fu movie. The only mark on him when he ran off was a small cut on his forehead.'

Bruce looked down, hoping that Zara couldn't see the scab through his overgrown fringe.

'Did they have any CCTV footage?' James asked. 'It sounds amazing, *whoever* that dude was.'

'Funny you should say that,' Zara said. She shuffled her papers and found another excerpt. 'This one comes from a man who worked in the office behind the hotel's reception area. *He looked very young, but I didn't really think about that at the time. He was stocky and quite good looking. He charged into the office, saying that he was a policeman and demanding all our surveillance tapes as evidence. I explained that the Leith Hotel's CCTV was stored on hard disks on a server. So he calmly opened the server cupboard, removed all the drives and took them away in a cardboard box.* Further down it says that he was wearing *Nike trainers, jeans and a baseball cap.*'

'Not much of a description,' James pointed out. 'Half the young blokes in the country wear jeans and Nikes.'

Zara smiled. 'But it somehow reminded me of the report John Jones wrote about your Brigands Motorcycle Club mission. Remember how the Führer would always try to switch off surveillance cameras before anything happened, or failing that remove them after the event? What did you do with the hard drives, James?'

James smiled uneasily. 'Hypothetically, if it *had* been me, I'd have taken the hard drives apart with a screwdriver, then put the magnetic platters in a bucket half filled with petrol and set it on fire. The heat would burn the magnetic coating on the discs, making them unusable.'

'But of course, it wasn't you, was it?' Zara asked.

Bruce was pretty sure that Zara could nail them if she wanted to: shoeprints, fingerprints, DNA, other surveillance cameras in the area. But he was getting a sense that she didn't want to.

'Do you want it to be us or not?' Bruce asked.

'God forbid that it was,' Zara said. 'Because *if* it was, I'd have to launch a full investigation against you two, plus Lauren and Kevin, and you'd all face expulsion. I'd also have to declare Kyle a security risk, ban him from campus and have him placed under surveillance. Then there would be a detailed report for me to write, explaining how a retired agent like Kyle was allowed to see a top-secret mission briefing. And I'd have to explain how the organisation I was running ended up in control of a mission where two of my current agents and one former agent were working for the other side and making friends with an investigative journalist.

'Finally I'd have to face the ethics committee, and explain myself to the intelligence minister in London. I'd probably have to resign from my job. The mission controller in charge of the operation would also have to resign from his job, and in case you haven't noticed that particular mission controller is my husband.'

Bruce's mouth dropped open. 'I never realised it would be that serious.'

'So even if it was us, and of course it wasn't,' James said, 'it would be better for *everyone* if nobody outside of this room ever found out what really happened?'

Zara nodded as she shut the folder. 'Don't spread the word on campus. Stay away from Kyle for a bit, he'll possibly be under MI5 surveillance for the next two or three months. Don't involve yourselves with Guilt Trips, Helena Bayliss and Hugh Verhoeven.'

'Can you help Kyle at all?' Bruce asked. 'Get him out of prison or whatever?'

'Absolutely not,' Zara said. 'Anything I do to help Kyle will flag up the fact that he's an ex-CHERUB agent.

He's a big boy now. I'm sure Guilt Trips and Hugh Verhoeven have enough money to make sure he's got a good lawyer.'

'And what can they charge him with?' James asked. 'He didn't hurt anyone, or do anything much else that's illegal.'

'I reckon he'll get a caution,' Bruce agreed. 'MI5 don't like having their dirty washing aired in open court.'

'So,' Zara said, sighing loudly as she stood up from her desk. 'That's about all I have to say on this. I expect you boys are hungry and I have a family to get home to.'

James and Bruce looked at one another and exchanged sly smiles as they stood up. Zara strode across the room and took her coat from the hat stand by the door.

'And there's one other thing I'd like to say,' Zara said. 'The world is a messy place. Sometimes it's hard to tell who the good guys and bad guys are, but I don't think there's much doubt that Tan Abdullah is one of the bad ones. You took some pretty stupid risks. As chairwoman I can't condone what you did, but as a human being with a conscience I can't condemn it either.'

December 2009

36. TERMINAL

James came through the arrivals gate at Heathrow terminal five. It was mid morning. He was eighteen years old and wore a red T-shirt with a Nike tick and the logo of the *Stanford Cardinals* American football team. His skin looked tanned, but he had bags under his eyes after the ten-hour flight from San Francisco.

'I missed you so much,' Kerry squealed, as she grabbed James and pulled him tight. Her fingers dug into flesh that felt a little thicker than usual. 'Letting yourself go a bit, Mr Adams.'

She didn't say any more because James plunged his tongue into her mouth and shoved his hand up the back of her mini skirt.

'Four months,' James said, with a tear welling in his eye. 'It's been *way* too long.'

An elderly woman tutted disapprovingly as the two

teenagers slobbered and groped. James needed a shave and the bristles irritated Kerry's face. She didn't care about that, but she did care when a lad of about thirteen whistled and shouted *nice bum* before getting a gentle clump off his mother.

'Everyone's staring,' Kerry protested, as she pushed James away.

'Let them,' James said. 'They can arrest us for gross indecency for all I care. We could find a toilet or something.'

Kerry started to laugh. 'James I'm not shagging you in an airport toilet.'

'I'm desperate,' James begged. 'It's a newish terminal. They're probably quite clean.'

'Or we could go to our room,' Kerry said, as she produced a credit-card-type hotel room key.

James broke into a huge smile. 'Oh god, I love you *so* much,' he gushed.

'It's pretty crappy,' Kerry said. 'Twenty-quid internet special, but it's got a bed and a shower. Thought we could hang out there for a few hours before we meet up with Lauren in town.'

'How far?'

'Ten-minute drive,' Kerry said. 'Can you control yourself for that long?'

'Just about,' James said, pretending to sulk.

But Kerry didn't twig that he was only pretending and panicked slightly, thinking he was upset because she didn't reciprocate his *I love you*.

'I love you too,' Kerry said. 'And I booked that room

because you're not the only one who couldn't wait until we got back to campus this evening.'

'All right!' James said enthusiastically, as he spun around looking for the exit. 'Why are we standing here?'

Kerry took James' hand luggage and they started to walk with a huge wheelie bag trundling behind. James put his hand up the back of Kerry's skirt again, but she shoved it away.

'Everyone can see my arse when you do that,' Kerry said irritably as they neared a set of automatic doors which led to the car park. 'You're an embarrassment!'

'You're easily embarrassed, aren't you?' James teased. He stopped walking and turned back so that he faced the huge and crowded arrivals hall.

'James what are you doing?' Kerry asked.

'This is my girlfriend Kerry Chang,' James shouted at the top of his voice. 'She's got a great arse, and I hope you've all enjoyed looking at it. Now I'm gonna take her to a hotel room and have a damned good sha–'

Before James could finish, Kerry had her hand clamped over his mouth.

'I'll murder you!' Kerry said, as James howled with laughter.

Kerry dug her hand under James' ribs and tickled until he collapsed on to his knees.

'I love her!' James shouted, as over a hundred people stood gawping and Kerry burned red with embarrassment.

They both ended up flat on the airport floor,

laughing helplessly as an airport security officer loomed over them.

'Act your ages,' the yellow-jacketed woman said. 'You're blocking everyone's way out.'

James pointed at Kerry. 'It was her,' he said mischievously. 'She started it.'

The officer didn't see the funny side and tapped a finger against her walkie-talkie. 'If you've got a problem you can explain it to the airport police.'

James and Kerry had tears in their eyes as they headed through the automatic doors leading towards the car park.

*

They'd arranged to meet Lauren outside East Finchley underground station at two, but James and Kerry couldn't prise themselves apart. They held on in the hotel for as long as they could and ended up being forty minutes late.

'Traffic was awful,' James lied, as he stepped out of the silver Mercedes that Kerry had taken from campus and gave Lauren a kiss. 'You've grown a couple of centimetres since I last saw you.'

'And you've got chunkier,' Lauren noted.

'Booze and parties,' James explained.

'Cuddlier is the word I'd use,' Kerry smiled.

'I've actually lost a bit now I've gone back to weight training and running,' James said. 'But when I first arrived at Stanford it was craziness every single night.'

The trio drove to the nearest Pizza Express and caught up over a late lunch.

'How was your first term at Stanford?' Lauren asked.

'They call them quarters, not terms,' James explained. 'The campus is quite like CHERUB, except you have to share a room and there's ten thousand people on the campus, instead of a few hundred. The work's pretty hard. I've never struggled with maths or physics before, but everyone in my classes has brains spilling out their ears.'

'What about your exams?' Kerry asked, as she bit a bruschetta.

'You don't take proper exams until the end of second quarter in March,' James explained. 'But you get continuous assessment. I've had all As and Bs, except you have to take at least one arts course in your first year. I picked Russian because I already speak the language, but you have to read *Crime and Punishment* by Dostoevsky, which is basically a six-hundred-page novel where absolutely bugger all happens.'

'So you said it's lots of parties and stuff?'

James nodded. 'It's wild. I mean, if you want you can go to a party every night. But you have to learn to balance it or you'd end up wrecked at every lecture.'

Kerry felt uncomfortable at the thought of all this revelry. She didn't doubt that James loved her, but he was also a randy git and she couldn't help wondering if he'd stayed faithful during four months living in a college crawling with eighteen-year-old girls.

'I've put in my application for Stanford now,' Kerry said. 'Meryl says it should go through on the nod.'

'Cool,' James grinned. The waitress arrived with two

pizzas and a lasagne for Kerry. 'So how's everyone on campus?'

'Pretty quiet actually,' Lauren said. 'Loads of people are off on missions. Rat's in Australia with Andy. Bethany got back with Bruce, but it only lasted three weeks. Jake Parker's been suspended from missions after he got Ronan drunk and dared him to take a crap in the campus fountain.'

'Kevin got his navy shirt,' Kerry added.

James smiled. 'That's cool, Kevin's a great kid. Who got my old room?'

'Some new grey shirt called James Watkinson,' Kerry said, as she blew on a steaming fork-load of lasagne. 'Pretty quiet, keeps himself to himself mostly.'

'It's weird,' Lauren added. 'Jake and Kevin used to be the youngest grey shirts. But now people like you and Shakeel are retired there's a new group who are even younger.'

'You forgot to tell him about the big huge enormous campus sex scandal,' Kerry said cheerfully.

'Oh god!' Lauren laughed. 'Meatball is a daddy. The couple who moved into Mr Large's old house have a little poodle and Meatball had his way with her.'

Everyone laughed until Kerry remembered something. 'And Joshua Asker said I have to tell you that he's a good swimmer now and that you have to go to the pool with him so that he can show you.'

'I saw my dad,' Lauren said.

Lauren dropped this in casually, but James almost choked. 'You saw Uncle Ron? How did he find out where you are?'

'He wrote a letter to Islington council, which was forwarded on to CHERUB campus. He's eligible for parole early in the new year. He wanted a character reference for his parole application, saying that he was in contact with his daughter and that I thought his release would be beneficial to me. Apparently having close family can help sway a parole hearing.'

James shook his head with contempt. 'I hope you told him to shove that idea right up his hairy crack.'

Lauren looked awkward. 'I went to see him. He's had treatment for cancer, he looks really thin and I think he's been beaten up a few times in prison. I said I'd write the reference, on condition that he didn't hassle me when he got out.'

James put his head in his hands. 'How could you?' he gasped. 'Ron used to hit both of us. He treated Mum like dirt and *you* grassed him up after he punched you so hard that you ended up with two huge black eyes.'

'I know,' Lauren said, with uncharacteristic meekness. 'But all that's ancient history and no matter what Ron did, he's still my dad.'

James shook his head in disgust, but didn't say any more. His return from college for Christmas was supposed to be a happy occasion, besides which Lauren was stubborn so he wouldn't win the argument if he pushed it.

'Have you thought any more about seeing *your* dad?' Kerry asked.

James nodded, then waited to finish his mouthful before continuing. 'It was freaky. On the first day of my course they gave everyone a list of textbooks we'd need. So I'm sitting in my room at Stanford, ordering all these books off amazon.com. And I see that one of the maths books is co-written by Professor James Duncan. My laptop almost fell off my bed and Chris my roommate is like *What's up with you?* And I'm like, *I think I just discovered that one of my maths textbooks was written by my dad.*

'It felt like a sign or something. Especially when I'd just arrived at college and was feeling a bit homesick. So I dug up my dad's e-mail and sent him a message. I got a reply a few days later and we've been e-mailing back and forth ever since.'

Lauren smiled. 'So you're going to meet him?'

'Yeah,' James nodded. 'And I've got a little half-sister Megan who's nearly four. And a baby brother called Albert – named after Albert Einstein apparently.'

'When will you visit?' Kerry asked.

James shrugged. 'We didn't set a date because I didn't know what was going on with everyone else. But I've got three weeks before I fly back to the States.'

'How will you explain your years at CHERUB?' Lauren asked.

'I've just used my standard background story, telling my dad that I grew up in a succession of foster homes after Mum died,' James explained. 'We worked the whole thing out before I left campus.'

Kerry smiled. 'So did your dad give you the answers to the questions in his textbook?'

'No,' James laughed. 'But he did help me once when

I got totally stuffed on a maths assignment. He seems like a nice guy. I'm really looking forward to going up there and saying hello.'

'So what else have you been up to in California?' Lauren asked. 'What's your roommate like?'

'You thought he was gay at one time, didn't you?' Kerry asked.

'Until I came back to my room and found him bonking away at this giant hippo. *Oh Chris, oh Chris, that's so gooooood!*'

Lauren and Kerry both laughed, and James felt good being back with them and having so much stuff to catch up on.

*

An hour later, Kerry stopped the silver Mercedes at the bottom of a grassy hill. She stayed a few metres behind as James squelched through the long grass, holding flowers in one arm and with the other around Lauren's shoulders.

Britain is a small country and Londoners are buried six to a grave, with a half-metre between headstones restricted to a maximum height of forty centimetres. They stopped by a lozenge made from pinkish marble, with the gold-leaf inscription already starting to peel:

Gwendoline Choke
May 1966 – September 2003
Sadly missed by James & Lauren

At the bottom of the stone was an engraved image of a cartoonish angel standing in front of a rainbow and blowing a bugle.

'I can't believe I picked that tacky bloody design,' Lauren said, shaking her head as she looked at the stone.

'You were only nine,' James said. 'If it was my choice, she probably would have ended up with the Arsenal crest.'

Lauren took a backpack off her shoulder and pulled out a bottle of soapy water and a sponge to clean the stone. James pulled a couple of weeds out of the ground before pressing the earth under his foot and laying out a bunch of sunflowers.

A bitter wind caught the cellophane James had peeled from around the flowers and he bumped into Kerry as they both tried to catch it. But it whipped high into the air and embedded itself out of reach in a nearby tree. When James got back he saw that Lauren had tears streaming down her face.

'Hey,' James said soothingly, as he went down on one knee. 'What's the matter? You don't usually get this upset.'

'I really miss her,' Lauren sniffed. 'And I missed you when you were in America.'

'I missed you,' James said gently.

'I'll probably go off to university in a few years,' Lauren explained. 'We'll live in different towns, maybe even different countries. I'll never just be able to go downstairs to your room and say hello, or come and see what you're up to when I'm bored.'

'Life's always sad when you look backwards,' James said, as his eyes teared over. 'When I think about Mum. Or when I realise that I'll never go on another training exercise, or see some of the friends I've made on my missions. But that's how life goes. Things have to move on.'

'I never met your mum,' Kerry said, handing over a tissue as Lauren stood up. 'But I bet she'd be really proud if she saw you both now.'

James smiled and pulled both Lauren and Kerry into a tight hug. 'You're my two best girls,' he said. 'We've got our whole lives ahead of us. Now let's get back to the car. I've got used to California and I'm freezing my balls off up here.'

EPILOGUE

The following updates were written shortly before the publication of this book in September 2010.

RALPH 'THE FÜHRER' DONNINGTON stood trial at the Old Bailey in London charged with weapons-smuggling offences and resisting arrest. He received a prison sentence of sixteen years. Fellow defendant DIRTY DAVE was sentenced to eleven years.

The vicious gang war between Brigands MC and the Vengeful Bastards continues to rage. In mid-2009 the UK Brigands upped the ante by recruiting more than two hundred members of subordinate gangs such as the Monster Bunch in a process known as 'patching over'. The Vengeful Bastards have also patched over more than a dozen gangs.

On the positive side, police believe that the arrest of

Ralph Donnington brought an end to the Brigands' weapons-smuggling operations and has significantly reduced the number of illegal weapons entering the UK.

ALISON and KAM LEE's Surf Club restaurant burned down under suspicious circumstances in November 2009. Police believe that it was a revenge attack, ordered by the Führer.

AIZAT RAKYAT's grandmother died in 2007 after which his younger sister WATI was taken in by friends living on the mainland who'd originally lived in Aizat's village.

Aizat was released from prison in Malaysia in October 2009. He completed a high-school education while in a young offenders' prison. Following his release he received a grant from Guilt Trips and now attends university in northern Malaysia.

His village on Langkawi island has now been developed as a luxury timeshare resort, linked to the adjoining Regency Plaza Hotel. A compensation case brought by villagers and funded by Guilt Trips was dismissed by a Malaysian judge on the grounds that the villagers had no legal entitlement to the land on which they had lived for generations.

HELENA BAYLISS continues to work as the global head of Guilt Trips. The organisation now has offices in eight countries and more than twenty full-time staff. She also writes articles on environmental and tourism issues for newspapers all over the world, and regularly appears as a pundit on British television.

In early 2010, Helena successfully appealed against her ban from Malaysia. She plans to travel to Malaysia in 2011, giving her son Aizat Jr a chance to meet his father.

Journalist HUGH VERHOEVEN's story on Tan Abdullah received limited media coverage in the UK. However, the story was a sensation in Malaysia and the bribery scandal was a factor in the collapse of the Malaysian government a few months later.

Verhoeven has returned to retirement and is currently working on a volume of memoirs about his career as a TV journalist.

Following the death of TAN ABDULLAH, a bitter fight erupted between JUNE LING, Abdullah's two previous wives and his nine children over an estimated $4.4 billion fortune. The disputes are expected to drag on for several years, spanning courts in Malaysia, Thailand and the United States.

After living briefly in New York with their stepmother, TJ and SUZIE returned to Malaysia to live with their biological mother.

Tan's oldest son is still governor of Langkawi island, and despite his father's controversial suicide he remains hotly tipped to some day become prime minister of Malaysia.

Following investigations in Malaysia and the UK, a slightly smaller £4.7 billion arms deal between the two countries was brokered by DAVID SECOMBE and signed in April 2010.

Following his arrest inside the Leith Hotel, KYLE BLUEMAN was briefly held at a central London police station and released without charge.

He is now in his final year studying law at Cambridge University and hopes to become a barrister. He continues to do volunteer work for Guilt Trips in his spare time.

MEATBALL has been banned from the next-door neighbour's garden. Lauren adamantly refuses to let anyone have him neutered. Three of his mongrel children live in the junior block on campus.

DANA SMITH dropped out of her London art college. She works part-time in an art gallery owned by her Ugandan boyfriend.

DANTE WELSH attended the Old Bailey to see the sentencing of Ralph Donnington and was delighted to see the lengthy sentence handed down. The ex-girlfriend of a Brigand came forward shortly afterwards stating that she was willing to testify that both she and her former husband had been involved in a clean-up operation that followed the 2003 murder of Dante's parents and two older siblings.

The murder trial is expected to take place in 2011 and Dante will be the star witness. If the Führer is convicted of the quadruple murder, he can expect to spend the rest of his life in prison.

Dante's younger sister HOLLY WELSH is expected to begin CHERUB basic training in 2012.

BETHANY PARKER was expelled from CHERUB after campus security discovered that she was engaged in a relationship with a boy she'd met during a mission two years earlier. This was regarded as a severe breach of security regulations.

She now lives near to CHERUB campus, lodging with the mission controller Maureen Evans.

Following the award of navy shirts, KEVIN SUMNER and JAKE PARKER are both fourteen and regarded as part of the latest generation of outstanding CHERUB agents. Jake occasionally visits his sister Bethany, but they still don't get on.

BRUCE NORRIS spent most of his last year at CHERUB on a mission in the United States. He plans to study journalism and photography at university after taking a year off to travel the world with identical twins CALLUM and CONNOR REILLY.

Bruce also has a long-term goal to bulk up and become an Ultimate Fighting champion.

KERRY CHANG was accepted into Stanford University and joined James Adams in Palo Alto California in August 2010. Despite her suspicions, James did not cheat on her during his first year at college.

Kerry's long-term best friend GABRIELLE O'BRIEN is studying medicine at the University of Sussex and hopes to become a doctor.

LAUREN ADAMS remains on good terms with Bethany Parker, and her boyfriend Rat. She is due to retire as a CHERUB agent in 2012.

Her father RONALD ONIONS was granted parole and released from prison in March 2010. At the time he was in the advanced stages of throat cancer. He died four months later in a North London hospice.

Lauren and her friends Bethany and Rat were the only attendees at his cremation service.

JAMES ADAMS is in his second year studying maths and physics at Stanford University and has achieved reasonable grades. He spent his summer break working as an assistant at the CHERUB hostel. He is in regular contact with his father and has visited him several times during holidays in the UK.

James is expected to live happily ever after.

Is this the end for CHERUB?

You've just finished reading James Adams' last CHERUB adventure, but have you read the rest?

1. The Recruit
2. Class A
3. Maximum Security
4. The Killing
5. Divine Madness
6. Man vs Beast
7. The Fall
8. Mad Dogs
9. The Sleepwalker
10. The General
11. Brigands M.C.

For exclusive content, including bonus stories, news, out-takes, games and downloads visit the essential digital destination for all things CHERUB at **www.cherubcampus.com**

Is this the end for CHERUB?

Robert Muchamore takes us back to World War Two, where the first CHERUB adventure is about to begin . . .

1. The Escape
2. Eagle Day
3. Secret Army

coming soon . . .

4. Grey Wolves

The British secret service is about to discover that kids working undercover will help to win the war.

Find out more about Henderson's Boys,
the original CHERUB agents, as well as news,
games and exclusive content at
www.hendersonsboys.com

IS THIS THE END FOR CHERUB?

Shadow Wave was James Adams' last mission as a CHERUB agent. So what's next? Find out what every CHERUB fan wants to know by following the link below!